NORTH WOODS UNIVERSITY
BOOK ONE

# THE BET

**USA TODAY BESTSELLING AUTHORS**

# J.L. BECK &
# C. HALLMAN

© Copyright 2019 Beck & Hallman LLC

Cover Art by: Black Widow Designs

Editing: Ellie McLove at My Brothers Editor

All rights reserved. This book or parts thereof may not be reproduced in any form, stored in any retrieval system, or transmitted in any form by any means —electronic, mechanical, photocopy, recording, or otherwise—without prior written permission of the publisher, except as provided by United States of America copyright law.

Dear Reader,

We're so happy that you picked up our newest book The Bet. We hope you enjoy it to your fullest and we cannot wait to read your reviews on it. However, we wanted to leave a little note at the start of the book to warn readers with sensitivity to dubious content, sexual themes, and verbal abuse that this book may not be a good read for them.

We also would like to say that while the book is entirely fiction we know that abuse, sexual, physical, and verbal is a very real thing in our world and that we do NOT condone any behavior of that nature, nor do we think that it's okay to treat someone that way.

Again, this is fiction and while we don't always agree with the things our characters do sometimes it makes sense for a story.

With love,

J.L. Beck & C. Hallman

# 1

## REMINGTON

*I* lick my lips, the busty blonde sitting beside me has my cock rock hard. I know I should be focusing on the shit that the professor is droning on about, but I don't care. All I can think about is the things she's going to do with her lips and tongue in about an hour.

A loud creaking noise fills the room interrupting Mr. Johnson, and momentarily pulling me from Layla, or maybe it's Lacy, I can't really remember. I look from the girl beside me and to the door.

Whoever it is, is going to get an ass-chewing. In college, the professors don't really care if you're late or don't show up, so I'm not really sure why Mr. Johnson makes a show out of those that are tardy, still, I don't hold my breath that he isn't going to start bitching in a second.

My entire world flips on its axis when I see the person entering the room. Big blue eyes, soft pink lips, and long blonde curls, just the way I remember them.

*Jules.*

My heart starts beating out of my chest with just one look. *No fucking way.* I must be dreaming, or high, or drunk, or all three combined, because there is no fucking way that she's really here, much less in this class.

I haven't seen her in three years.

Three. Fucking. Years.

The memory of her is like a hot branding iron on my skin. The day she left was the day I lost a piece of who I was...a piece I tossed over my shoulder and never cared to find again. I grit my teeth, my jaw flexing with the pressure.

Mr. Johnson spins around, finger already raised as if he is about to snarl at her, but when he sees the sweet angel standing in the middle of the room, his face changes, morphing into something else. Even he can't bring himself to yell at this sweet creature.

*Sweet creature.* I almost snort. This girl, well, clearly a woman now, given the curves she's hiding and the tight jeans showing off her full ass broke me.

"I'm sorry. I didn't mean to interrupt. I just had a hard time finding the room," she whispers, her sing-song voice filling the room. She bats her long eyelashes at him innocently and all he does is clear his throat and motion for her to sit down.

Most of the assholes in this room are probably thinking she is acting, playing the innocent act, the woman who can do no wrong, but I know better. Everything about her is sweet and gentle. She wouldn't hurt a fly. She never saw anything as a nuisance, not even me.

Jules has always been the sweetest person I know...until the day she ripped my heart out of my chest and left, taking the shredded pieces with her. Her sweetness turned sour the day she moved away, and all because she wanted to please her father. She didn't even fight. Didn't fight for us, for our friendship, for the chance of love.

She just left...left when I needed her more than anything, more than air, more than life. Losing her was like losing a piece of my soul, it killed me, but I survived. I built myself back up and became the man I am today.

"Excuse me," she whispers, walking down the middle aisle getting closer and closer to me. Every step she takes angers me. I don't want her near me, let alone to be in the same room as me. She spots an open seat in the row in front of me, and slides into it, but not before lifting her eyes to survey the room.

The professor has already started talking again, and most of the room is focused on the board, scribbling down every little word that's written, so no one notices her stares. She tucks a curled lock of blonde hair behind her ear and then as if the entire fucking universe wanted to damn us, her eyes lock on mine.

Those big blue eyes, once so full of life, of wonder, of love for me, for *us*. In that instant, the entire fucking world could blow up around us and we wouldn't notice. She seems shocked to see me, about as shocked as I am to see her, and then a tiny smile pulls at her plump lips.

"Remington..." the girl beside me whines, rubbing her manicured hand against my thigh, and suddenly my cock has deflated. I feel sick to my stomach, my insides twisting, all because of Jules.

She gives me a tiny little wave and then settles into her seat.

*What the fuck?* What the hell just happened? Did she seriously just wave at me? Red hot anger zings through me. Who the fuck does she think she is? Waving at me, acting like she doesn't know what the hell she did. The hour seems to drone on, and with every ticking minute, my anger seems to grow. I feel like a boiling pot of water. One single second away from boiling over.

"Do you still want to hang out after class?"

"No," I grit out.

"Why? Don't tell me it's because of that girl that just waved at you. Who is she anyway?" Using my hand, I brush hers off my thigh and grip my pen with enough strength to snap the damn thing. Maybe I should tell her, yes, but the blonde with a sweet smile and soft heart just ruined my fucking day, year, hell my life.

"She's no one. I don't even fucking know her, so stop acting jealous," I whisper when all I want to do is yell. I wonder if Jules can hear me, I sure fucking hope so. I don't want her to try and reach out to me, try and talk to me. I don't want her to have a damn thing to do with me.

"Okay, so why then?" She pouts, and I twist away from her.

This classroom is too small, filled with too many people, and I feel like I'm suffocating. Her mere presence makes it feel like my heart is being ripped out of my chest all over again.

*"I have to go, Remington."*

*I shake my head, not comprehending what she's saying.*

*"What the fuck, Jules? Why?" I know I shouldn't swear at her, but I don't understand. I already lost my mom. If I lose Jules too, I'll risk falling off the deep end.*

*She worries her bottom lip between her teeth looking at me as if she doesn't want to say what she's going to next.* "You knew my parents were getting a divorce, and my mom, she's too busy with work for me to live with her. You know she travels all the time and really, I want to move with my dad."

*I blink.* "Move? Like, leave?" *My lungs deflate, my heart cracks down the middle.*

"Yes." She frowns. "I just rather go with my dad, Remington. You know I don't get along with my mom all that well and my brother is going to live with my dad too."

I understand what she is saying, but all I can feel is pain, anger, heartache.

"You're my best friend, Jules. I need you." My voice cracks, my insides twisting painfully.

"I know." Tears glisten in her big blue eyes. "We have the phone. I can call you, check up on you. I can come and visit."

I tighten my hand into a fist. I'm angry, at Jules, at her parents, at my own mother for choosing fucking liquor over her children.

"You know what, don't worry about me. Go and live with your daddy." My words slice through her, and I can tell they hurt. She reaches for me, her hand landing on my bicep, but I shrugged it off. If she cared about me as much as she said she did, she would find a way to make this work.

"Don't act like that. It's not like I want to hurt you." I can hear her talking, but all I can feel is the betrayal. If she's leaving, if she's not even going to be here anymore, then I should just end this, rip out my own damn heart instead of letting her do it.

"Go away, Jules. Go pack your shit and get out of my face. I don't ever want to see you again." I barely get the words out. God, does it hurt to say them, it hurts so damn bad.

"What? You don't mean that." She makes another grab for me, but I take a step backward, putting space between us.

This is it. The end.

"I do. I never cared about you, about our friendship. You mean nothing. Just like my mother. Nothing." I punctuate the words, staring down at her. Her pink lips tremble, lips I've thought of kissing my entire life, her hands shaking, and when the tears start to fall, I turn away.

"You...you can't..." she starts, but I whirl back around, stepping into her space. I've never hurt her, never wanted her to be scared of me, damn if that is the last thing I ever wanted but seeing her right now with tears swimming in her eyes, looking like she's the one that has a right to be heartbroken angers me. There are only two women I've ever loved in my life, and I've already lost one, now I'm losing her too.

Leaving me with no one...

"I do not care about you. Leave. Now. You've ruined us. Our friendship."

"I'm sorry, but can't change this, Remmy."

"Neither can I. Now get out of my face. I never want to see you again."

Her mouth opens as if she's going to say something, but I shake my head, giving her a warning look. I don't want to hear another word come out of her mouth. I don't want to see her pink lips, big blue eyes, or soft blonde curls ever again.

"Remington," someone calls my name, pulling me from the memory, and I blink letting the image of Jules' tear-stained face disappear from my mind. I realize then that people are starting to shuffle out of the classroom. *Fuck.* My eyes move to the seat in front of me, the one that Jules was in before I spaced out. It's empty now, thank fuck. Now all I have to do is get rid of this chick and I can get out of here.

"Look, Lacey..." I start, pushing from the table.

"It's Layla, actually," she sneers, displeasure appearing in her eyes.

"Uhh, yeah sorry, anyway...I've got shit to do. I'll text you later?" I shove all my shit into my backpack and start down the stairs, refusing to let her even talk. As soon as I step outside the classroom, I see her.

*Jules. My heart. My fucking best friend.*

Her eyes connect with mine, a smile pulls at her pink lips, and she takes a step forward. I tighten my hold on my backpack, every muscle inside my body tightening.

What the fuck?

What the actual fuck does she think she's doing?

# 2

# JULES

My heart beats so furiously inside my chest I think it's going to break free from my body and run down the hallway. It's been three years…three long years since the day he took my heart and ran it through the proverbial blender. I take a step forward, my feet moving all on their own.

He's so different now, bigger, taller, so much taller that I have to look up at him. My eyes roam over his body, it's toned and muscled, just like an athlete's. My mouth waters at the sight.

The ripped blue jeans and a white t-shirt he's wearing do nothing to hide his chiseled body. His dark russet brown hair is still as unruly as ever, going in every which way. The only thing that seems to not have changed is his dark green eyes that are currently piercing mine, a furious fire flickering in their depths. He holds his head high, an arrogance oozing from within.

There's a scowl on his face, and instead of looking happy to see me, he looks angry, impossibly angry. He still can't be angry over me moving away, can he be? No, there is no way. The Remington I knew never held a grudge.

Still, I remember the things he said that night the last time I had seen him. Even then, I never believed that he meant the words he said. How could he? We had been friends since grade school, you couldn't just forget about someone...you couldn't just start hating them for something that wasn't really their fault.

My body reacts to his presence just as it always did when we were kids and I find myself taking a step forward, and then another until I'm in front of him wrapping my slim arms around his middle.

"Remmy," I sigh, feeling a little too happy to see him. For a split second, everything is right in the world again. My father isn't dead. My mother is happy. Remington and I are friends again. I lean against him, closing my eyes, and letting his warmth seep into my bones, into every pore on my body.

He still smells the same, like soap and mint. His body, though harder, still feels the same too, and I smile against his chest. I can't believe he is really here. I didn't expect to see him, not today, and maybe not ever again.

Then the moment passes, and I'm dragged back to reality when someone pulls me off of him. My eyes fly open and I realize that no one has pulled me off of him, but instead that he is pushing me away. My mouth opens and I'm about to ask him what's wrong when I see the anger reflecting in his eyes.

His fingers wrap around my upper arm, his grip hard as steel as he starts down the hall while dragging me behind him. I can barely keep up with his fast pace, his height making his steps bigger than mine. Apparently, I'm not the only one confused because everyone we pass looks just as shocked and flabbergasted about what's happening as I am.

We round the corner and he opens the first door we pass, pushing me inside of the room. I stumble over my feet and grip onto a table to balance myself when he releases me with a shove. My heart is in my throat, and my lungs burn, refusing to fill with air. I look around the empty classroom, wondering what the hell is going on when he opens his mouth and starts yelling at me.

"What the hell do you think you are doing? You can't just waltz in here pretending you know me," he seethes, his words feel like a dull knife slicing through my chest.

*Pretending to know him?* I don't understand what he means, nor do I understand why he is so angry, so hateful. We used to be best friends, certainly, he remembers that, right? Was there some accident while I was gone? Did he get hurt and hit his head? Does he not remember who I am?

"Don't fucking talk to me, don't wave at me, don't even breathe in my direction and definitely don't call me *Remmy*! My name's Remington. No one calls me Remmy anymore, especially not you," he barks, exhaling a ragged breath, his gaze darkening.

"Just stay the fuck out of my way, and away from me. I want nothing to do with you."

His dig about me not being his friend snaps me back to reality, and suddenly I'm angry too, more than angry. "You can't possibly still be mad about something that happened three years ago," I huff, bitter laughter on the tip of my tongue.

He takes a step forward, his body looming over me, his eyes are dark, so dark they almost appear black. I've never been afraid of him, never in my entire life, but right now, there is something so unnerving, so intimidating about him that I almost want to make a run for the door.

"Oh, believe me...I'm not angry. I never even cared about you. I was glad you moved away, that I was finally rid of your whiny ass. I only ever hung out with you because of Jackson," he sneers, grinning down at me and I don't think he even knows how badly his words hurt me, he couldn't, he doesn't know what happened to my brother.

The reminder of my brother is more than I can handle at this moment, the wounds of his loss still fresh, still raw. I can't do this with him, not without having a mental break down. I shove past him and pull the door open, thanking God he doesn't try and grab me.

I can barely see where I'm going as I speed walk down the hall, running into several people on my way out. I have to get outside...I need some fresh air. I feel like I'm suffocating, my lungs deprived of air, no matter how many times I inhale and exhale.

Once outside, I force air into my lungs, breathing in and out a couple of times to stop the panic attack that was on the fringe of coming.

Hugging him was a bad idea, talking to him probably even worse of an idea. I was wrong to think that he wouldn't hold a grudge from that day. I was hurt, torn up over losing him, over the things he said, but I never would've treated him the way he just treated me.

Pressing a hand to my chest, I push away the thoughts of my brother and father. Losing them was hard, and the only reason I'm here now. Never in my wildest dreams would I have suspected Remington would be here too. I thought he'd get as far away from his family as he could, and yet he stayed right under their noses.

Pulling my phone from my pocket, I check the time. *Shit!* My little conversation with Remington put me behind and now I'm going to be late for yet another class. I shove my phone back into my skinny jeans and start running across campus. My next class isn't nearly as far away and by the grace of God, I somehow make it to the classroom only a smidge late. The teacher is already talking when I walk in and of course, just like in the last class, all the other students are quietly sitting in their chairs.

All eyes are on me as I try to sneak into the room and find a seat. My cheeks heat at all the eyes scanning over my body…It's the middle of the semester, so anyone who is new is going to draw attention, at least that's what I tell myself so I don't spend the entire day feeling self-conscious.

I sit down in the first free seat I find, trying to gather my thoughts enough to at least listen to what the professor is saying. I pull out a pen, and notebook, and ready myself to learn.

"Tough day, huh?" someone whispers beside me. Turning my head, I lock eyes with the guy next to me. *Do I really look that exhausted?* I eye him curiously. He's attractive in that all-American boy way, definitely nothing like Remington, that's for sure. I push that thought away. I shouldn't be comparing anyone to that asshole.

"Yeah, you could say that," I answer, giving him a small smile before turning my gaze back to the front of the room where the professor starts to draw a diagram on the board.

"I'm assuming you're new here since I'm sure I would remember seeing such a pretty face in this class."

"Thank you, and yes, I am new. Is it that obvious?" I wipe a strand of hair from my forehead and watch as the guy scans my face.

"Not really, but like I said, I'm sure I would have noticed someone as attractive as you walking into class."

I give him another little smile, not wanting to be rude, even though I don't care for his compliments an awful lot, especially not after the day I've had so far. I open my book and try to concentrate on the material in front of me, but I just keep replaying all the horrible things Remington said to me. It's like my mind wants to torture me, making me relive that moment over and over again.

I thought maybe, just maybe he would be happy to see me, whenever we saw each other again but I thought wrong. Still, even if he didn't want to see me, I didn't expect him to treat me so shitty. I'm so engrossed in thinking about Remmy that I almost don't notice the guy beside me staring. Why is he staring at me? Is there something on my face?

Tapping my pen on my notepad impatiently, I wait for the class to be let out. I try to ignore the feeling of his eyes on me and focus on the board for a few more minutes. The professor says something about an assignment he'll be sending to our emails, and then everyone starts moving, shuffling out of the classroom. I blink, slowly realizing I just daydreamed through an entire class.

"It's Cole, by the way," the guy who has been staring at me for at least the last ten minutes finally says. He holds out his hand right as I stand and like the people pleaser I am, I take it, shaking it. I know it's a strange thing to do, but I'm old-school like that. He oozes confidence that's almost contagious.

"Jules," I tell him as he holds on to my hand a moment longer than necessary, bringing it to his lips as if he's some Romeo. He plants a soft kiss to the very top of it, and I shiver a moment before he releases me.

"Jules. Mmmm, that's a beautiful name." He smiles, showing

me his perfectly straight, white teeth. "Would you like to come to a party tonight, Jules?"

I clutch my notebook to my chest and consider his question.

*Would I like to go to a party?* It probably wouldn't be a bad idea for me to go, to get out and socialize but after the day I've had, I think I'll pass.

"Oh, no, thank you. I just moved here. I haven't even unpacked yet and I need to catch up on the classes I've missed. Homework doesn't do itself." A bubble of laughter slips past my lips and I realize just how dumb I sound. This day has gone to shit, and truthfully, I just need to go back to my room, lay down and read a book. There's nothing that a good book can't cure.

"Sounds like coming to a party is exactly what you need if you ask me. You look stressed and like you might need to relax for a few hours. Find something to distract you from all the craziness." He pauses briefly, his green eyes moving to my lips. "You know, forget about your problems?"

*Relax? Find a distraction?*

Maybe he is right, maybe I need to do something to distract me.

"I'll think about it."

"Cool. Let me give you my number. You can text me if you decide to come. I'll send you the address." I chew on my bottom lip for a moment, a nervous habit of mine. Do I really want to give this guy my number?

In the back of my mind I know I should do it...I'm young, and new here, how the hell am I going to make friends or enjoy college if all I do is stay in my room? If I don't give my number out, or hang out with anyone? What do I have to worry about? Deciding against the paranoia, I decide to give him my number.

"Sure." I smile, and pull my phone out, watching as his eyes light up. A warm feeling tingles through me as he rattles off the number and I type it into my phone. Then I send him a quick text with a smiling emoji so he knows it's me.

"Thanks, Jules, and seriously, consider coming out tonight. I'll introduce you to everyone, show you the ropes." He winks, and I find myself grinning.

It's so strange to smile and laugh when I feel like I shouldn't be.

"Alright, Cole." I bat my eyelashes at him, and we walk out of class together. It almost feels normal to be talking to a guy. Up until today, I never really took notice of men.

Not that I didn't notice them, but more like I kept them at arm's length. Losing Remington killed me and pushed me to focus on nothing more than my grades. Love, boys, relationships, totally out of the question. At least until now.

"Where are you headed?" Cole questions as we walk down the sidewalk.

"I'm just going back to my room for a couple of hours. My next class is at two," I divulge. The sound of laughter ahead catches my attention and I lift my gaze, my eyes landing on a group of guys, four of them to be exact, one of them being Remington. My feet feel like cinder blocks and I stop dead in my tracks, while Cole continues walking forward until he realizes that I'm no longer beside him.

"Jules?" He says my name like he's been saying it his whole life. His eyes move between me, and where I'm looking. Remington's gaze is fire and fury, and I can feel it penetrating my skin, looking right through me even from this distance.

"Uhh yeah, what's up?" I force my gaze back to him, avoiding

Remington's stare at all costs. Cole continues looking at the group of guys, and it feels like he's piecing something together in his mind, then he blinks, and looks back down at me, a smile on his lips.

"Text me, okay?" he asks and I nod, watching him walk over to the group of guys.

For a moment I just stand there staring, my eyes bleeding into Remington's. Eyes that I remember being filled with so much happiness and excitement...eyes that belong to someone that I thought would be my best friend forever, and maybe lover?

Shaking my head, I tell myself to let it go, before releasing a sigh. Then I turn around, deciding to take the long way around campus, and back to the house I share with the two other girls that go to school here, two girls that would probably die if someone like Cole looked at them. Two girls that aren't me.

I thought going to a new college would be rough.

I never expected Remington to be here though.

## 3

## REMINGTON

Seeing her with Cole Robson shouldn't have bothered me, not really. So why the fuck did it feel like someone was stabbing me in the heart over and over again with a fucking fork? I tried to ignore the pain, but it was far too noticeable, and that only annoyed me more.

Knowing she's here, at *North Woods,* at my fucking school, irritates me beyond belief. I want to tell her to leave, to turn the fuck around and go back to wherever she came from, but I won't. Instead, I'm going to do the next best thing and make her life a living hell.

The odds of me getting her to leave town on her own is slim to none, but if I push her, force her out of this town with tear-stained cheeks I doubt she'll return ever again.

The music from the party downstairs vibrates through the walls and the floor. Fuck, the frat house is packed tonight. Alan sure spread the word about tonight. The first huge party of the semester and we were going to do our legendary bet tonight.

"Heard you fucked Layla again?" Thomas nudges my arm. Fucking the same woman twice wasn't really my thing. I rarely ever had sex with the same woman, however, there weren't a lot of women as good at blow jobs as she was. Still, I hadn't had sex with her more than once. If she referred to blow jobs as sex, then that was all her doing.

"I didn't fuck her. She sucked my dick, there's a difference," I chide, taking a long pull from the bottle of beer in my hands. After finding out Jules was here...I'm going to need a lot more beer and a lot more pussy.

"Alright boys, you got your picks ready?" Cole questions with excitement handing out a stack of square pieces of paper and pens after setting the *NWU* hat in the center of the table.

"You know the rules. The girls must be present at the party," I announce, giving Thomas a knowing look. He's notorious for dropping names of girls into the hat that don't even show up at parties, making it ten times harder to win. Not that winning gets you much of anything other than bragging rights, it sucks when you don't get any pussy for six weeks though. I take another pull from my beer bottle, letting the cold liquid cool my heated insides.

"Shut up, Rem!" He rolls his eyes, taking a chug from his glass. I chuckle and write the first three girls' names down that came up and talked to me, then I toss them into the hat. Kia, Thomas, Cole, and Alan do the same, and soon the hat is full of unsuspecting partygoers names. Names of women that won't even realize how much their lives are going to be changing in the next six weeks.

"So remember, if she's a virgin, you get more points. Anything other than sex isn't fulfilling the bet. Winner takes bragging rights and doesn't have to do any house party cleaning for the next six months. At the six week point, you have to break it off with her and let her know it was nothing more than a bet. If you can't do it, or you fail to do it, then you forfeit your bet and lose."

"Thank you for explaining the rules, Captain Obvious." Though a refresher on said rules never hurt anyone.

Alan gives the hat a good shake, almost losing some pieces of paper in the process. A nervous kind of energy runs through me. Why the fuck do I feel so nervous? I have no reason to be...I've done this many times. Plus, it's just fucking. Completely harmless, all fun.

One by one we each pluck a single piece of paper from the hat. I unfold mine in my hands, not caring for any dramatic splendors and stare at the name.

*Fuck no!* Not even fuck no. No way in hell. That can't be right. She's not even here, is she? I look up and around the group, thinking this must be a joke, but no one in this room knows about my connection to her so there is no way one of these assholes did this to be a dick. No, this is fate, karma kicking me in the balls.

I look back down at the paper, my hand shaking, hoping that maybe the name has magically changed in the last few seconds, but even after I blink, I see it hasn't.

*Jules Peterson* is still the name scribbled in blue ink. I feel sick to my stomach. Not only did she ruin me once before, but now she's reappeared back in my life to do it again. The muscles in my jaw jump as I try to figure out what the fuck I'm going to do.

"Who did you get, Rem?" Cole asks, frowning at me.

Apparently, he didn't get the girl he wanted either.

I turn the paper around and hold it up so he can read it.

"Shit! That's who I wanted," he whines. *Who he wanted?* For a moment, I think about what I saw this afternoon. Them walking together, her smiling up at him, seemingly happy. I should've realized what was happening then. It was obvious Cole was chasing tail, claiming her as his next conquest.

"Here, you can have her." I flick the piece of paper at him and snatch the piece he's holding in his hand.

"Fuck yeah!" He almost jumps from excitement. "This is going to be so fucking great. She won't even know what hit her," he snickers. "She's already given me her number, getting inside those virgin panties shouldn't be too hard now."

A lump forms in my throat at his words. *Virgin.* No fucking way is Jules still a virgin. She might act innocent and even come off as pure, but there's no way her cherry is still dangling between her legs. No. I can't think about Jules and sex in the same sentence. Let him break her heart. She deserves it.

Frustrated, I stomp out of the room without even hearing what names the other guys drew. I'm fed up already, and she's only been here one fucking day. Thrusting my fingers through my hair in frustration, I clomp down the steps, stopping when I reach the bottom of the staircase. I tip my beer back, emptying its contents into my throat before scanning the crowd.

*Weak. She makes me weak.* My eyes immediately seek her out, like she's a magnet that I'm drawn to or something. It doesn't take me long. Three seconds tops to find her golden blonde curls calling out to me like a beacon in the room. She's wearing makeup, not much, but enough to make her eyes pop, and the same pair of skinny jeans from earlier, the ones that show off her perfect ass.

An ass I'd love to sink my teeth into...

Fuck, why does she have to be beautiful, and perfect, and... *No!* She's nothing to me. Trash, garbage, scum beneath my feet, that's what she is. I take a couple calming breaths reminding myself that she's the reason we're here. She's the fucking reason I'm the way I am. Shaking my head, I read the new name in my hand.

*Cally Brice.* I try to rack my brain, connecting the name to a face. Redhead, I *think*. I look around the room once more until I spot the girl I think is Cally.

She's standing in the opposite corner of the room, away from Jules. *Thank God,* I need to be as far away from her as I can get. Cally spots me as I start to walk over to her, her eyes light up. She's pretty enough, big green eyes, looking at me all googly eyed. This is going to be a cakewalk...I'll have the bet won by tonight.

"Hey, Cally, right?"

She blinks at me like she can't believe I just said her name. "Umm, yes," she stutters, and I grin.

"You look beautiful tonight." I lay it on thick, knowing just what to say to charm her panties off. I'm so good at it, the boys once told me I could charm the panties off a nun if I tried. I didn't, in case you were wondering.

She tucks a strand of red hair behind her ear. "Thank you...it's nothing really, just a little makeup, and..." Out of the corner of my eye, I spot Cole walking up to Jules. She's smiling, and laughing, still having not seen me yet.

I warned her, told her I'd ruin her if she didn't leave me alone, stay out of my way, and still, she found her way to my house, to my party, into the lion's den. She's got a brain inside that head of hers and if she was smart, she would've tucked tail and ran the other way by now.

Cole stands close, too close, leaning in to whisper something into her ear. Her eyes widen and she nibbles on her plump bottom lip that is painted red this evening.

Those lips, her hair, that fucking body. In my mind, I can see her writhing beneath me, her tight little cunt swallowing my cock. I've always wondered what she would look like as she falls apart, as she squeezes my cock with her tightness. *Jesus.* There's a pounding forming behind my eyes, warranting the onset of a fucking headache.

Fuck Cole. Fuck her. He can rip her heart out...rip it out and break it into a million pieces. Inhaling through my nose, I reason with myself. She doesn't matter, she's no one, nothing. *She broke your heart.* I remind myself.

Yeah, she broke your heart, but you can't stop thinking about her. Being with her, inside of her. My hands curl into fists, forgetting about the girl in front of me, the party, the fucking people around me. But for some reason, I can't erase her. When he leans in a little closer, and his lips almost touch hers, I lose it. I fundamentally lose it and find my body reacting to what's happening without even thinking of the consequences.

"Hey..." Cally calls out after me, but I brush her off like a gnat. Inside my head, I tell myself that I don't care about anything, nothing at all. Only making the girl in front of me feel the same kind of loss I've felt for the last three fucking years. She doesn't get to come here and have the time of her life.

"I've changed my mind," I growl at Cole and grab Jules by her slim arm. Her skin is warm, soft, and she smells like vanilla and sugar. The scent slams into me, hitting me like a ton of bricks right in the gut. Pulling her toward me, I watch as her face morphs from laughter and happiness, to anger and confusion in an instant.

"Cole?" She looks between us with a puzzled expression.

"Rem," Cole warns, his eyes almost pleading as if he knows what I'm going to do. I shake my head, stopping him from saying anything. I don't give a fuck what he says. She was mine first, and always will be, and we have a history. She's mine to ruin, mine to break. When I don't say anything, she starts to struggle in my grasp.

"Let go of me," she growls through her teeth, trying to sink her feet into the floor. Does she think she's strong enough to fight me? I'm nearly a foot taller than her, much stronger and if she wants to get technical about it, I have no problem proving it to her.

Grinning, I hone in on that simmering pain that eats, breathes, and lives inside of me. "Nope. I warned you, Jules, told you that if you didn't stay out of my way, there would be consequences. It's not my fault you're a shit listener."

"You don't own the school, Remmy! Plus, I was invited to this party. Why can't you just leave me alone? You can't control me, or tell me where I can and can't go, you aren't a damn god!" she yells over the music blaring through the house.

Her feistiness turns me on as much as it angers me. I tug her through the crowd, and she loses her footing a time or two, but with my hand on her arm, she manages to stay upright. Once I reach the edge of the room, I open the back door and pull her out into the dimly lit backyard. The cold air bites into my skin, but it's a welcoming feeling with the rage boiling inside of me.

Once outside, I release her like her skin is on fire and shove her against the side of the house. Touching her reminds me of the times when we were kids... when I held her hand and walked with her. It reminds me of the person I was before she broke me.

"Invited or not, I told you not to show your fucking face around me." She looks back toward the door as if she thinks Cole or someone else will come rescue her. Stupid. So stupid. I bear my teeth, feeling the need to shake some common sense into her. She doesn't know me anymore, the man I am, the person I became because of her.

I don't hurt women, not unless you count breaking their hearts as hurting them, but I want to hurt Jules. I want her to feel my pain…I want to own her body, her heart. I want her tears, her misery. I want to feel all of it.

Leaning into her face, I say, "If you're waiting for a knight to come and rescue you, you'll be waiting a long time. Cole won't save you from me. He's not dumb enough to stick his nose where it doesn't fucking belong, and nor would he try. I'm the king of this campus. It's my playground and I fuck and take from those that I want to."

"What happened to you, Remmy?" Her voice cracks, her eyes soft, pleading even. Like she doesn't know what she fucking did to me, how she destroyed me, broke my heart. She wants to play stupid, the victim. I'll show her what it's like to be the victim.

"It's Remington," I yell, watching as she shudders. "And you can drop the innocent little act, like you don't know what the fuck you did."

She shakes her head, sending blonde curls flying, and I can't stop myself from doing what I do next. I'm an asshole, a bastard, a fucking douchebag, but I am who I am, and Jules had her chance to save me, to be mine, now she's nothing, nothing but a fucking bet.

"I don't understand, I never…" she starts, but I don't want to hear her excuses. I don't care about anything she has to say. Her words are nothing but lies. She gasps at my sudden movement as I advance toward her, trying to press herself against the house to put more space between us.

"Get on your knees," I order.

Her expression turns from puzzled to fearful and though my stomach twists and knots and it feels like I might throw up, I'm enjoying this, my blood singing, the monster inside me gobbling up the exchange, fueling the beast inside of me.

"What? No way, this is not happening Rem..." Too many words are being said, her excuses only angering me further. With both my hands, I push down on her shoulders, forcing her to the ground and on her knees. She cries out as if I've hurt her, but I know I didn't. I've barely touched her, *yet*.

"Consequences. For everything you do, there is a consequence. Now yours is to suck my dick like the good little whore you are, or I'm going to ruin your entire existence here. I warned you, Jules. I fucking warned you, but you didn't listen to me. You didn't take me seriously, but maybe next time you will." I snarl, reaching for the button on my jeans. How fucked up is it that I'm hard? That my cock is screaming to take her?

"Don't do this, Remington. Please don't..." she begs, tears glistening in her eyes. And I think back to that day, the day that I fucking needed her. I would've done anything and said anything to keep her with me then. My begs, my pleas went unnoticed, uncared for.

Shoving my pants down, I take sick satisfaction when her lips start to tremble. I'm so caught up looking at her face and her big blue eyes that I don't notice her pulling her fist back until it's too late. Her tiny hands land against my ball sack, and all the air in my lungs dissipates. My stomach churns and I fall to my knees as she moves away from me and onto her unsteady legs. A lightning bolt of pain passes through my balls.

"Don't touch me, and don't fucking threaten me again. You've changed, *Remington,* and the person you are and the person I am, are no longer people that run in the same circles. I don't know you anymore. The Remington I knew never would've done what you just did. Touch me again and I'll find a way to make you pay."

And that's the truth, the fucking truth. Never in a million years would I have put my hands on her like that. I never would've been excited to see fear flicker in her eyes, but I wasn't that person anymore. This was the new me, and the only version she was going to fucking get.

"I'll break you, Jules. I'll make you pay for this," I bite out each word, holding onto my balls, my entire world spinning out of control. One fucking day, one day is all it took for her to come back into my life sending all the perfectly constructed walls surrounding my heart into a crumbling mess. One day is all it took for her to make my stupid black hole of a heart beat again.

"I look forward to it," she sneers, walking back into the house, leaving me alone outside with nothing more than the sick feeling of what I almost did to her, and the reality of the man I've become.

# 4

## JULES

*T*wo days. That's how long it's been since Remington showed me a side of him I never plan to see again. Every time I close my eyes, there he is, an image of his angry eyes. All I can see is him forcing me to my knees, ordering me to suck his dick. I can't help but cringe. Who the hell does he think he is? He never put his hands on me before, and though he didn't hurt me, not physically, he definitely wounded me emotionally.

"Which movie do you want to watch?" Cally, my roommate, calls from the living room.

"I can't watch a movie right now. I've got like three assignments due tomorrow," I huff, trying to forget about Remington, about the party, and the entire events from that night. I'd have saved myself a lot of time had I not tried to make friends and just stayed home and did my homework.

"I thought you had someone coming over?" Bridget, my other roommate, appears in the kitchen. She's got her long blonde hair in a messy bun, and a pair of glasses sit on the tip of her nose. Like me, Bridget is all about her grades, and less about the drinking and boys. College is nothing more than another step in her life.

"Well, I did...I don't know if he's coming now." She pouts, plopping down onto the sectional before pulling out her phone. That explains why she's dressed like she's going to a party down the block.

Bridget grabs a bottle of water from the fridge and smiles at me. "How are classes going?"

"Good, just trying to figure out where everything is located."

"Yeah, the campus is huge, but you'll get used to it. Just like anything new. It takes time."

I smile, feeling thankful to have met Bridget.

She's kind and soft-hearted and offered to let me stay here rent-free, at least until I can get everything switched around with the colleges. My mom's trying to help me, but with her working non-stop, it's hard enough just to get her on the phone, let alone to help with anything.

"For sure, but I'm enjoying it."

"Yeah, she went to a party with me the other night," Cally pipes up from the couch, and Bridget smirks.

"She's already corrupting you, isn't she?"

I shake my head.

"No. I actually invited her to come with me. I was asked by someone I had just met and didn't want to go alone. But I won't be going again. I realized that parties aren't really my scene."

Bridget nods as if she agrees with me. "Mine either. I'm a homebody. All I need is a glass of wine and a good book and I'm good for the night."

"Boring," Cally snickers from the couch. Just then, the doorbell rings. Cally scurries from the couch like there's a fire and I start to pick up my books deciding that studying in my bedroom is a much smarter idea right now.

I don't care to watch Cally have sex with someone on our couch, not that I think she would, but I don't plan to stick around and find out. Bridget must feel the same way because she turns with her water bottle in hand and starts back down the hallway toward her bedroom. I load up all my stuff in my arms and turn to walk toward my bedroom, but my body freezes up when I see who it is that's at the door.

*Remington.*

The blood in my veins turns to ice and I can't get my stupid feet to move, it's like they're cemented into the floor or something. As soon as he spots me, his eyes turn from playful, a look I know all too well, to downright disgust and hate.

*Why does he hate me so much?*

I don't understand, and still a part of me wants to. I want to go to him, wrap my arms around him and will him to tell me what happened. But I'm afraid, afraid of what he might do, and even worse how I might react.

We're no longer best friends, were no longer anything, and that means there isn't anything stopping him from hurting me. There are no lines, nothing to be crossed because in Remington's mind everything is fair game.

He doesn't care for a damn thing, which is so unlike him. It's dangerous, and a game that I don't want to play. Cally closes the door, and the tension in the room grows thick. I can taste it on my tongue.

I don't think she knows what's going on, and even though I should probably tell her, being she's my roommate and all I know, it wouldn't change anything. Remington Miller is a North Woods god, and I'm just some transfer without a name. She would probably kick me out of the house if he asked her to.

"I'm so happy you showed up. I was just going to start a movie, want anything to drink?" Cally asks, oblivious to the daggers he's throwing at me. Somehow, I know this is bad, him knowing where I live, who my roommates are.

*You'll pay for this.*

His words ring in my ears. I can still feel the venom in his voice, clinging to my skin. I'm a nobody in his world, a nobody at this college, and he's a god with women throwing themselves at him and men wishing they could be him. Making me disappear wouldn't be too hard. Destroying me even easier.

"Cally, babe, mind if I have a short little chat with your friend." His deep seductive voice gets the blood pumping in my veins. I find myself shaking my head without thought. Scurrying from the living room, I all but run down the hallway and to my bedroom.

His heavy footfalls fill the space behind me, and I know there is no way I can outrun him. I should've listened. I shouldn't have pushed him. Reaching my door, I open it, throwing my books to the floor. Just as I turn to slam it closed and lock it, his booted foot wedges into the door jamb. My gaze falls to the spot. He still wears combat boots which is a strange thing for me to be thinking about at this moment when he's so close and clearly wanting to snap me in two.

"Didn't I tell you... warn you?" His voice is deadly, and I shiver, wondering if it's out of fear or something else. Since that night when he pushed me to my knees and ordered me to suck his cock, I've been feeling things, things I shouldn't be for a man as mean and scary as Remington.

I shove against the door, trying to shut it, but it only takes one tiny push for him to overpower me. He opens the door and saunters into the bedroom, *my bedroom,* his eyes never wavering from mine, fire and rage simmering in his green depths.

Why does he have to look so gorgeous, and angry, and mean, and no, I cannot be thinking about him like that right now. He isn't the same person I once knew.

His huge hand grips onto the edge of the door and then he's shutting it. Trapping us both inside I take a step back, the room feels smaller than usual now that he's in it. The sound of the lock clicking into place sends my heart into overdrive. It beats so loudly all I can hear for a moment is the swooshing of blood in my ears. Can he hear it too? How hard my heart is beating?

*What happened to the boy I loved?*

"Get out," I whisper, my voice weak, my body weak. I should've listened to him, listened to his stupid warning. Never before was I a rule breaker, but Remington's rules are dumb, more than dumb, they're asinine.

"Nope. I'm here to show you a lesson," he smirks, but it's not his usual smile, no this smile promises heartache. His eyes move up and down my body, and I feel like I'm under a microscope.

"I didn't do anything..." My lips tremble giving away my emotions, and I hate that he gets me to react this way. He takes a step forward, his body looming, rippling with anger, with a vengeance, and I know the boy I loved once, the boy who was my best friend, my everything, is no longer inside him.

"You fucking exist, and that's enough of a reason for me."

I don't even get a chance to respond, before he's on me, his fingers digging into my skin roughly. This time I know I won't get to punch him in the nuts, but that doesn't mean I'll just let him hurt me. I kick and claw at him, but he overpowers me as if I'm nothing but an annoying fly.

He pushes me down onto the bed face first, his knee pressing into my lower back to keep me in place. My face is in the bed sheets, and I struggle against his hold. Fear claws at my insides when I hear the flick of the button on his jeans. He isn't...he wouldn't? Would he?

"Remington, stop it," I order him, tossing my head to the side to get a much-needed breath and to make certain he can hear me. I feel his hands slip into the waistband of my yoga pants.

"You have no idea who the fuck you're messing with. Who I am now. I own this school...girls want me to fuck them, guys want to be me, and I run the place like a king. I could kill someone, and no one would care, no one would even bat an eye."

Panic grabs onto me, refusing to let go. He owns this school, and all the people in it, everyone except me. *He doesn't own me.* I let that sink in giving me the courage I need to fight him off. I squirm, bucking my hips and rolling them, doing whatever I can to throw him off.

"Fight me, Jules, fucking fight me. It makes all of this that much more exhilarating."

"You don't own me..." I choke on the rest of my sentence when I feel the cool air against my panty-covered ass. He shoves my yoga pants down my thighs and sinks more of his body weight into mine.

Even though I'm scared, terrified of what he's going to do, a part of me is tempted to give into the darkness inside of him, to let him unleash it on me. I wonder if I gave myself to him, if I let him have me, if it would change anything. If it would bring him back to me.

"We'll see about that."

I can feel his hot breath against my ear. Before I can gather my wits, he's ripping my panties down my legs, the effort it takes for him to do so is pitiful. My chest heaves as I try and catch my breath. He's not really going to do this, is he? He wouldn't rape me. That's not him, even as angry as he is, he wouldn't cross that line.

Then I feel him...and not just him, but his cock, it's huge, and it slides up and down my ass crack, making me shiver with fear, but there is more than fear simmering in my belly. There is something else entirely. Warmth fills my being, sending rivulets of pleasure straight to my core. I'm confused, completely fucking confused. I shouldn't want this, and strangely, I do.

I've imagined sex with him ever since I figured out what it was in seventh-grade health ed class. But never, ever did I imagine it being like this. I had always assumed he would be my first, but I thought it would be sweet and gentle, not this raw, dirty, roughness.

Remington's hand palms my heated flesh, his touch surprisingly gentle as he slides his cock between my ass cheeks, up and down, up and down. I can hear him inhale and exhale as if he's trying to calm himself. My own breathing is out of control and I wonder if this is it. If this is where he claims me.

"Should I fuck your pussy or your ass?" I start to squirm again, wishing I could at least see his face, try to find the boy inside of him I once knew.

"Let me go...you've proven your point," I croak, pleasure swirling between my legs.

"No, I don't think I have yet." His hand travels from my ass cheeks around my body and snakes between my legs. His fingers are thick and my body is having a hard time separating the things he's doing to it from the person he is now.

These are all things I wanted once upon a time, his hands on me, his lips on mine, and maybe part of me still wants them, but not with the man he is right now. I want the old him, the boy who held my hand, who smiled at me and wiped my tears away. I want my best friend back.

Without warning, he starts to rub gentle circles against my clit.

"Maybe I'll fuck both. Tell everyone you were a whore that begged me to take both of your holes."

My body reacts to his touch, even though his words are cruel, and his voice angry. I want to speak, to say something but I'm afraid I'll moan instead, so to save face I press my lips together.

He keeps rubbing me, teasing my clit and it's driving me insane.

"Remington," his name falls off my lips dripping with need and I could kick myself for not being able to keep my mouth shut.

"Mmm, your pussy is already wet. You like this, don't you? I bet you aren't even a virgin. I bet you've slept with tons of fuckers just like me. Slept your way through life."

"No," I cry out, just as he plunges two fingers inside my channel. I wince, my entire body locking up as pain and pleasure mix together.

"Fuck...you're so tight," he hisses, his fingers stilling inside of me. I whimper into the sheets, and he eases a little of his weight off my body before he starts moving again, thrusting his fingers deep inside me. He's knuckles deep, rubbing at a magical spot. A spot I didn't even know existed until now. The pleasure builds, bringing me closer to the edge. This is insane, wrong, so wrong but it feels right. I can't hold my moan in any longer.

"Perfect, absolute perfection," he whispers, most likely not wanting me to hear him. He presses a kiss to the back of my head as he fucks me with his fingers, spearing me, breaking my heart and body all over again.

It doesn't take long for me to grow wetter and wetter with need, my entire body shaking, my legs trembling as an impending orgasm sneaks up on me. I've only ever made myself come, and it's never felt the way it does now, earth-shattering, consuming every single cell in my body. All I can feel is his fingers sinking deeper and deeper into my flesh until I feel nothing but blissful pleasure rippling through my body.

My pussy quivers around his fingers, my muscles tightening, trying to push him out as my release gushes out of me and onto his hand.

"Such a pretty little pussy. I never would've expected you to be so responsive to my hate, I guess we're both full of surprises."

I bite my bottom lip hard enough to make it bleed, and cringe at the copper tang of blood against my tongue. When Remmy withdraws his fingers, I'm left reeling, my body missing his touch, the fire he sparks inside me.

He remains on top of me, just lying on my body, breathing heavy, as if he is the one needing a minute of rest after what just happened. Once his breathing is under control, he finally lifts his body off mine, the absence of his touch leaves me feeling cold. I crave his touch, his words even though cruel. All over again, I'm that little girl falling for her brother's best friend.

Before I can say or do anything, he pulls my pants all the way off, throwing them on the floor beside the bed. He flips me over onto my back and then he's back on me, his whole body pushing me into the mattress. In this position, I can see him, see what he's thinking, what he's feeling. Peering up into his hardened face, I wonder what he's going to do next, and even worse, if I'm going to let him do it.

My heart is racing, and my breathing is shallow now that we're face to face. He's still angry, nothing but hate and sadness reflecting in his eyes. It's then looking at him, seeing those emotions swirl that I realize I'm not mad at him. I don't hate him for doing this.

I couldn't, not even if I wanted to. Instead, I feel something entirely different...I feel remorse. I feel sorry that this is what he has turned into, sorry that there is no love in his life, that he's lost the light, the kindness he once had.

Feeling a need to bring back that man, I grasp onto his shirt, grabbing a handful of the fabric, pulling him even closer while lifting up my head from the mattress. I don't think. I simply press my lips to his and kiss him. His lips are warm, and I inhale his scent, diving headfirst into the emotions he's pulling deep from inside me.

My mouth fuses to his, a hunger clawing at my belly. The sweet innocent kisses we shared before when we were kids is nothing compared to this kiss. This kiss holds a need, a possessiveness I want to grab onto.

Remington deepens the kiss and for a moment, I forget about how hurt we are, how angry we've been over losing each other. For a moment, we're the same people we used to be using the strength of our kiss to say things neither of us ever could.

But the moment passes just as quickly as it started and within seconds, he's pulling away, his lips swollen, his chest heaving. I catch a flicker of confusion that mirrors my own in his eyes before he jumps off the bed, immediately turning his back to me. I can hear him fastening his pants back up. I'm shocked, my thoughts disheveled, but one thing sticks out in my mind. I don't want what we just shared to end already.

"What are you doing?" I ask, my voice weak. I don't want him to go, I don't want him to run away from me, not after I've caught a glimpse of the boy I once knew. I stare at his broad shoulders, his muscles rippling beneath his shirt, his body full of tension.

He wasn't expecting the kiss, or my reaction to him and maybe that's what he needs, to be shocked. I don't really know, but I can't let go of what happened. I'm waiting for an answer, but it never comes, and though I'm not surprised, I am hurt.

"Don't go!" I order, but he's already out the door, slamming it closed shut behind him, leaving me sitting on the bed naked from the waist down with nothing but the memory of his lips on mine. What did we just do? When I feel like my legs are steady enough to hold my weight, I slide off the bed and pick up my discarded clothes. Just as I'm pulling my panties up, the door flies open again.

Cally stands in the doorway her mouth gaping open, betrayal and hurt in her now cold gaze. "You knew I liked him! How could you do this to me? I thought you were my friend."

"It's not like that, Cally." And it's not. She wouldn't understand that though. No one would. No one knows of the past we share.

She crosses her arms over her chest, and I can tell she doesn't believe me. I reach for my yoga pants, feeling slightly exposed and a bit humiliated. I start to pull them on when she starts to talk again.

"Yeah, right," she scoffs. "Because he was in here a really long time, and you're missing a lot of clothes for someone who didn't just get laid. I really thought better of you, I guess I was wrong."

She turns around and leaves and for a second time tonight, my door is slammed shut.

I sag back down onto my mattress, feeling as if I'll never do anything right again. Remington is out to break my heart all over again and Cally thinks I betrayed her.

I shake my head, thinking of my brother and father at that moment. I wish Jackson was still alive. He would give me the advice I need, he would kick Remington's ass for acting the way he is. But he's gone and so is my father, and with nowhere else to turn, I do the only thing I can do...I cry.

## 5

## REMINGTON

*I* speed-walk across campus, even though my heart is racing as if I'm running at full speed. My mind reeling, my thoughts in complete disarray.

*What the fuck just happened?*

I don't understand. I was there to teach her a lesson, to hurt her, to rip her heart out like she ripped out mine. Everything I did, everything I said to her, was supposed to lead to her hating me as much as I hate her. I wanted to see the same pain in her eyes that I'm feeling...that I feel every single time, I look at her. Instead she looked at me with pity and regret.

Then she kissed me, fucking kissed me.

And the worst part of all...I kissed her back.

I fucking kissed her. I haven't kissed anyone in three years. I can't count how many girls I've fucked in that time, but I have never kissed a single one of them. Kissing is too personal, it's what people do when they want to get close, remember the person and if there is one thing I don't want to do with anyone, it is to get close...and especially not with her, not again.

*Why the fuck did I kiss her back?*

I hate her, don't I? My brain tells me I do, but my heart tells me different. My heart tells me I'm angry, confused... but not that I hate her. I lick my lips, her taste still lingering there. My mind wants to scrub that taste from my mouth, while my body wants to revel in it. My thoughts are cluttered with images of her and I need to clear my fucking head and get her out of my mind once and for all.

I try and think about anything but her lips, her eyes piercing mine, the way her pussy clenched around my fingers so tight I thought I was going to die. I crossed a line, one I never crossed with any woman before tonight. I never forced myself on someone, not that I really had to force myself on Jules, it was clear she was more than interested in me, it just was the way I went about it, taking from her, using her body without permission.

It was wrong. It was right. It was fucked up.

As much as I wanted to hurt her, there was no way I could've fucked her without her permission. I wanted to hurt her, rip her heart out, but I didn't want to commit a crime to do it. I liked my women willing, but she didn't have to know that, she could've been thinking I was going to do it the whole time, and she probably was, up until she flipped over and looked into my eyes. She always had the power to see right through me.

*Fuck.* I fist my hair in my hands in frustration, pulling tightly at the locks wishing they could give me the answers I need. Why can't she just go away? Her memory haunts me and now she's more than a memory, she's here, right under my nose ruining me all over again.

I pull out my cell, the group chat with all the guys pops up telling me I have over twenty missed notifications, but I don't care. The bet is the last thing going through my mind right now. I want to win, but I'm concerned about the effect that Jules has on me, and I need to get that shit in order before I even try and fuck her.

The thought of fucking her turns my cock to steel. I've wanted her since we were teenagers, and I could've had her so many times over. I wanted her to be my first, my last, my always. I grit my teeth. I need to find a way to forget her, to forget her memory. I've tried everything over the years - pussy, beer, weed. Nothing has ever dislodged her from my mind.

Focusing my attention on my phone, I find Cally's name and shoot her a text. I know she's not my bet, but finding out she was Jules' roommate only added to the fun. Now I have an in, into Jules' life, into making her as miserable as possible. I ask Cally to meet me at the diner for breakfast tomorrow and to no surprise she replies right away, telling me she would love to.

When I get to the house, all the guys are in the living room drinking beer. I grab two from the fridge, chugging one right away to settle my nerves, while sitting down with the second one. I'm consumed with a need to find a cure for her memory. I have to let go of the past we shared, and I can't think of a quicker way than getting hammered drunk with the guys. It's not a cure, but it will do for now. I down the second beer, and then another, and another until I'm five beers in a buzz finally starting to kick in.

"You okay, Rem?" Thomas asks, concern etched into his features as he eyes the beer cans sitting on the table in front of me. Typically, I don't drink that much, and especially not on school nights, but tonight I need all the beer I can get.

I nod my head, hating that for once I'm forced to lie to my friends.

"Never been better, Tom. Never been better."

∼

There's a throbbing behind my eyes that refuses to go away. It feels like I got ran over by a truck last night, and then it backed up and drove over me again. My muscles are stiff, and my stomach is churning. Drinking half a fridge full of beer probably wasn't the best idea but it sure as shit got the job done. By the end of the night I wasn't thinking about Jules, matter of fact, I didn't think about anything because it wasn't long until I was blacked out on the living room floor. Not one of my most flattering moments, I suppose.

After a quick shower, teeth brushing and change of clothes I'm feeling better. I walk into the diner and cringe, the bell above the door seems ten times louder today than it ever has before. Surveying the booths, I spot Cally sitting at a table by the window, she lifts her gaze to me, a bright smile on her lips. I walk over to where she is sitting and slide into the seat across from her.

"Hi." Her high pitch voice pierces my ears and I bite my tongue withholding the need to tell her to shut up. That, of course, wouldn't help my cause so instead I fight through the throbbing in my head and pretend to be interested in whatever she has to say.

"Hey, sorry I stormed out last night." I give her a soft smile. I need her to believe that I'm sorry that I intended to come over to see her and not Jules.

"Oh, it's okay," she says, but the frown on her face tells me she is anything but *okay*.

"Did Jules say something? About what happened last night?"

Cally's frown deepens further and it's painfully obvious she doesn't want to talk about her roommate with me. But being the asshole I am, I couldn't care less what she wants.

"She didn't say anything last night, not really. We kind of had a falling out. I guess she wasn't as good of a friend as I thought she was." She sighs, shrugging her shoulders as if she's disappointed.

*Don't I know how that feels.* I don't say shit though. My beef with Jules is mine alone, and if anyone gets to hate her, it's me.

"It's just shitty since we even let her stay for free with us. I should kick her out, but I would feel horrible doing so since her brother and father just died..."

*Wait, what?* That catches my attention and I slowly blink, trying to comprehend what I just heard. Cally continues talking, but I can't understand the words that are coming out of her mouth, not after what she just said. For a moment I'm frozen in my seat, and everything around me blurs.

*Jackson. Her father. Dead.*

"Are you okay?" Cally drags me back to reality after a moment. "You look a little pale."

"Did she say that?" I almost yell at Cally, but somehow keep the tremor out of my voice. She doesn't need to know the effect Jules has on me.

"Say what?" She wrinkles her nose.

"Did Jules tell you that her brother died?" I clarify, speaking slowly so she can understand me better.

"Ah, yes, that's why she moved here after the semester started, at least that's what she told me. Wouldn't be surprised if she's lying though, since talking to her yesterday..."

"Do you know where Jules is right now?"

"Bio lab, I think, why?"

I slide out of the seat and start walking away.

"What...what are you doing? What's wrong? Did I say something? Don't tell me you called me here to get closer to her," Cally calls after me, frustration coating her words, but I don't bother turning around. I've got all the information I need from her. She's Cole's problem now.

As I walk out of the diner, all I can think is that she is lying.

Jules is lying, she has to be. Jackson isn't dead...he can't be. I hated them both equally when they left but finding out your ex-best friend might be dead. Yeah, that's a kick to the fucking balls, and because of this little stunt, Jules has earned herself another session with me. I jog across campus to get to the biology building. I need to confront her right fucking now I don't care if she's in class, fuck I don't care if she's in the middle of her fucking final.

No one will pay me any attention. I do what I want when I want. The professors turn a blind eye to all the bad shit I do, and believe me, I do a lot of bad shit. But what teacher in this school wants to lose out on all that extra cash my dad is pouring into this place.

By the time I get to the lab, the anger inside of me has built up and I'm damn near ready to explode. I rip the door open and stomp into the lab. I scan the classroom. I can feel eyes on me, but I only care about the big blue ones, connected to a heart-shaped face, framed with blonde curls in the last row.

"Why would you fucking lie about something like this?" I curl my lip and stomp through the classroom heading straight for her. Her eyes go impossibly wide and her expression holds nothing but confusion. Always lying...always playing innocent. One day it's going to get her hurt... one fucking day.

# The Bet

"Telling people your brother is dead? What kind of sick fucking joke is that? Why the fuck would you lie about something like that?" Steam is billowing from my ears, and I want to smash my fist through something, destroy the room, break a desk or three. This woman brings out the worst in me, the absolute worst.

She gets up, gathering her things, ignoring me as if I didn't just yell at her in front of an entire classroom full of people. Hushed whispers fill the room as silence blankets us.

"Answer me," I shout, slamming my fist down on the first desk it connects with. Gasps fill the room and I see the professor out of the corner of my eye watching me. If she's smart, she will keep her fucking mouth shut.

Jules starts walking toward me, and I have to remind myself to calm down. Breathe. Don't react. Just breathe. She pushes past me and walks out of the building and I let her, afraid that if I grab her now, things might end badly. Following behind her, my feet slap against the pavement.

*Who the fuck does she think she is?*

She makes me insane, with need, with anger...I'm losing my damn mind because of her. It doesn't take long for me to catch up to her and when I do, I can't stop myself. I grab her by the shoulders, my fingers wrapped so tight around her slender arms I'm sure I'll leave bruises.

I don't want to hurt her, not physically at least, but she's driving me mad. She closes her eyes as if she can't fathom looking at me, but I need her to fucking look at me. I need to see the look in her eyes when she tells me the truth.

"Open your fucking eyes and tell me why you would lie? Why would you make up something like that? It's fucking pathetic, even for someone like you." I shake her small body, her silky blonde curls escape from behind her ears and her big eyes blink open.

Her gaze locks with mine and that's when I see it. The pain, the anger, and loss all staring back at me. It's heartbreaking the way she's looking at me and I want to pull her into my arms, kiss her and tell her everything is going to be okay.

"I didn't lie, Jackson is dead," she says quietly, her voice breaking at the end.

I can feel a wave of grief and sadness building up, ready to crash over me, but I push it away. Not ready to face all of that yet, I let anger overcome me instead and I release her with a shove. She stumbles backward and I almost reach out for her again to steady her, but instead, I shove my hands into my pockets to stop myself.

"And you didn't think that I deserved to know? Why wouldn't you tell me that my best friend is dead?"

She laughs, but it's not laughter she's emitting, it's pain, thick and heavy. "Oh, when would you have liked me to do that, Remington? When you ordered me to stay out of your way and you acted like we didn't know each other or maybe when you told me not to call you by the name I've called you since I was five? Oooo, maybe when you had your fingers deep inside me or when you all but told me to leave you the fuck alone or face the consequences? Please, tell me, which time should I have dropped that fucking bomb on you?"

My teeth grind together, and for once in my fucking life, I don't know what to fucking say. I've been beating her down with my words, trying my best to make her feel as weak as she makes me feel, and this whole time she's been suffering the loss of her brother, my best fucking friend. Losing Jackson was almost as tough as losing Jules, she had my heart, had me wrapped around her tiny little finger.

"He was my best friend..." I say more to myself than her.

"Yeah, so was I but you seem to have forgotten that part of your life." She shoves at my chest to get me out of the way, her touch zings through me, restarting my heart and I listen to her feet, every step, as she walks farther and farther away from me.

Her footsteps sound just like they did all those years ago when she walked away, hollow, leaving a gaping hole inside my chest.

It takes me a long moment to regain my composure. Tears sting my eyes. I look around wiping at my eyes. I don't fucking cry, and I haven't since the day they both left me. I think about Jules, about the pain I'm causing her, about my revenge, about my own selfish needs. I've only ever loved her...her and my mother, and my mother never came back for my brothers and me, she's never even fucking called.

Jules, she's here now...but how can I forgive her for leaving me in the first place?

I've never been so conflicted in my life...so out of control.

I can't let go of the pain. I can't be weak by giving into her touch, her tears, her angelic face. But the thought of hurting her more than she's already been hurt sickens me.

I hate myself for doing this to her...for doing this to me but had she not left me, had she not shattered my heart, we wouldn't be here right now.

## 6

## JULES

*I*'m so freaking tired I can barely put one foot in front of the other. I've never been so exhausted, mentally and physically. I didn't sleep a wink last night and I couldn't bring myself to eat anything this morning either. I spent most of the last twelve hours crying and I'm sure it still shows in my face now. At least that's why I hope everybody is looking at me with a disgusted expression on their face.

I try to ignore all the stares and whispers everywhere I go, but it gets exponentially harder to do so when I get to calculus and the whispers start to sound more like screams.

"She lied about her brother being dead…who does that?"

I don't even turn my head to see who is talking.

"I heard she did it for sympathy, so she could stay somewhere for free."

I should have known that what happened yesterday in bio would spread through the gossip web like wildfire. And it should come as even less of a surprise that everybody thinks I'm the bad guy. Of course, Remington can do no wrong, god forbid the asshole take responsibility for his actions. I mean who calls someone out like that in front of a whole classroom full of people? A bully that's who.

Tears prick at my eyes thinking about him.

*No, I'm not going to cry again.*

"I bet she didn't even have a brother..." someone whispers behind me and somehow hearing those words hurt more than any other comment I've heard today.

Call me a liar and a cheater. Call me a bitch or a whore, but somebody telling me that my brother never existed at all is too much. All I have left of him are memories and for someone to say that those are not real, causes the hole in my chest to ache so badly I can barely breathe. I get up from my seat and walk out of the classroom before the professor even opens his book.

I can feel eyes on me, and it literally has my stomach churning, acid rising in my throat with every step I take. I don't care if I fail every single class right now.

All I want to do is curl up in my bed and cry my eyes out. I don't want to be around these people or listen to their pitiful rumors. It doesn't take long for me to make my way back to the house, and the second I walk in the door, things get even worse.

"Jules, we need to talk," Cally says while glaring at me.

"Cally, please, I can't do this with you right now," I choke out, pushing past her. I walk into my room hoping she doesn't follow, but of course, I wouldn't get that lucky.

"Listen, I think you should find a new place to stay, this isn't working out."

I fight back the tears, trying to hold them in. This entire day has been shit, and now I come home to this.

"Okay, I'll pack up my stuff," I tell her just so she will stop talking to me. I close my bedroom door in her face, and sag down onto the bed, placing a pillow over my face. The tears fall, and they just keep coming with no end in sight.

How can one person have so many tears?

*"Jules!" Remington called my name. I could hear the laughter in his voice. "Come out." My heart was racing out of my chest. I had never remained hidden this long.*

*"Did you find her yet?" I heard my brother ask.*

*"Nope...she's switched up her hiding spots." His words made me smile. At the end of each day, I went home with my cheeks hurting from smiling so much. The sound of branches breaking off in the distance told me my brother was walking away to look elsewhere.*

*I nibbled on my bottom lip and waited with bated breath for Remington's footsteps to follow. My brow furrowed after a few minutes, and I popped my head out from behind the tree I had been hiding behind for the last ten minutes.*

*As soon as I did, I spotted Remington, his big green eyes dazzling in the summer sun.*

*"Found you!" he yelled, and a pout formed against my lips.*

*"I would've won if you just walked away." I knew I shouldn't be mad, it wasn't like they never let me win, but I was so close to doing it on my own this time. If only I had more patience.*

*Remington crossed the ten feet that separated us, his hands reaching for me out of instinct. He always protected me, cherished me, and I would consider him to be like another brother if I didn't always picture myself kissing him.*

*"If it helps any, I had no idea where you were hiding, Jules. I just knew I couldn't leave you out here alone." And just like that, I wasn't*

upset over losing anymore. I licked my lips and peered up in Remington's eyes.

"Looks like you lost again." Jackson's teasing voice filled my ears, and Remington pulled away as if he knew that my brother would kick his butt for touching me. It had happened before, they fought a couple of times over boy stuff, stuff they always told me was none of my business.

"Shut up, J," Remington growled, and I merely snickered.

I was pretty sure I loved Remington Miller more than ever that day.

The memory from that day and all the other happy memories seem as if they're from a distant world, a different life, one that is fading away with each passing day. I lean over the edge of the bed and grab the box from underneath it. Setting it on the bed in front of me, I take a minute to ready myself to open the lid. I already feel broken, Remington, taking the last of my whole pieces and shattering them with his assault on me yesterday.

I open the box and stare at the picture laying on top. I take a moment to stare at it, to feel the memory from that day. It's Jackson on his most recent birthday, he is smiling at the camera, not a worry in the world. His smile is infectious, bright, and he looks happy, beyond happy.

His blue eyes gleam, and I'll never forget what he said to me that night. He hugged me, kissed me on top of the head like he always did. Had I known it would be my last hug, my last conversation with him, I would've hung on a little longer. I tell myself over and over again that there was no way we could have possibly known that this was the last picture we would ever take of him? Or the last time we would ever see him alive.

With shaking hands, I grab the stack of pictures and spread them out on the bed. Most of them are of Jackson and me, but there are a few of all three of us and some of just Remmy and I.

One picture is of us laying in the grass, we are both looking at each other with nothing but love. I remember the way I felt that day, the emotions coursing through my veins.

I thought I would be with him forever. I thought he would be my first, my last, my everything. We look like different people in those pictures and not just because we have grown up since they were taken. It's more like the things that have happened to us changed us. Changed the way we feel and think...changed how we look at the world.

I don't know how long I stare at those pictures, wishing with everything inside of me that I could go back to those days, and that they weren't just a memory.

I wish I could see my brother again, see Remmy again...the Remmy I know...the one that loved me and cared for me. God, do I wish he was the same person. I don't want to admit it, but I need him. I need him so badly right now.

A knock on the door pulls me from my fantasy world. This isn't going to be good. I look up, just as the door comes swinging open and Cally walks in. I wipe the tears staining my cheeks with the back of my hands as if that would make them disappear. Anybody with eyes can see I've been crying from a mile away and that I'm on the verge of a mental break down.

"I thought you were packing not looking at pic..." Her words catch in her throat when she looks down at the pictures spread out across my bed. Her green eyes go wide with shock and maybe even a little confusion and for a moment she just stares with her mouth gaping open.

"Is that...?" She closes her mouth and blinks as if she can't really believe what she was just about to ask, or what she's seeing.

"Cally...I never meant to hurt you. I know you like him...it's hard not to, believe me, I know, but I've loved Remmy since we were kids... since before I knew what love even was."

"You've known him since you were kids? And you really do have a brother?"

I nod my head in response.

"These pictures are from when we were growing up. We used to be neighbors. He was best friends with my brother and me. There was a time when I couldn't even imagine not having them in my life and now, I have neither of them."

"What happened?" Her question is like a knife to the gut, and I find myself gulping, for air, for words to answer her question, for a damn reason as to why it all fell apart.

Is there really an answer to what happened? I've always looked at it as a learning curve to life. I couldn't stop my parents from getting a divorce, from my mother working, or my father moving away. I couldn't stop our friendship, or mine and Remington's love from crumbling to pieces. There was literally nothing I could do to save us, and I think he knew it too. I think he knew it and so he hurt me before I could hurt him.

"We moved, is the short answer. My brother is a story for another day." I give her a sad smile. I don't dare mention the fact that Remington's mother leaving only made matters worse. She chose liquor over her children, and the person it hurt most was Remington because when no one else in their family believed she would get better, he did. He believed so much he thought he could make her better, he thought he could fix her...but, in the end, he couldn't.

"Well, that explains a lot, I guess." Her tone tells me there is more to what she is saying, and I can't help but wonder what I am missing.

"What do you mean?"

She looks at me sheepishly. "Well, Remington texted me to meet up with him yesterday. I thought he wanted to hang out, but he wouldn't shut up about you. I figured it was because of what happened earlier that day... I mean, I like him, Jules, but having a crush on someone and loving them are two completely different worlds."

*And boy did I know that.*

When I don't say anything she says, "I'm really sorry, I didn't see this before."

"I don't blame you, you didn't know, and I don't expect you to understand. I just don't want you thinking I was trying to steal him out from underneath you. I'm not like that. The only reason I didn't say anything is because chances are Remington and I will never be anything more than enemies now. He hates me, and he's pretty close to achieving his goal of making me hate him back."

Cally frowns. "Since he started school here, he's been lost, angry at the world. He's a really sweet guy sometimes, but only when he wants something. But if he's not fucking you, then he generally doesn't want anything to do with you."

"I know. I discovered that really quickly. I made the mistake of hugging him on my first day. He doesn't like to be touched..."

"Looking at these pictures, it seems he didn't always used to be that way. I mean he's hugging you and holding your hand in quite a few of those images." She pauses, smiling at me, and I know we're back to being on the same page again.

"I don't know if it's true, but I heard a rumor that he never kisses the girls he screws. Maybe that has something to do with you?" She lifts her eyebrows in question, like I could provide her with an answer.

A nervous knot forms in my belly. I doubt what she is saying is true, how could you have sex with someone and not kiss them, *ever?* Remington doesn't take me as the type of guy to not kiss a woman. Then I think back to his reaction from when I kissed him... how cold he was at first...how unresponsive. I thought maybe it was because he didn't want to kiss me, but now maybe it was because of something else entirely.

"How do you not kiss someone the entire time you're having sex with them?"

Cally grins and I feel like I'm giving myself away and the fact that I'm still a virgin. "It's easy. Just do them from behind and you don't have to worry about it. If they can't see you, and their lips are nowhere near yours, then you don't risk them touching. And like I said, the rumor is strong around here, since that's something he does often."

I don't say it out loud, but that seems so cruel, so unkind, not that doggy style is bad, I'm sure it's great. I mean, I don't have any experience myself, but it seems to be popular enough. I still can't imagine the intentions behind the position, why he would choose it...that's cruel.

"That seems like an asshole thing to do," I mutter, picking up the pictures and placing them back inside the box.

Cally watches me for a long moment, and I'm thankful to have her as a friend today, as someone I can confide in.

"Well, Remington is kind of an asshole, and obviously nothing like the person you used to know... and I know you know that Jules, but something tells me he won't change simply because you showed up."

She doesn't have to tell me that.

"I know, believe me, I know. I'm confident the boy I fell in love with in those pictures is nothing but a fading memory, one that will eventually be washed away and replaced with the cruel man he blames me for becoming."

"Don't let him blame you. In the end, we all have our own choices to make. He chose to become the person he is today, and no matter what, he can't put that hate on you. Life goes on, and it's obvious he's still living in the past."

"I won't. I haven't let him blame me thus far." I give her a smile.

"You don't have to move out. I mean unless you want to. I was just being a bitch, but I don't want you to move out. Bridget and I love having you here."

"Thank you," I whisper. Moving back in with my mother would suck, but I would do it if I had nowhere else to go. My father left everything to my brother and me, but since my brother is gone now, it all fell into my lap, the house, the life insurance.

"Take all the time you need, and if you ever want to talk, you know where my room is. I'm sorry for being an asshole. I liked Remington, I really did, but after seeing all of this, I know I don't stand a chance." She gives me a reassuring smile before slipping out of the bedroom, leaving me alone with my thoughts.

I should tell her I don't have a chance in hell either.

Remington isn't my savior, my white knight anymore. He's a man now, cloaked in darkness, drowning in the waters of his past, and if I'm not careful, he'll drag me down with him.

## 7

## REMINGTON

Sleep doesn't come easy, and I find myself tossing and turning in bed all night, making classes almost unbearable the next day. I watch for Jules at every corner, even as I meet up with the guys for breakfast. Ever since she kissed me, I can't get her taste off my lips. Every time I close my eyes, I feel her soft body against mine, my fingers deep inside her.

When I walk into English the next day, the first thing I do is look for Jules. It's stupid I know, since I hate her and all, but I can't stop my body's reaction to her. I need to see her, make sure she's still mine to torment.

When I find her, I almost grin, the energy inside me sizzles and expands outward. My heart starts to beat out of my chest, and the heavy air surrounding me that sticks to my lungs, making it hard to breathe lifts.

I take my seat in the row behind her and tap my pen against my notebook. I have no intention of paying an ounce of attention to the teacher today. I'm simply here for Jules. My leg starts to bounce up and down as more students filter into the room, and Layla shoves down into the seat beside me.

Jules got me right in the fucking emotions when she told me her brother died. Jackson was one of my closest friends, the only one that seemed to matter beside Jules. Since her confession, I haven't been able to sleep, or even eat. I feel out of sorts which isn't normal since I don't generally give a fuck about anyone or anything.

"Rem," Layla greets me, resting her hand against my thigh. I give her a chin nod, but keep my eyes on Jules' blonde curls. I wish I could've seen her face when she fell apart on my hand the other day. *No.* No, I don't. I don't want to see her happy. But I do... My heart and my brain are waging war on my body, and I don't fucking know who is going to win.

"I missed you. You never texted me," Layla whines in my ear.

"Sorry, I forgot." I grin, even though I feel annoyed. I'm good at hiding my emotions, at getting what I want.

"It's okay...I forgive you." She nibbles on her bottom lip and leans into my face. Before Jules showed her face here, all that would've mattered was finding my next lay, or getting my dick sucked, but now I'm more annoyed with Layla's presence than I am turned on by it.

Layla's fingers move over my jeans until she reaches my cock. I don't stop her, what's the point. If she wants to touch me then great, so long as she keeps her fucking mouth shut.

"I want to suck your cock, Rem," Layla purrs in my ear. But all I can hear is Jules tapping her pen against her notebook angrily. She can hear Layla, and I'd bet anything that's annoying the fuck out of her.

*Hurt her. Break her.* The words bounce off my skull inside my mind.

"Jules," I whisper her name, watching as her back straightens at the sound of my voice.

She can hear me, I know she can, and I wonder what she's thinking. I wonder what my voice does to her. Do I make her as insane as she makes me? Does she want to throttle me and kiss me all at the same time?

*Kiss me?* I sneer at myself. *No.* No kissing. Not even Jules.

"Jules," I taunt once more. "I know you can hear me..." I watch her tiny hand clench into a fist. Good...so fucking good. Her reaction to me makes my dick hard.

I continue taunting her, all while ignoring Layla's incessant whines in my ear.

"Jules...are you thinking about my fingers...?" I lean forward, and whisper, my breath fanning against her ear. She smells like vanilla and sugar, so fucking warm and inviting, so fucking much like the Jules from my past. "Do you think about my fingers deep inside you...?"

"Stop." She breaks, swiveling around, her voice snapping through the air, and much louder than a whisper. Mr. Johnson turns from the board, his eyes on Jules.

"Jules, is there something that you would like to share with the class?" At her name being called, and all eyes turning to her she shifts in her seat, turning back around, but I can't miss the soft blush that starts to rise in her cheeks at being called out.

"N-No...I'm sorry..." she says, trying to make her voice strong.

"Good. If you didn't come here to learn then you can leave," he announces, his tone pissing me off instantly. It's bad enough he called her out in class, but now he's fucking being a dick by insinuating that she doesn't want to fucking learn.

"Lay off," I growl at him, slapping my palm on the table. "She was just answering one of my questions."

"Mr. Miller, it's so nice of you to join in on the conversation. Maybe you would like to take you and your attitude out of my classroom."

Now I'm more than pissed...I'm fucking angry.

"Excuse me?" I growl.

"You heard me. Out. And when you come back into my classroom, you better have a better attitude."

I blink, my jaw flexing. Did this bastard just fucking talk to me like I was dirt beneath his feet?

*What the fuck!*

"Whatever." I roll my eyes and grab my shit, walking out of the classroom, while feeling every pair of eyes on me. He's not worth the fucking paperwork or ticket. I rip the door open, and then I slam it closed as I walk out, making certain I've made a fucking scene.

Once in the hall I try and take a couple calming breaths. What the hell is wrong with me? I stuck up for Jules without even thinking about it. I shake my head and thread my fingers through my hair.

*She's nothing.*

*She's everything.*

My heartbeat thunders loudly in my ears. She's lost everything...

Every-single-fucking-thing.

I try and reason with myself. Maybe I can't forgive her completely, but I could stop being a fucking asshole. I could try and make her life easier. I can't deny that I want her body. I want every fucking chick's body, but... friendship, anything close to it, is a no. It has to be. When the doors open and students start to filter out, I realize I've just stood here for the last five fucking minutes internally battling with myself.

*Talk to her.*

Fuck, okay. *I'll talk to her,* I tell myself. I shove my hands into the pockets of my jeans and wait. This is a bad idea. But all I'm doing is talking. Layla appears, a sneer in her eyes. She's pissed, I could tell without even looking at her. A second later, Jules walks out, and for a moment I do nothing but stare at her.

Her blonde locks are curled at the ends like always, she's wearing a pair of killer skinny jeans and thigh-high brown boots, with a cream-colored blouse that makes her eyes pop. Her face falls the moment she spots me looking at her, but I don't care. Running from me isn't an option and I hope she fucking gets that now.

"Jules," I say her name, and it almost comes out like it used to, need and care woven through each letter of her name.

"What do you want, Remington?" She whirls around on me, fire in her blue orbs. "Did you stay back to taunt me some more? What could you possibly have to say that you didn't already?" I'm taken aback by her anger, by the sadness she emits. Give me her fire, her fear, any day, but sadness, no, I don't want her fucking sadness.

"No. I just wanted to talk. I'm sorry about that back there." Her eyebrows lift in surprise.

"Sorry...wow..." She seems as taken aback by my apology as I am.

"I just wanted to talk...wanted to..." The words hang between us. I don't actually know what I wanted to do. I hadn't thought this far ahead.

"What do you want to talk about? How to torment me the best? Get me in trouble? Yell at me? Blame me for your own fucking problems?"

Her response pisses me off. If she's looking for a verbal fight, she's seconds from getting one.

"Watch it, Jules. I can and will still crush you. Don't take my kindness for weakness." I say the words even though I know I'll never be able to follow through with them. Finding out about her brother changed something inside me. It lessened the fucking hate I have for her somehow.

She shakes her head, and I want to grab onto her and pull her into my chest, whether to hug her or crush her to death, I haven't decided yet.

"You know what, Remington? I've come to the conclusion that you're beyond saving. The person I used to know, the man that never would've taken from me, or hurt me, no longer lives inside of you, and that's sad, so fucking sad."

My nostrils flare and I feel the fury brewing inside me like a storm whipping across the plains. She knows just what to say to set me off.

"I should've fucking known talking to you was a mistake. You're nothing but a fucking ice queen." I shake my head, but I can't seem to dislodge her stupid fucking words.

"Yup, cold as fuck..." She walks up to me and I have half a mind to grab her, to force her to listen to me. "And all because of one fucking boy who ruined me."

"Ruined you?" I laugh, and this time, I do grab her. She gasps as my hand circles around her arm and I push her forcefully against the brick exterior wall. Then I cage her with my body, making certain she can't escape me. She looks like a damn doe caught in the headlights of a car that's seconds away from taking her life.

I lean into her face, hating how intoxicating she is, the way that my body reacts to hers. I hate that even after all this time she still has power over me.

"All I was doing was being nice, and you had to go and be a bitch..." My eyes move to her throat. I can see her quickening pulse. *Is she scared?*

"No, you weren't trying to be nice. You were trying to get me in trouble. You were being a heartless prick."

I pull back, one of my already clenched fists tightening as anger pumps through my veins.

"Don't turn this around on me," I croak.

"Why not?" She tilts her head, somehow gaining the strength to smile, and I want to hurt her. I want to hurt her as she hurt me. "All the choices you made in your life led to this very moment, Remmy. They all lead to this. You're trying to blame me because you can't handle that you are the one responsible for your own life. You chose this."

And just like, that she's provoking me, pushing me over the edge, mixing the already out of control fire with gasoline, making the flames bigger, the fire roar. I raise my fist and slam it into the wall right beside her head. The pain of the hit vibrates up my arm, making my teeth rattle inside my head. I'm seething now, my nostrils flare, and I sneer, staring down at the once strong woman who now looks like she might piss her pants.

"Do you want to see me lose control? Do you want me to hurt you?" I barely get the words out. Why does she have this much control over me? I slam my fist against the brick wall again, and she flinches like I might hit her.

*Would I?* The thought terrifies me and for a moment all I see is me losing my cool with her, me putting my fucking hands on her. I want to hurt her...but not like that... Seeing the fear in her eyes makes me pull away. I want her fear but not this way and within seconds, she's scurrying away, leaving me in the same spot she left me the other night.

"Weak," I grit out. "She makes you fucking weak." And then I let the rage consume me. I pummel the wall letting my fists scrape against the unforgiving brick. My knuckles bleed, my bones ache, but the fire inside me is still burning hot, it roars, and the flames flicker up toward the sky.

*All I wanted to do was talk.* I squeeze my eyes shut, wishing she never showed her face here. I know I'll have to talk to her, eventually...I can't stay away from her, she's like a bad drug. She'll ruin me if I let her, she's already done so once before, and yet I'm still dumb enough to try and talk to her, to try and reason with her.

Maybe I could get her kicked out of school? Do I really want to go that far? I turn around and start walking back toward the frat house. Instead of pissing my brother off by showing up at his office, I pull out my cell and dial his number.

"Shouldn't you be in class?" His deep voice resonates through the phone.

"What are you, my gatekeeper?" I scoff.

"No, but I am your brother, which is kind of like the same thing." His response makes me laugh, lightening the feeling Jules left me with.

"I have a question."

"If it's about her, I don't want to hear it."

"What? Wait, you knew she was here?" My mouth pops open and I stop dead in my tracks. I should turn around and go to the administrative building just to slug him in the face.

"I work for the college, Rem, yeah I knew she was here. I just didn't think you would notice or care since you haven't even talked to her in three years. You're way too busy with other stuff, I figured she would sneak right under your nose."

"While you thought fucking wrong," I growl, feeling betrayed by my own blood. I know I shouldn't be mad, because honestly, it's not his fault, but I am furious, and I have to take it out on someone.

"Did you do something? Is that why you're calling? I swear, Rem, if you did something, I'm telling Dad. She just lost her brother and her dad." And just like that, my heart cracks in two.

"You knew that too..." The words come out in a whisper.

"Well yeah, her mom told me, not her. She came in and helped Jules do some paperwork. Anyway, you didn't answer my question...did you do something? Why are you calling? You never call unless you've done something."

I shake my head and squeeze my cell phone hard enough to break the thing. "Never mind. I'll deal with it."

"Deal with—"

I cut off his question by hanging up the phone. I can't have Jules removed from the school, and that only seems to irritate me more. My brother knew about her brother before even I did. My brothers have always loved Jules, my father cherished her like the daughter he never had, which of course made losing her hurt ten times fucking harder.

I tip my head back toward the sky, wondering what the fuck I'm going to do? I have to talk to her, try and create some type of truce, but even I don't really want that. It's the stupid fucking organ throbbing in my chest that wants it.

"Jules," I say her name, letting it roll off my tongue like it used to all while wondering if I'll ever be able to look at her and say her name without feeling heartbroken.

# 8

## JULES

Up and down, up and down. That's what my chest does as I try and calm my erratic breathing. Refusing to let Remington's anger toward me ruin my day. I grab a latte from the coffee shop at the corner before my next class. The caffeine gives me the buzz I need to get through the afternoon. I do everything I can to forget about him. I can't care about him. Not when he's being the way he is. When I arrive for my last class of the day, I spot Cole. He greets me with a smile as soon as I sit down.

"Jules."

"Cole," I respond with the same cool tone. I remind myself that he is friends with Remington and that anything I say to him may find its way back to him.

"How are you?"

"Peachy," I respond, taking a sip of my once warm coffee. The professor starts talking, saving me from any more conversation. I focus on taking notes, jotting every little thing down. By the end of class, I have two pages full and I feel like I'm more on track to being my normal self. My phone chimes in my pocket as the professor gives us our assignment, an essay of course.

"This blows. I fucking hate homework," Cole announces.

"I don't think anyone likes homework." I laugh, pulling my phone out, noticing it's a text from Cally. "I don't know about you, but I've never heard someone say 'yay homework, I'm so glad I have to spend three days writing a paper.'" Sarcasm laces my words, and I become distracted with the text from Cally.

**Shark week. Pick me up a piece of chocolate lava cake from the diner, pretty please?**

I stare at the screen smiling for a moment before I type out my reply. I feel eyes on me and look up to see Cole staring right at me. He smiles, but it doesn't reach his eyes, telling me it's a forced smile rather than a genuine one.

"Where you headed?" he asks nonchalantly, shoving his hands into the front of his jeans.

"Diner. It's shark week in our house so…" I trail off and he chuckles.

"I'm headed that way too. I'll walk you." He sounds like the perfect gentleman and maybe he is, I don't know, but I do know that if he's friends with Remington, there has to be something wrong with him.

*You were his friend once too.* My subconscious rears its ugly head and all I can think is they're not the same people anymore. The Remington he is now is no one I would call a friend.

"Sure. That would be nice." I smile politely. The least I can do is be nice to him and give him the benefit of the doubt.

Unlike Remington, he's never given me a reason not to like him.

We walk to the diner making friendly small talk. Cole asks me questions as if he is trying to get to know me, things like what I do for fun, my favorite animal.

He seems really sweet, but somehow, I can't shake the feeling that it's all an act. Maybe I just have trust issues now, mainly thanks to Remington, or maybe my gut is just telling me what I'm not really wanting to see.

We walk into the diner and Cole spots some people who must be his friends. They're already waving us over, and I feel a nervous knot form in my throat.

"Come sit with us." Cole reaches for my hand, attempting to pull me in the direction of his friends.

"I was just going to get something to go. Remember...homework?"

"Come on, just for a minute, you can meet Thomas and his girl. Then you can order from the table." He gives me a dazzling smile and I feel like I should at least go say hi since he did walk me down here.

"Okay," I say, already regretting that I let myself be talked into this.

Cole introduces everybody and as we sit down, I try to smile and not show my lack of interest in them. It's not in me to be this hateful, to not want to get to know someone when I meet them. But I don't have it in me to pretend.

I order a few pieces of chocolate cake to go as soon as the waitress comes by, hoping to just get out of here as fast as possible.

A bad feeling sinks into my stomach, and to make matters worse, Cole lays his arm on the back of the bench behind me, making my skin crawl.

It feels too much like he has an arm around me, and I don't like it. I can feel his body heat close to my shoulders and unlike when Remington touches me, I don't enjoy this. My body is screaming that this is wrong.

I'm completely zoned out of their conversation and when I finally come back to reality, I realize that all three of them are laughing. Even though I have no idea what we are talking about, I chime in laughing too.

I try not to meet their eyes and give away how fake my laughter is, so instead I look out the window. My breath hitches when I see someone walking away from the diner.

I don't see his face, but I don't have to, to know that it's him. Maybe he was meeting them here? I don't think too much into it. I can't allow myself to dwell on thoughts of him without becoming consumed.

"Chocolate cake to go?" The waitress comes out of nowhere, setting a bag on the table in front of me.

"Thank you." I get up from my seat and grab the bag.

"Sorry to rush out but my friend is probably waiting at the door for me...well, for the chocolate cakes," I joke. All I can think about is escaping this diner, and Cole and his friends.

"No worries, Jules. Maybe we can hang out sometime?" Cole says, there's far too much hope in his voice.

I bite the inside of my cheek. *No.* "Sure, maybe...I'll see you around. Bye guys." I give them one last smile before walking out of the diner and back to my place. The walk back to the house doesn't take long, and I actually enjoy the fresh air. It helps clear my head, and for the first time in a long time, I feel like I can breathe, like really breathe. When I finally reach the house, I almost frown, wishing the walk could last forever. I'm not even in the door and Cally is all but ripping the bag out of my hand.

"Bridget, cake!" Cally yells down the hall. I smile...the first genuine smile today as she sits down on the couch and starts gobbling down the cake like she hasn't eaten in years. By the time Bridget and I sit down and get our pieces out, she's already halfway done with hers.

"How was your day?" Bridget asks me in between bites. I tell her about the whole Remington thing that took place last night. I prefer not to keep secrets, and since Remington's hate for me is known campus-wide, it's not like I'm not telling them something they couldn't find out via the gossip circles.

I open my mouth to ask her how her day was just as a knock on the door, interrupts me.

"I'll get it," Bridges says, already on her feet and walking to the front door. With her hand on the knob, she turns to look at me before opening it. "If it's him, I'll send him away unless you want him to come in?"

"I don't want to see or talk to him," I tell her, and she nods before opening the door. I watch her face as she looks at the person behind the door. I see nothing but surprise on her features and I wonder who the hell is on the other side of that door.

"Oh, hey…"

"Hey, is Jules here?" I hear a familiar male voice, but it's not Remington's. I put the slice of cake down on the table beside me and get up from the couch. I know that voice, and the man it belongs to, and I won't believe he's really on the other side of that door until I see him in person.

Bridget gives me a confused look, and I know she doesn't understand if she should slam the door in his face or open it and let him in.

"Let him in," I tell her while I'm already halfway to the door. She swings the door open all the way and Sebastian walks in with a huge smile pulling at his lips when he sees me heading straight for him.

"Hey, little sis." He grins, stepping closer, holding his arms out to me. I close the distance between us with one more step and throw my arms around his middle. Just like Remington, Sebastian towers over me. He engulfs me in one of his famous bear hugs and for a few moments, I forget that any of my troubles exist.

Unlike Remmy, Sebastian hasn't changed much, he's still the same brown-haired, cheesy grinned boy I remember and if he wasn't buried in work all the time, I would have asked him to hang out with me already. He presses a kiss to the top of my head before releasing me.

His hands grab my shoulders, and he studies me, his hazel eyes roaming over every inch of my body as if he is looking for some invisible injury. I stare up at him, the resemblance between him and Remington is almost identical, so close they could almost be twins.

"You look terrible." He frowns. "What did he do? Tell me now, so I know how hard to punch him in his ugly mug."

I sigh. "I see you Miller boys haven't changed when it comes to settling your arguments. Still using your fists to settle everything?"

Sebastian grins at me. "There are other ways to settle arguments?"

I can't help but smile. "Come on in, sit down, and have some cake." I usher him inside and close the door giving him no chance to escape. This is exactly what I needed right now, even more so after all the bullshit with Remington.

"Okay, you had me at cake." He snickers and follows me to the couch where Bridget and Cally are eyeing us curiously.

"Oh, gosh. I'm so sorry…this is Sebastian, Remington's older brother," I explain. "He just started working here, at the dean's office. Seb, these are my roommates Cally and Bridget."

He gives them a small wave. "I'm the better brother." He winks, and Cally coughs, while Bridget rolls her eyes.

"Not hard to be the better brother," Cally says between bites. "No offense but your brother is a major dick."

"None taken, but in his defense, he's a little lost. A little conversation with my fist should straighten him out."

They both look at him like they don't believe him, and I don't blame them, because honestly, I don't really believe him. Remmy is too far gone for his brothers or father to bring him back.

"It was nice to meet you Sebastian, but I have loads of homework to do, so I'll take my cake and leave you and Jules to catch up," Bridget says before getting up and making her way to the bedroom.

"So you came here to tell me you're going to beat up Remmy?" I grin.

"No, I came here to check up on you, which I've been meaning to do since you got here but I've literally been working ten hours every day. Also, I came here to let you know that you are coming to family dinner on Sunday."

"I don't think that's a good idea," I say, shaking my head. "It's not like it used to be. Remmy hates me, and I do mean literally hates me. I don't want to ruin your family dinner."

He gives me a deadpan expression. "Dad wants to see you. He's been asking about you all week and you know if you don't show up, he'll come here himself and get you."

I chew on my lip. It's not like he's lying. Papa Miller will absolutely come here and get me.

"Come on, it's family dinner," Sebastian coos.

"Exactly, *family* dinner..." I say out loud even though I didn't mean to.

"Don't even, Jules. You know you'll always be a part of our family. It's not our fault Remington is a dick. Dad loves you, I love you, we all do, and you know it." His words are bittersweet, and I know he doesn't know how much I need to hear them right now.

But he talks of a time in the past, a time when we were like family and I wish more than anything that I could go back to that. I just don't see how we can, not with all the scar tissue, with all the hate pulsing between Remington and I.

Sebastian's phone starts to ring then, and he rolls his eyes as soon as he hears the ring tone. "You gotta be fucking kidding me." He pulls his phone from his dress slacks and looks at the screen, his frown deepening. "It's fucking work."

He gets up, shaking his head, anger filling his features. "I'm sorry, Jules, I have to go. I'll pick you up at six Sunday night, so please be ready, otherwise I'll send Dad instead," he orders, pointing a finger at me.

He gives me a quick hug and walks out the door a moment later. Only when he is gone, do I realize Cally's still sitting quietly on the couch next to me. She's curled up in a blanket, licking her fork.

"So is he single?" She wiggles her eyebrows, and I shake my head, a laugh emitting from my throat.

"Do not even think about it." I give her a warning look.

"Aw come on, Jules, he's cute."

"Cally..."

She pushes off the couch, her now empty cake container in hand. "Okay, okay. But he's seriously cute."

"He can be cute, and still be left alone. You don't want to get mixed up with those boys." I sag into the couch, trying to think of how I'm going to get out of Sunday dinner with him. Remington will kill me if he finds out that I'm going to be there.

"Of course I want to get mixed up in boys...I just won't get mixed up in that one." She snickers and walks out of the living room.

*What the hell am I going to do?*

The last thing I want to do is see Remington...but I can't let my fear of seeing him stop me from seeing his brothers, from seeing his father. I want to be happy, even if Remington doesn't want me to be and I guess that answers my question.

I'm going to do what Jules wants...

I'm going to make myself happy.

## 9

## REMINGTON

*I* feel like a fucking idiot sitting on the couch waiting for Cole and Thomas to come home so I can ask them what the fuck I saw back at the diner earlier. I know rationally I have no right to be mad at Cole. He's done nothing wrong. She isn't with me now, and he has no idea about the history we share, but that doesn't stop the jealousy from spreading through my chest like a lethal venom.

When the door finally opens and the guys walk in laughing and smiling, I have the urge to jump up and yell at them, what for...I have no idea. I'm acting so irrational it's not even fucking funny.

"Hey, Rem," Thomas greets me, and I give him a head nod.

"Hey," I reply. I have to bite the inside of my cheek to keep from asking them right away what the hell was going on. I don't want to seem like I'm overly curious, or anything, because it's not like me to want any more than a one time fuck.

A lot of the women I've fucked have also fucked all my roommates. It's not unlike us to share, what is, is for me to act jealous. And since I know what that would look and sound like, I hold my tongue. I wait until they get some beer out of the fridge and settle down onto the couch.

*Seems like a good amount of time has passed now.*

"I saw you at the diner. I was walking by, but I didn't want to interrupt your little...whatever that was," I say, keeping my voice flat and uninterested when in reality I'm so fucking interested I want to scream from the rooftops.

"We were just on a little double date, no biggy," Cole says nonchalantly. I grip my beer bottle so tightly I think it might break in my hand. *What the fuck?* I don't understand why it's bothering me so much. Actually I do, but I'm not ready to admit it to myself.

Allen and Kia walk through the door not long after, tossing their backpacks by the door doing the same thing that Cole and Thomas did when they walked in. They each grab a beer from the fridge before settling down onto one of the couches.

"How is everyone's bet going?" Cole asks.

"Well, my chick is immune to bad boy charm." Thomas frowns.

"Mine hissed at me the last time I tried to talk to her." Alan chuckles. "I'm sure when I get her into bed though she'll be nothing but a purring little kitten."

"Way to turn a bad into a good." Kia fist bumps Alan across the living room table and they both break out into laughter.

"Mine's being a bitch. Having a hard time getting her to drop her panties," Cole shakes his head in frustration. "I'm pretty sure she is interested in someone else."

I roll my neck, the tension is thick inside my body. I haven't had sex in days, and my emotions are spiraling out of control, that has to explain why I'm filled with this...this jealous rage.

"How is yours, Rem? I bet you already bagged her, didn't you?" Thomas questions, with a grin on his face.

"Damn fucking straight I did," I grin, and they all hoot, and holler. I don't tell them that I didn't actually fuck Jules, they don't have to know that. All they have to believe is what I tell them.

"Well, where's the proof?" Alan asks, taking a sip of his beer. The thought of them hearing Jules' soft whimpers makes me sick to my stomach. I grit my teeth and shove my pathetic feelings to the side. Jules didn't care when she broke my heart, when she shattered it into a million fucking pieces. She didn't care when she went on a date with Cole... or when I tried to fucking talk to her. She doesn't care about me, or anything that I have to say.

She's the bet, nothing else, nothing more.

"As if I wouldn't get proof..."

I pull out my phone and go through the voice recordings. I find what I'm looking for right away, but my finger hovers over the screen for a few seconds. There is a distinct sick feeling floating around in my stomach even before I hit play. That sick feeling is accompanied by a nagging feeling in the back of my mind telling me that I'm about to make a horrible mistake. *No. Think of your broken heart. Of how badly she hurt you. How much you loved her....and how she didn't stay.*

I shove that feeling down and bury it under a truckload of anger. I concentrate on that feeling, letting it fester, and eat away at all the good inside me, and nothing else, and that's when I hit play on the recording.

We hear my voice first.

"*Should I fuck your pussy or your ass?...Maybe I'll fuck both. Tell everyone you were a whore that begged me to take both of your holes.*"

"*Remington.*" Jules' voice comes from the speaker for the first time and the guys start cheering a little. I feel that sick feeling eating through the anger, through the pain.

"You fucking asshole, why didn't you tell us you already hit it?" Allen whispers while everyone else is still listening.

"*Mmm, your pussy is already wet. You like this, don't you? I bet you aren't even a virgin. I bet you've slept with tons of fuckers just like me. Slept your way through life.*"

"No," Jules says, her voice tiny, weak and the guys cheer again, their grins something I previously would've enjoyed but now I can't see the fun in any of this.

"I knew she was a fucking virgin..." Thomas snickers.

"*Fuck...you're so tight.*" I hiss out and Jules' quiet moans come through next.

I place a hand to my stomach, afraid I might vomit all over the fucking floor. Suddenly I've had enough. I can't listen to this anymore and I definitely can't sit here while the guys listen anymore.

Turning the audio off, I rush from the couch and into the bathroom. I slam the door closed behind me, and barely have a moment before the vomit starts coming. My heart pounds inside my chest as I grip onto the toilet, the sickness pouring out of me. Shivers rack my body, and it feels like I'm actually sick.

Jules will never know what I've done, but it doesn't make it any better, it doesn't change that I took that one single moment between us and turned it around, shared it, just to win a stupid fucking bet and all because I was angry, jealous.

Her words from earlier play on repeat inside my head, "*You know what, Remington, I've come to the conclusion that you're beyond saving. The person I used to know, the man that never would've taken from me, or hurt me, no longer lives inside of you, and that's sad, so fucking sad."*

Tears sting my eyes...she's right, she's so fucking right and I don't know how to fix this. I don't know how to let go of the pain. I thought doing this would make me feel better, maybe even free me from the pain completely. I thought I would be happier knowing that I hurt her, but instead I feel only more pain...I feel like a piece of shit, like I've harmed an innocent individual.

I shake my head, there is no going back now. She is right. I'm fucking doomed. Way past saving. She has no idea how fucking sad my life has become, how lost I am without her. I've lost my one single reason to breathe, and now I'm suffocating, slowly losing the best parts of me.

"You okay, Rem?" I hear someone at the door and wipe at my face with the back of my hand. I can't answer the door like this. I can't let them know how weak I am for this girl.

"Oh, uhhh yeah." I try to keep the pain out of my voice. "I had some Mexican earlier. Pretty sure it's running through me," I lie, knowing I can't go out there right now. I can't face them or let them see me this way.

"Okay, man, just making sure." After what seems like forever, I flush the toilet, wash my hands and walk out of the bathroom.

I grab my phone off the couch and walk into my room. I sink down onto the mattress and stare at the ceiling, wallowing in my pain, wondering how I got to where I am? How I let things get to this point?

∼

THE GUYS and I walk into the house down the street, the party is already in full swing with the island in the kitchen as a makeshift bar and the living room as a dance floor. Thankfully the party isn't at our place tonight. I'm not sure I could handle it if it was.

It's been torture since I shared the audio with the guys. Days have passed, but the sick feeling clings to my bones, my insides like the plague. What I did was wrong...it was wrong with any other girl, but it was really fucking wrong where Jules was considered.

Some loud rap song starts to beat through the shit speakers, vibrating right through me, making the slight throbbing I already have behind my eyes worse.

Thomas grabs me a beer and I open it, taking a small sip. Normally I would be getting shit faced and finding something to sink my dick into, but tonight, the beer won't even be able to numb the pain, and no amount of slickness from another chick is going to help me forget the one person I truly want.

I nod, smile, and talk to people, acting like nothing is wrong, all while I'm slowly being eaten alive inside by guilt. Jules' image haunts me every time I close my eyes, and when my eyes aren't closed, she's right there in real life fucking with my head and my heart.

I've regretted hitting play on my phone so many times that I wished I could go back in time and punch my fucking self for being such a selfish prick. It didn't matter how many times I tried to swallow down the pain she had caused me. I had only hurt myself by letting others in on my sick need to hurt her.

"Oh, hey Rem, I didn't know you were here." Layla saunters up to me, her hips swaying. She wraps her hand around my forearm and leans into me. "It's really loud in here, wanna go upstairs?" she coaxes, batting her eyelashes at me.

"I just got here, maybe later."

She gives me a disapproving pout and before I can stop her, she reaches out, wrapping her other hand around my cock. My dick twitches, but not because of Layla's hand, no, it's because at that exact second, I spot Jules across the room.

"Feels like he wants to go upstairs," Layla coos, stepping even closer while rubbing my dick more vigorously. Of course, in that same moment, Jules looks up and sees me with Layla glued to my side like a leech. Even from across the room, I can see the anger simmering in her eyes right below the hurt and disappointment.

She expects better of me, hell I expect better of me.

When Cally sees me, she takes Jules' arm and pulls her away, and together they disappear into the kitchen. I push Layla off of me and head that way. Now's my chance to apologize for being a fucking asshole over and over again. I weave through the crowd, trying to get to her, but it seems like the forces are fucking against me. When I catch a break in the crowd, I take it, but I make it all of two steps before Cole's frame steps in front of me.

"Hey dude." From his tone alone, I can tell he's nervous. I've known Cole since we started college. There was nothing particularly special about him, but I did consider him to be a friend, at least until he started hanging out with Jules.

"What's up?" I keep my eyes on the entrance to the kitchen.

"Listen." He scratches at the back of his head nervously. "Since you are done with Jules and the bet is over, I'm going to try to get with her," he starts to explain, and already I can feel the jealous rage beating at my chest, waiting to be unleashed.

He smirks, and I want to punch that fucking look right off his ugly face. "I went on a few dates with her and I'm pretty sure I'm going to get some tonight. All I'm asking is, please don't mess this up by pissing her off. She really hates you, man, and I don't want her in a bad mood. Can't get laid if she leaves the party."

"Who said I was done with her?"

Cole's eyebrows lift and he gives me a surprised look. "No one, but I mean it's kind of your thing. You fuck them and leave them. I've never seen you with the same girl twice."

It's not like he's lying. I've never had sex with the same girl twice, and because of that stupid audio, I all but shoved Jules into Cole's and any other asshole's lap.

I shrug, taking a drink from my beer. "Maybe her pussy is just that good."

"I guess, but seriously...not tonight, Rem. I want her. I've worked really hard, and you already won the bet. Let me at least try." Desperation coats every single word, and I don't know why I really care. I can't stop Jules from doing something she wants to do.

She doesn't belong to me, hasn't for awhile. If she kept going on dates with him, she must actually like him. Maybe seeing her want someone else is what I need.

"Sure. I won't interrupt," I grit the words out. Cole gives me a nod and a slap to the back as if I just did him a favor or something.

"Thanks, Rem. I owe you."

Bringing the beer bottle to my lips, I tip it back, guzzling it down. I need all the fucking alcohol I can get if I'm going to be subjected to sitting here, and watching Cole seduce the only girl I've ever loved.

He walks away and in the direction, I was just going to go. I didn't expect her to show up here, parties don't really seem like her thing. I had tried to drag her to a party or two when we were teenagers. She went once and never accompanied me to another.

Like an idiot, I stand there in the middle of the crowded living room staring at the doorway leading into the kitchen.

"Yo Rem! Beer pong?" Alan yells over the music, and I twist around to see the bastard. I find Thomas, Kia, and Alan of course staring at me waiting for my response. I sigh, what the fuck else am I supposed to do? I don't want Layla, and drinking isn't doing it for me tonight. I guess I could leave, but there's no way in fucking hell I'm leaving Jules here, at least not until I'm one hundred percent sure she's hooking up with Cole.

"Rem, you going to play or what?" Thomas yells this time and I shake my head, pulling myself from my chaotic mind.

"Yeah, give me a fucking second," I yell back and walk into the kitchen to grab another beer. As soon as I enter, I feel her eyes on me...they blaze a path of fire up and down my body. I do my best not to look at her, but the pull she has on me is magnetic. My heart literally fucking beats for her, it always has.

I grab a beer from the fridge and look at her out of the corner of my eye. Her and Cally sip on their drinks, laughing at something Cole says. The bastard takes that moment to wrap an arm around Jules, pulling her into his chest. Her body language is off, making it seem like she doesn't want him to touch her, but her smile, the way she's looking up at him as he talks, says otherwise.

*Fuck it.* I toss the cap to my beer over my shoulder and walk back out into the living room to find the guys. I don't deserve Jules anyway...not that Cole does either, but I'm not going to meddle in her life anymore. I've hurt her enough and hurt myself in the process. I can't look at her without feeling like I betrayed her, like I fucking physically slapped her. This is what I get...to be eaten alive by guilt, to be suffocated with shame.

Deep down I know she's right...

I'm not worth saving...

I'm not worthy of her, or love.

I'm just Remington now.

Not her best friend...or her love...not even Remmy.

Just a heartless bastard who took his need for revenge too far.

## 10

## JULES

The music is loud and while the drink in my hand is cold, it does nothing to cool me off. Sweat slicks my body, there are tons of people in this house, that has to be why I feel like I'm literally on fire. My jaw feels funny and I have this constant need to lick my lips for some reason. I have no idea what is going on, but I'm thinking I've had too much to drink.

I look around the crowded room trying to find Cally. She was with me just a little bit ago, or at least I think she was. I set my drink down on the counter. I shouldn't drink any more tonight, in fact, I'm certain I should go home. I feel so off, and unlike myself and I don't like it. My eyes scan over all the faces surrounding me, but none of them are Cally, or even someone I know. The only familiar face is Cole's, and he is standing right next to me. Our eyes lock and a warmth washes over me.

I blink, unable to make the warm feeling go away. Then I smile, and for some reason, I'm just over the moon happy to see him.

"You look like you should sit down, let's go upstairs for a bit," he tells me while his hands run over my lower back. His touch is warm and soothing and sends an electric current of pleasure straight through me. I've never felt anything like this before and all I want is more of it. I nod my head, agreeing and let him usher me up the stairs.

He wraps his arm around me, and I lean into his body wanting more of this weird connection I'm feeling. Earlier, Cole was the last thing I wanted, but now he's the only one that seems to matter. He leads me into a bedroom and deposits me on a bed. In the back of my mind, a tiny voice whispers...telling me I should be scared, that I shouldn't be letting this happen... but the feeling to those emotions never comes, and I don't want to give up the happiness and warmth encompassing me right now.

"You look like you're burning up, are you hot?" Cole's voice has changed slightly. It's darker, but I can't latch onto it, because all I feel is joy with him.

"Yeah." I'm so freaking hot right now I could take an ice bath and still not be cooled off.

"Want to take off some of your clothes?"

His question surprises me. I swallow, but my throat feels like gritty sandpaper.

"I don't know..." I respond, but Cole is already helping me out of my top. I should tell him to stop but his touch feels so amazing and when my shirt is finally off and the cool air washes over my blazing hot skin my need to tell him to stop vanishes.

"Doesn't that feel better?" Cole whispers while slipping my bra straps down over my shoulders before reaching around me to unhook the clasp. I press my hands to his firm chest, but I don't know if it's to push him away or pull him closer. There's this dizzying need, and pressure deep between my thighs that begs to be touched.

"Just relax, baby. I'll make you feel real good. Just relax and lie back," he coaxes gently, pushing me against my shoulders until I'm lying flat on my back, the sheets scratching against my inflamed skin.

"Hot. I feel so hot," I mumble.

"I know, that's why I'm helping you out of your clothes, silly." He flicks the button on my jeans and pulls them down my legs. It feels so great to be free of the harsh fabric, that a moan escapes my lips as soon as they're gone.

"Yeah, that's better." I think I hear him rasp, but I can't be sure. "Why don't you close your eyes for a minute and just enjoy how good this feels?"

I do what he tells me and close my eyes, only instead of the darkness that usually accompanies closing your eyes... I see hundreds of colors dancing across my vision.

When I feel the bed dip next to me, I pry my eyes open and find Cole lying down on the bed next to me. Confusion mars my features... I don't know when he took his clothes off or even how long we've been lying here, but he's shirtless, showing off his toned chest. I look down and find he has also stripped off his jeans.

He's wearing his boxers, and I can feel the soft cotton of my panties against my hips, confirming that they're still there. I open my mouth to say something, but the words never come, and the next thing I know, Cole is crawling over top of me.

Using his knee, he nudges my legs apart before he settles the full weight of his body on top of mine. He feels good, sparks of pleasure rocket through me, but my mind is still confused, telling me I shouldn't want this. It's almost like my body and my mind are not on the same page anymore.

"I think I should go home," I whisper, looking up into his eyes, but they aren't the same eyes I've come to know. They're darker and hold a darkness. I wait for the fear to come, but it never does. I don't understand why I'm not scared, why I'm still lying on the bed.

"No, you don't, you like this. I know you do. Just let me make you feel good and then I'll take you home, promise." His voice drops. His lips find my skin and he peppers sloppy kisses against my throat. His lips on the tender skin is overwhelming my senses, but the voice in my head is nagging, telling me that this is wrong, and it's getting louder with each kiss he gives me.

He grinds his pelvis into my center and I can feel his hardness rubbing between my legs. Why does this feel so good when I know it shouldn't? My body is telling me to give in, to just take this mind-blowing pleasure but my mind, my brain, is fighting back, demanding I stop this.

Cole lifts his head and tries to kiss me, but I twist my head just in time so his lips press against my cheek instead. I know I don't want to kiss him. I've only ever wanted to kiss Remmy.

My best friend. My protector.

*Remington.*

Something inside my brain snaps. I don't want this...I don't want Cole. I've only ever wanted Remington.

"Stop! I don't want this." My voice is much smaller now than I want it to be, but Cole doesn't stop touching me. This is wrong, so wrong.

I shove at his chest, but he doesn't budge, in fact, he uses his weight to press me farther into the mattress, making it hard for me to breathe. His fingers dig into my flesh, holding me in place, making it impossible for me to escape. He's holding me hard enough to leave bruises, but I feel no pain. I feel nothing but this deep primal need to let him keep going. But this isn't me, and he isn't who I want.

"Please, stop," I try again, wishing that Remmy was here now.

I don't want Cole all over me, but I don't have the strength to push him off. I whimper, struggling once more against his grip. His teeth sink into my earlobe and I shove him again.

Suddenly, I hear what sounds like a door opening. My vision is blurry, and I can't tell who it is that's stepped into the room. In the next instant, Cole's body is ripped away and for once I feel like I can breathe. My gaze swings around the bed, trying to figure out what's happening. *Where did Cole go?*

As if my silent prayers were answered, Remmy appears before me. He's standing next to the bed looking down at me with nothing but pure rage in his beautifully haunted eyes. I should probably be scared, but for some reason, all I can feel is an enormous relief. He looks like a Greek god, and normally I would be hating his presence but, in this instance, I just want to wrap my arms around him and ask him why he hates me so much.

"Did you give her something?" His voice sounds like a thunderstorm and the lightning in that storm is about to strike Cole dead.

"I just gave her a little E."

"You gave her ecstasy? What the fuck is wrong with you?" Remmy's voice seems to grow louder and louder with every word he says.

"What's it matter? She wanted it. She was pawing at me, asking to come up here."

Remmy's eyes move between Cole and me, and I wonder what he's thinking. His gaze rakes over my naked body. I should feel the need to cover up, but I don't. I don't understand what is wrong with me, all I know is that there is in fact something wrong with me.

"Is this what you wanted, Jules?" Remmy finally breaks the silence.

"No," I answer honestly. "I asked him to stop, but he wouldn't." Then as if my confession has sparked a forest fire inside Remmy, he's on Cole, his fist smashing into his face. I watch emotionlessly as Remmy pummels his face into the floor, never giving Cole a chance to come up for air.

"I'll fucking kill you for touching her...kill you," he growls. "You're nothing but a piece of shit, a fucking rapist."

"Remmy!" I call out to him, but he's still caught up in his aggression, so I get up from the bed, and pad over to him, my body zinging with pleasure as I grab onto his bulging bicep. My eyes move over Cole's bloody and bruised face, but no emotions come. I should care, it's not like me to not care, but I don't.

"Remmy!" I say his name a little softer this time and he releases Cole, letting him slump against the floor. A moment later he's whirling around on me. The look in his eyes is wild, feral... and I want him. Only him. Always him. I shiver, reaching for him once more. He looks like he might ravage me, and right now, I would let him. I'd let him have me over and over again.

"I want you," I whimper. The look in his eyes diminishes almost instantly, and before I can say another word, he's gathering up my clothes and grabbing a blanket off the floor.

"No, Jules. I'm not fucking you with that drug in your system. I'm an asshole, a monster even but I will not take your fucking innocence like this." His response is almost like a slap to the face, and I want to fight him on this, tell him how much he means to me, but the stupid words won't come. In fact, nothing will. I feel lifeless, like I'm floating on a cloud in the sky.

"Come on, you need to get dressed," he says, already pulling my shirt over my head. I awkwardly pull my arms through and a shiver runs down my spine when the fabric runs over my bare nipple. I forgot he took my bra off. My hands move all on their own and I reach out for Remmy, letting my fingers run over the hard planes of his chest. The need to touch him far too much to ignore. My pulse quickens, and a throbbing begins between my thighs. *This*...this is what I should've felt with Cole.

His chest rises and falls so rapidly I know he wants this too, so why isn't he reacting to me in the same way I am him. He takes a couple deep breaths and kneels down in front of me. I look down at him, confused until I realize he is holding out my jeans for me.

"Step in," he orders. I almost fall over when I lift my foot to step in, but he grabs my hip and steadies me. His hand against my bare skin is like heaven and I moan out in pleasure. "Hold on to my shoulders." His words are restrained.

He doesn't have to tell me twice. I grab his shoulders with both hands, enjoying the feeling of his muscles flexing beneath his shirt as he moves. Sucking in a deep breath, I inhale his scent. The smell of beer is on his breath, but his natural scent, the one that makes him, him is what I really smell...soap and just Remmy.

"We're going to walk out of here like nothing is wrong, okay?" He pulls my jeans up and over my ass and zips up the zipper. I'm too focused on his hands against my most sensitive areas to remember what he's saying.

"Okay?" he repeats, and I see something inside his eyes, something that looks a lot like shame, and maybe even pain. I want to ask him what's going on, why he feels the way he does, but I just can't bring myself to do it. I just want to kiss him, feel his hands against my skin.

"Okay," I murmur, just as he straightens. My hands are still on his shoulders and suddenly the touch isn't enough., I need more. Snaking my arms all the way around his neck, I lean into him, my head coming to rest against his chest.

Pressing my ear to his chest, a smile tugs at my lips at the steady beat of his heart. I'm sure he's going to push me away again at any moment, like he did when I hugged him last time, so when he doesn't, I lean in even closer, pressing my front against his, until we're so close I can feel every inch of his muscled body against mine.

We stand there, him letting me hug him, and even resting a hand on the small of my back. I don't tell him this, but if I could stay like this forever...I would. Apparently Remmy can't though because just as soon as I start to close my eyes, he starts to pull away, pushing against my shoulders gently, holding me at arm's length.

"We need to go, Jules." There's an urgency to his voice.

I don't want to go, and anywhere I go I want him to go too.

"Are you coming with me?"

"I'll take you home if that's what you mean."

"I don't want to go home. I want to go with you." I frown, or at least I think I'm frowning, I don't really know.

"Jules." His tone holds a warning, but I still don't feel scared. This is Remmy...the real Remmy, not the facade he puts on display for this stupid college or his friends. This is the boy I fell in love with, the boy who kissed my boo-boos and put ants in my pants, the boy that laughed at me when I cut my bangs for the first time, making myself look like a boy.

"Please? I don't want you to go. I don't want you to hate me. Can we just be friends again? I miss you, I miss you so much," I start to mumble, my knees wobbling with weakness.

"That's the drug talking. You don't mean anything you're saying right now." He looks like he wants to believe me, but I can understand why he doesn't.

"I don't want to be alone. I want to be with you...please, Remmy...please?" My fingers grip onto his shirt, not caring that I'm begging him. Fisting the fabric in my hands, I'm willing him to see through all of this and to the real me.

"Fuck, Jules," he growls in frustration. "Let's go. I can't risk getting another suspension from fighting." And just like that, I'm reminded that Cole is lying in a heap on the floor.

"Will he be okay?" I finally ask Remmy as he starts to guide us out of the bedroom and out into the crowded hallway.

"If I could kill him and get away with it, I would. But since I can't yes, he will live."

I shrug, hoping tomorrow I can make much better sense of all of this.

We make our way through the house, Remmy navigating the crowd, pushing through it until we reach what looks like a back door instead of the way I came in.

I'm having a hard time putting one foot in front of the other, my body and mind not fully connected. Remmy must notice too cause his arms tighten around me. He's basically holding my entire weight up while we walk. I'm reminded then that I never want to let him go again. We finally make it outside, the cool air kisses my skin, and I shiver.

"Are you sure you want to come back to the frat house with me?" he whispers into my ear and I sway unsteadily.

"Yes...I told you I miss you and want to be best friends again."

Remmy doesn't respond to anything I say and instead continues walking. We walk to the front of the house and start down the sidewalk. In a blink, we're at the entrance of the frat house. I attempt to walk up the steps, but I can barely lift my legs now.

Remmy sighs, and picks me up, gently placing me over his shoulder. He opens the front door and walks inside. His booted feet pound against the stairs as my body is jostled back and forth with the movement. When we reach the top of the stairs, I feel like I might throw up.

"Remmy..." I almost whine. He stops at a door, pulling out what sounds like keys. Before I realize it, he's gently placing me back down on my feet, my body sliding down his front until my feet touch the floor.

Looking up at him, I see every ounce of the person I wanted to see when I first showed back up here. Remington Miller. My best friend... my lover...the man I planned to marry and have babies with.

I lick my lips and we stand there for a long moment.

Word vomit. Oh lord. It's coming. It's rising in my throat. There's nothing I can do to stop the words from coming.

"I love you, Remmy," I whisper, pressing my heated cheek against his chest.

## 11

## REMINGTON

"I love you, Remmy." I can't breathe. I can't even fucking respond to those four little words. I know Jules has no idea what is going on, but I can't help but feel like this is some sick joke. Like I'm on an episode of Punk'd. The one words I always needed her to say, and she says them now, after we've already fallen apart, after I've already broken us.

"Come on, let me get you a shirt to wear." I clear my throat, feeling like there's a bowling ball size of emotions lodged in it. *It's the drugs talking,* I have to remind myself. She doesn't really mean any of this. Tomorrow morning she'll be back to hating me again, and I'll be back to loathing myself.

"You'll stay with me, right?" She can't really mean what she's asking me. She doesn't want me within fifty feet of her any other day, but suddenly she wants me right beside her. No, she doesn't want me. She doesn't. We're just like fire and gasoline to each other. Explosive, powerful, and if you get us too close to each other, we'll burn everything to the ground.

What we had before is gone forever, nothing but a distant memory, something that we can never go back to. Still, I can't help but let tonight be what it is. I can't help but pretend like we are still the same two people, so hopelessly in love. For her...tonight I'll pretend like I'm still the same, like I haven't lost myself.

"If that's what you want?" I guide her back toward my bed, a place I've never had a woman before. This is my room, my space to relax, my sanctuary. I've never brought a girl up here, no matter how much they begged and whined.

So I guess in a way, she might not have been the first girl I had sex with, God knows I fucked my way through high school and college, but she's the first girl to be in *my* bed, *my* bedroom. She holds so many of my firsts though.

My first date, even if it was nothing more than a tea-party set up in the backyard. My first kiss, under the big oak tree at the park. My first dance at homecoming, where I begged and pleaded with her to go because, in my mind, she was the only girl worthy of dancing with.

She was the first girl I've ever loved, actually the only girl I ever loved, and I can't imagine that would ever change.

Nodding her head, she lets me push her back onto the mattress. I can see her hardened nipples poking through her shirt and I have to stop myself from reaching out and running my fingers over them. I wonder if she would push me away if I go too far, tell me no like she told Cole. Cole. *That fucking bastard.* I didn't think I could hate someone more than I hate myself, but that fucker takes the cake. The fact that he drugged her and took her up into that bedroom like she was some cheap lay makes me rage like a volcano.

Leaving her on the bed, I go to my dresser digging down to the bottom of my t-shirt drawer. There I find the t-shirt she would always wear when she spent the night over at my house, on the nights her parents fighting made it impossible for her to sleep. It's got a faded Mickey Mouse logo on the front of it, and the cotton is worn, but it's still in one piece, and still hers.

I'll never admit it, but when she first left, I held onto that stupid shirt, using it like a fucking security blanket so I wouldn't ever forget the way she smelt.

Eventually her scent faded, along with her, but I couldn't ever forget her. I was so connected to that shirt that any time I tried to destroy it, I would see Jules in it, looking at me with a smile, a halo of blonde curls hanging down her back, her big blue eyes piercing mine, seeing a part of me that I never allowed anyone else to.

Turning around, I hand it to her, watching as an indescribable emotion overtakes her face. The drugs must be wearing off a little bit since it seems she's able to smile again.

"You kept it? Oh my god, Remmy. I looked everywhere for this t-shirt when we moved, and I couldn't find it. I thought it got lost, ended up in the donate box by accident."

"It's just a t-shirt, Jules." I shrug, knowing damn well it's far more than that.

"*Just a shirt?*" She pushes up from the bed, her body swaying with the motion. I'm grabbing onto her by the hips without thought, steadying her as she looks up at me, her white teeth sinking into her plump pink bottom lip. I lean away from her knowing how close I am to losing control, to kissing her. With her, nothing is normal, what it should be.

"Come on, let's get you into bed." I make her walk backward until we reach the edge of the bed. She grabs the hem of her shirt and pulls it off, leaving her naked from the waist up. I gulp. I saw her half naked earlier, but I was in such a fury then, that I didn't take the time to really look at her, but now without any barrier between us, I can.

Of course her tits are perfect, just the right size, full but perky, with soft pink nipples hardened to a point, all but begging to be sucked on.

Perfect...just like everything else about her.

She just sits there looking up at me, her eyes silently begging me to touch her. *It's the drug.* She doesn't make a move to put on the shirt, so I grab it from her and for the second time tonight I help her into a shirt.

Then as if she's somehow realized she was just sitting before me doing nothing, she starts fumbling with the button on her jeans. Her hands are clumsy, and she blows out a frustrated sigh, that makes me grin. *Adorable.* That's all I can think. On her third attempt at unbuttoning the button, I bend down and unsnap the thing.

"Charming me right out of my pants." Amusement twinkles in her eyes. She has no idea. There would be no charming with her. She's mine, she has always been mine, every single inch of her. I just never took the time to let her know how much I wanted her in that way.

Even though I shouldn't, I watch her as she slips her jeans off, while I start to strip out of my own clothing. By the time I'm down to my boxers, she's finally managed to get her jeans off. I walk around the bed and lie down on one side, leaving her enough space to lie on the other side. But when she crawls back onto the bed, she comes straight for me, trying to get on top of me.

"Jules, stop, you don't want this." I grab her waist and force her to lie down next to me.

"Please, I want this, I want to touch you," she whines while reaching for me, her small hands landing on my arm.

"And I want you to touch me."

*The drug, it's the drug.*

"Don't you want to touch me, Remmy?" She's taunting me, making it hard for me to say no to her. I never say no to any willing woman, but Jules isn't a willing woman, not tonight.

"Jules, stop," I warn, barely restraining myself from rolling over, grabbing her and caging her with my body, from claiming what's always been mine.

She must sense the tension in the air because she frowns.

"Will you at least hold me?"

If my heart wasn't already broken, it would crack right through the middle now. Her voice drips with desperation as if she thinks she'll die if I don't hold her.

"Alright, I'll hold you, but that's it. Nothing else, Jules, and I mean it." I barely say the last word before she is snuggled up into my side. She hugs my chest with one arm and throws her leg over mine, her knee getting dangerously close to my steel hard cock. My eyes move to her bare legs, and over her creamy white thigh.

*She doesn't really want you.*

My body is tense, every muscle, every cell begging for me to give in to her wants, to my own selfish needs.

"I miss you," she purrs into the side of my chest, her curls tickling me.

"You've told me that already." It's still a lie. "Just go to sleep. You'll feel different in the morning, trust me."

"Why do you hate me? You hate me when I love you? That's not how it works." Her words slur a little.

"Jules, please, just go to sleep." I can't talk to her about this, not now, maybe not ever. I can pretend I'm the old me tonight, but that doesn't change who I am now. I close my eyes, hoping she doesn't say anything else, my heart has endured enough of a beating tonight. When she doesn't speak after a short time, all I can do is thank the Lord. Her breathing evens out after awhile and I open my eyes one more time to look at her.

She's clinging on to me like she actually wants me, *no*, like she needs me and with everything inside of me, I wish that it wasn't a lie.

∽

ADRENALINE PUMPS THROUGH MY VEINS, dragging me out of a shallow sleep when a loud noise hits my ears. *Jules.* My first and only thought. I look at the empty space beside me before I quickly scan the room. Our eyes meet and relief floods me. She's still here, and she's okay.

"I'm sorry I didn't mean to wake you. I was just trying to go to the bathroom," she says from the floor beside the bed. "Then I tripped." Her voice is raspy as if her throat is dry. I bet anything her head is throbbing too. She didn't drink that much last night but coming off ecstasy in itself is like a hangover.

"Are you okay?"

"Yeah, I'm fine." She gets back up onto her feet and scurries into the small bathroom attached to my room. I get up from the bed and pull on a t-shirt and then a pair of sweatpants. Mentally I have no idea what the hell I'm going to say to her. She's not high on the drugs anymore, which means everything she says, her reactions, it will all be honest, the truth.

She comes back out a few minutes later, her eyes on the floor as if she's lost in thought. Her gaze lifts as soon as she sees me standing and leaning against the dresser. She opens her mouth as if she's about to say something, but I cut her off before she can even get out the first syllable. I'm not sure I'm ready to hear her tell me how much she hates me for everything that happened last night.

"Don't! Just don't say anything right now," I order, trying to keep any emotion out of my voice. Her eyes go wide, confusion written all over her beautiful features. I just can't hear her say it. I can't listen to her admit that I was right and whatever she felt last night was a reaction to the drugs that were in her system.

"Rem—"

"I said don't," I cut her off again, but even I can't miss the hurt in her eyes. "Let's just forget last night ever happened. Just take your things and get out." I brush past her and go into the bathroom, closing the door behind me.

Last night was the first time in a long time that I slept all the way through the night, and the first time I slept with a woman for more than just sex. Gripping onto the edge of the sink, I notice my swollen and beat up knuckles. I grin, wondering how the fucker's face must look right now. I hope he's in pain, that his nose is broken, and his eyes are swollen shut, then again if they aren't, I suppose I can show him another lesson.

Air fills my lungs and I exhale it out. I do this a few more times letting the fury from Cole simmer. My thoughts shift back to Jules. I just told her to forget about last night, as if that was so easy, as if I could do so myself. I shake my head in disbelief and lift my gaze to the mirror. I feel like a drug addict who used for the first time after being clean for several years.

I reach for my toothbrush and when I pick it up, I realize that it's wet.

*Did she just use my toothbrush?*

Shaking the thought away, I brush my teeth and wash my face. I have to tell myself a thousand times that I'm not what she wants, and her behavior last night was nothing but a reaction to the drugs Cole gave her, but there's a sliver of hope inside me wondering if maybe it wasn't just the drugs...maybe it was what she really wanted.

When I emerge from the bathroom, I find that the room is empty. Relief and disappointment both crash into me all at once. This room has never seemed so empty before, and because she was here, it no longer feels like it's *mine*, and mine alone.

Glancing over to the bed where just ten minutes ago she was in my arms, sleeping, not arguing with me or telling me she hated me, but sleeping peacefully, I wish for the moment to return. My heart and mind are racing at the same speed. The room still smells like her, vanilla and sugar... or maybe I'm just imagining that. It wouldn't surprise me if I was.

Shit. I need to clear my mind and get some of this pent-up energy out. There are a couple of different things I could do to help but sleeping with someone else and fucking up Cole's face again aren't really all that appealing to me, even more so since the only person I want now is Jules. Eyeing my Nikes near my closet, I decide to go for a run.

Maybe if I run long enough, fast enough, I can outrun the problems overtaking my life.

## 12

## JULES

Humiliation. It bleeds into every pore on my body as all the memories from the night before surface in my mind. Cole, the things he did to me. When I arrive at the apartment, I take an hour-long shower scrubbing at my skin to rid the feeling of his hands, and his lips from my body. Then I cry...I sob against the tile for being stupid, for letting myself be alone with Cole, for letting him slip drugs into my drink. It was my fault... all my fault, I should've been smarter, but seeing Remington at the party, it just pushed me, it pushed me to act out.

And act out, I did. I hold my head in my hands. I'm so disappointed in myself. The only good thing to come from last night was Remington. It felt like he was his old self, like he was *my* Remmy again. He held me in his arms and defended me. He made my heart beat like crazy, my stomach fill with butterflies. Then this morning, he didn't even let me thank him or apologize for how I acted. He just brushed it off like nothing ever happened.

*"You'll regret this in the morning, trust me."*

His words had never been more false. I didn't regret what happened between us. In fact, I wanted to relish in the memory of it, because I was certain it wouldn't happen again. A throbbing begins behind my eyes and I cringe, remembering how I threw myself at him. How I wanted him so badly, I would've given myself to him in the state that I was. But he didn't want me back, he doesn't want me like I want him, not anymore.

A knock on the bathroom door drags me from my pity party of one.

"Jules, are you okay?" Cally's muffled voice comes through the door. She sounds concerned and now I feel bad about that too. I told her I was okay when I stormed in here, but of course she doesn't believe me. We got separated at the party last night, and she knows I didn't come home, which means she's assuming I slept with someone.

"Yeah, I'll be out in a minute."

"Okay, are you sure though? You didn't come home last night. I was really worried about you. If something happened, you know you can tell me, right?"

Something inside my chest tightens. Lots of things happened last night, lots of things, and none of them are something I want to talk about right now.

"Nothing happened, and I'm sorry for worrying you. I'll be right out." I hate lying to her, but I don't want to explain the Cole thing, or how Remington rescued me, not right now at least.

"Okay, just making sure." The tone of her voice tells me she doesn't believe me, but I'm just thankful she doesn't push for answers, because I have nothing to give her.

Standing from my seated position, I gather my stuff, and open the bathroom door, scurrying across the hall and into my bedroom. I toss my dirty clothes into the hamper and put my bathroom bag on my desk. Then I sink down onto my mattress and grab my cell phone.

There are tons of texts from Cally, and then a couple from Cole, which I delete right away. But it's the one from Sebastian that leaves me with a sick feeling in my stomach.

"Fuck," I mutter to no one but myself, burying my face in my pillow. I forgot about family dinner. After everything that happened yesterday, I now have to face Remington all over again. This is a nightmare, a complete nightmare, and one that I continue to star in.

My stomach churns thinking of what his reaction will be when I show up at his house tomorrow. Will he tell me to leave? Will he end up fighting with his brothers all over again? What will his father say? All of these questions are hurting my head more. I can't focus on them, not right now. Plugging my cell phone into the charger, I lie down, curl into a ball and wish like hell that I was back in Remington's arms, with his warm body pressed against mine.

*"I love you..."* I told him, and the words were still true...I did still love him, and probably would die still loving him. But Remington was like Pandora's box, and every time I opened him up, I wasn't sure what I would get. Closing my eyes, I wish for sleep to come...but it never does.

∽

"How was your weekend?" Sebastian asks from the driver's seat of his SUV. Music from the radio filters quietly through the speakers, but all I can do is focus on the tightening knot of fear in my belly. Am I about to ruin everything by going to their house for dinner? Remington hasn't messed with me in days, didn't even attempt to talk to me until yesterday and now... now I was going to be giving that up for a visit with his family.

He would retaliate, lash out and hurt me.

"Fine." I shrug, refusing to talk to him about the party, or any topic remotely close to it.

"Fine? That's it?" He gives me a look that all but calls me a liar. "You never were a very good liar, Jules."

My cheeks heat, knowing he can see right through me. Each of the Miller boys are good at that, seeing right through your bullshit.

"It was fine," I say, trying to make it sound a little more believable.

Sebastian rolls his eyes. "No offense, Jules, because you're beautiful no matter what, but you look like you went through a blender. There are bags under your eyes, and you just seem so heartbroken. Is Remington still messing with you?"

*How did he know Remington was messing with me?*

"He's going to be so angry...angry that I showed up, angry that I'm ruining your dinner." I break, letting a sliver of my fear and worry out.

"So this is about him?"

"What...no...it's not. I mean kind of, but not really. He's just...he's Remington and we don't exactly have a good history."

Sebastian rolls his eyes. "Your history is fine. Rem is just an idiot who is too dumb to admit what he wants. He's hurt and like a typical male, the first thing he does is run, and ask questions later."

"He literally hates me, Seb."

"No, he doesn't. He wants you to think he hates you. There is a difference, sis." It's my turn to roll my eyes, and I do, because as much as I love Sebastian, he has no idea the shit storm I have had to endure when it comes to his brother. Sebastian has loved only one girl in his life, and she's dead now, so his advice, though sweet isn't helpful.

If Remington ever loved me, even a little bit, I wouldn't ever be able to tell, at least not since last night. Everything he does is to hurt me, in one way or another.

"What do you know about relationships? I haven't seen you date a woman since—" My words cut off. His hands tighten on the steering wheel and for a moment, I think Sebastian might be angry. It's very rare that you see him mad, mad enough to snap.

"You're right. Dating isn't really my thing, but that doesn't mean that I don't know what I'm talking about. I know my brother. I know you. I know that you both are still very much in love with each other. He just needs to let go of the past, let go of what you did to him."

My head snaps to the side. "What I did?" I'm kind of angry now. "I didn't do anything. My parents forced me to move. I wanted to try and make things work...as friends. I didn't know he wanted to be together like that, we hadn't talked about it yet."

But we often acted as a couple, at least now that I think back on it. There were many times when I thought we would be more, but we never actually went further than some innocent kisses and I know that was all mostly my own doing.

I was afraid...of love, of falling for my best friend.

"He wanted you, even then, hell even now. It was always you, Jules, and it will forever be you. The heart wants what the heart wants, and Remmy wants you."

"He couldn't have fooled me with the way he's been acting."

I know Sebastian isn't lying. It was very clear to me that Remington wanted something more, but I was always so afraid of losing him as a friend that I tried to ignore it. He never went on dates, or even out with his guy friends and when he did, he always brought me with. Up until the day I left, we were best friends, and deep down, I knew we were in love. But I still didn't understand how in his eyes this ended up being all my fault.

As soon as we pull into the subdivision, everything inside me starts to twist. My heart hurts, my lungs won't fill with air. I don't know what the hell is happening, but I want it to stop. Sebastian's face fills with concern as he looks between me and the road.

"Are you sure you're okay, Jules?" I can't answer him. I don't know what to say. I'm okay, but am I really *okay?*

"I'm just nervous. I don't want to make anyone mad or ruin your Sunday dinner. I know how important these things are to you guys."

Sebastian gives me a knowing grin. "It'll be fine. Dad is so excited to see you, I think he just about had a heart attack when I told him you were coming."

I playfully punch him in the arm. "Don't say that."

"What? He did...I was actually worried, and then he started talking again and I knew he was fine." We both laugh, and then the laughter ceases when we pull into the driveway.

Sebastian puts the SUV in park and kills the engine. I stare at the house. The large brick house looks the same as it did the day I left, the outside still the same natural stone, the door the same dark cream color. There's even a weathered welcome sign stuck to the garage. The cracks in the driveway are still there, it's the same driveway I colored with chalk on so many years ago. The memories this place holds almost bring me to tears.

"Everything will be fine. It's just dinner."

I know it's just dinner, but is it really? At the end of the day, this is Remington's family, not mine. The sound of a door opening catches my attention and I realize Sebastian is already getting out of the car.

*Shit.* This is it. The moment where I put a target on my back again. I climb out of the car. My legs are shaky, the nervous knot inside my belly unraveling, leaving a trail of fear behind. I walk around the car where Sebastian is waiting for me.

"I'm nervous," I blurt out right as his hand grabs onto mine.

"Don't be. I'll kick his ass if he says anything." I give him a weak smile, and together we walk up the driveway and to the front door. Sebastian doesn't knock, he twists the knob and opens the door. As soon as the door opens, I'm pulled back in time to one of the many memories I shared with Remington in this house.

*Opening the sliding glass door, I tiptoe into the house. Remington. That's who I need right now. I know Papa Miller isn't home, he's on a business trip which means Alexander would be watching over his brothers if he was even home. Remmy said that he went to a lot of parties.*

*"You're a cheater, a fucking cheater..." Sebastian's angry voice fills my ears, and I hurry to see what is going on. As soon as I enter the living room, I find Remmy grinning like a fool at his brother. They're playing on the Xbox. As soon as Remmy notices me, he bounds from the couch and over to me.*

*"What's wrong, Jules?" His eyes bleed into mine, and concern etches into his features. His hands reach for me, pulling me into his chest like he*

knows what I need, probably because he always knows what I need. Tears start to fall from my eyes without hesitation.

"I'm going to bed, Seb," Remmy announces.

"Is she okay?" Sebastian's tone tells me he too is worried. It isn't often I come over here crying or after ten pm.

"She will be," Remmy answers, and picks me up like a small child, carrying me down the hall and into his bedroom. I feel so safe in his arms, not that I wasn't safe at home, my parents never hurt me, but their fighting was constant, and it wracked every nerve ending in my body. As soon as we're alone in his bedroom with the door closed, he places me on the bed. I can hear him rustling around, probably looking for PJs or something.

"What happened?" he asks a moment later.

I bite my bottom lip and wonder if I should really tell him. He's my best friend, yes, but he's always teasing me and making fun of me. He would probably just call me a baby, tell me to grow a thicker skin.

When I don't answer him, he turns on the bedside lamp, a soft glow of light blankets us and my cheeks heat when I see that he's taken off his shirt and slipped into a pair of flannel sleep pants. My eyes roam over his body, his muscles are toned, more definite. He's changed so much over the last two years and I would be lying if I said I didn't notice it.

There were many times I wanted his hands on me, in much different ways.

"Jules, what the hell happened?" he asks again, this time with more urgency.

"My parents. They're fighting again. I can't sleep, and I don't want to be alone." I feel the stupid tears stinging my eyes.

"Where's Jackson?"

I shrug, "I don't know. He doesn't want to be home any more than I do. *The only difference is he can drive, and I can't.*" My response must suffice enough because he doesn't say anything else about it.

"*Scoot over.*" *He nudges my PJ covered legs and I do as he says. My heart starts to beat out of my chest as he crawls into the bed and turns off the light.*

*When he reaches for me and pulls me into his side, a zing pulses through me. Why is this so different tonight? We've done this numerous times since we were small kids.*

"*You'll never be alone, Jules. Never,*" *he whispers into my hair and I swear I feel his lips against my forehead. His skin is so warm, and I burrow into his side, wrapping an arm around his middle, relishing in the feeling of his bare warm skin against mine.*

"*Why's that?*" *I whisper back, already knowing his answer.*

"*Because you'll always have me,*" *he whispers.*

"Jules? You okay?" Sebastian's voice finds me through the foggy memory. I gulp, realizing we're standing in the foyer.

"Jules? You seriously brought her here?" Remington's deep, very angry voice finds me next and when I lift my gaze from the floor, I see him, standing there, an angry Greek god, with piercing blue eyes and dark brown hair.

He hates me...he hates me because he loved me, and I left.

## 13

## REMINGTON

Of course they would fucking do this, Sebastian of all people. She always had him wrapped around her finger. Turning on my heels, I go straight to the fridge for a beer. It damn near killed me not to go to her Saturday. I texted Cally instead asking her if Jules was okay. She told me she was but that she had stayed in her room all day.

I wanted to go over and comfort her, but I didn't have it in me. I couldn't give into the reemerging feelings that were trying to take root inside my heart.

"Remington. You will keep your mouth shut, and behave like a gentleman, do you understand me?" My father's deep voice vibrates through me, clearing the angry fog from my mind. My father was one person I respected, never fought with, and not just because he was my father. I watched him work tirelessly nearly all my life to give us a good upbringing, even when my mother was constantly drunk. He stepped up to be two parents when all he had to do was really be one, and I loved him more than I could ever put into words for that. But that didn't mean I had to like what was happening here tonight.

They fooled me, convinced me to come to family dinner knowing damn well that Jules would be here. My jaw tightens, my teeth grinding together as I nod my head. Having her here brings back memories, memories I longed to forget a million times over.

While she moved on with her life somewhere new...I was forced to relive every fucking little moment, every kiss, whimper, every smile, and tear. I was forced to relive the pain of what she had done, every single day inside the walls of this house.

"Where is my girl?" My father shoves from the recliner and walks through the living room and to the foyer where she's standing with Sebastian. As soon as she sees his towering frame, she's running toward him, wrapping her arms around his middle. He picks her up and hugs her like he always did, her feet dangling off the floor.

"Papa!!" she calls out. "I can't breathe." A soft chuckle emits from my father's throat and he places her back down on her feet. My father is built like a brick house, his frame looming over Jules' much smaller one. I'm positive some days that's the only thing we got from him - our statures and our determination to never give up.

"How's my sweet girl doing? You've grown so much in three years!" Excitement riddles my father's voice. "Let me look at you." He releases her just so he can look at her face again. His features turn from elation to sadness in an instant.

I can see him reminiscing of how it used to be. He always loved Jules, she was the daughter he never had. He loved having her come over, that's why he never said anything even though he knew she was sneaking in at night.

Most parents wouldn't allow a boy and girl to sleep in the same room, or spend as much time together as Jules and I did, but my father knew I wouldn't hurt her or take advantage of her. He knew that I was feeling deeper things for her. We never talked about girls, but that's because there was nothing to talk about.

It was always Jules, always.

"I'm so sorry about what happened to Jackson and your father...so sorry Jules," he tells her, his voice almost shaking with emotion. "If there is anything I can ever do for you...anything you ever need, I'm always here, okay?"

Jules nods, wrapping her slim arms around his middle again. Dread and guilt consume me in an instant. This is what normal people do. This is what she needed when her brother and father died, comfort, compassion, someone to care about her.

She tried to hug me the first day she saw me, and I pushed her away. I made her feel even worse, I kicked her when she was down, when she was grieving the loss of the two people she loved most.

"I'm holding up. Right now, it's mainly learning to deal with them not being here anymore. Dad's life insurance policy paid for the funerals and left me with enough money to finish college. He was so excited about me going to college, I knew I couldn't just drop out." She smiles, but it's filled with sadness.

"Well, if you need anything else, you know where to go. Our door is always open for you. Always." He presses a kiss to her forehead, and I squeeze the beer bottle in my hand.

I'm such a fucking asshole. I should just punch myself in the face for treating her the way I did.

"Thanks, Papa." She releases him and takes a step back, swiping at her eyes.

*Is she crying?*

"Alright, it's dinner time." My father claps his hands together. Sebastian is already in the kitchen sampling the tacos I helped my father make.

Dad turns and walks toward the kitchen giving me a knowing look, one that all but says *do something stupid and I'll beat your ass all over this house.* But what he doesn't know is there isn't any fight left in me, not when it comes to her. I won't hurt her, not ever again.

Jules stands there for a long moment, and I can't bring myself to look away from her. She's still her and I'm still me, but we're miles and miles apart from being the same people we used to be and the realization of that hurts, it hurts so fucking bad.

"Come on," I urge her, taking a sip of my beer, before nodding toward the kitchen.

"I'm sorry...I wasn't..." she starts, but I press a finger to my lips. She still hasn't moved, every fear and emotion she's feeling painted onto her features.

"Not tonight, Jules. Tonight we pretend we didn't lose each other. That you didn't break my heart into a million pieces, and that I didn't hurt you back."

She nods and I can see the tears glistening in her eyes. She's hurting, falling apart and I can't stop myself from walking over to her. I can't stop myself from grabbing her hand, from holding it in mine.

My reaction to her has nothing to do with my father's warning, and everything to do with the fact that I am truly weak for her. She is my drug, my kryptonite, she makes my blood sing and my heart beat. Her hand feels small in mine and I squeeze it giving her a knowing grin, one that used to make her smile.

"Let's just eat, okay?"

"I don't want you to be mad at me for coming here..."

I blink, realizing now why she's so nervous looking, why she seems as if she might barf at any given second.

"We can't do this right now, Jules, soon, but not right now. And I'm not mad at you for coming here. You were invited." I'm not ready to hear her excuses, or how much she regrets telling me she loves me or misses me from the other night. I guess in my mind, I'm not ready to let her go, to let go of the pain. Her big blue eyes pierce through mine, making the air in my lungs still.

"We'll talk later, okay?" I tell her and my statement causes her to perk up. She nods once more, her whole body relaxing, her jaw goes lax, and the scowl on her face dissolving. The thought of how scared she was just now, of how worried she was over my reaction of her being here is like a punch to the gut.

This house used to be her safe haven and today she was afraid to even come here, and all...because of me. I'm such a fucking asshole. I force myself to think about something else, something like the fact that a truce seems to have taken place between us, at least for right now.

I'm still angry and upset, but the pain is so much more bearable with her by my side. Knowing we're on the same page, even if it's just for tonight, makes it easier for me to breathe again. She lets me guide her into the kitchen and as soon as I release her hand from my own, I feel lost.

My father eyes me closely as we enter the kitchen but as soon as he sees the small smile on Jules' pink lips, his own face lights up. We each grab a couple different items and bring them to the table in the dining room.

"Dig in, guys," my father announces, but Sebastian and I are already one step ahead of him. We have family dinners almost every Sunday, but I can't remember the last time it felt like we're an actual family.

"Anything new going on with my boys?" dad asks, dabbing at his mouth with a napkin.

"Nope," Sebastian chimes first, before taking a drink of his soda. "Just pushing a bunch of papers around an office dealing with assholes every day." He grins at me and I roll my eyes. It's not like he has to deal with me *every* day. Just the ones that end in *y*.

"What about you, Rem? Anything new?"

I shake my head, shoving a chip into my mouth, chewing it and then answering him. "No. Same old, same old," I lie, everything has changed since Jules came back into my life. It's like she turned my entire world upside down...or maybe it's just been up upside down this whole time and her showing back up turned everything right side up?

"Well, Alexander called me the other day," he says, directing his attention off of me and I almost sink into my seat.

"There is nothing new with him either, or at least nothing he can tell me about, I guess. He's still somewhere in the desert, in Iraq and he still isn't sure when he'll be home next. He did tell me to tell you all he said hi, you too Jules."

I glance over to the picture of my brother in his dress blues hanging on the wall. I haven't seen Lex in over a year. He was only supposed to be deployed for seven months, but the idiot extended his tour. Typical of him. He always did want to save the world.

"Tell him I said hi back next time you talk to him," Jules murmurs with a mouth full of taco.

"Jules, what about you, how are your grades? Still kicking ass, I'm assuming?"

She grins. "Of course, Papa. Grades are the most important thing. It's been a little rough getting used to things, classes, and figuring out where everything is, but my grades aren't reflecting the mass chaos taking place in my life."

"Good. I'm glad to see at least one of you have your head on straight."

"Seriously, Dad?" Sebastian mumbles through a mouth full of food.

"What? It's true. You know they say it takes men longer to mature than women? I'm starting to believe that statement."

I roll my eyes but smile. For the first time in a long time, the storm inside of me calms. It isn't wreaking havoc on my body. For the first time since Jules left, I can breathe, laugh, smile, enjoy the moment for what it really is.

We finish eating and then clean up in the kitchen like we used to. Once we're all finished, we head into the living room. Dad takes the recliner as usual while Sebastian, Jules, and I pile onto the leather sectional. Somehow Jules ends up sandwiched between us. Seb turns on a movie, but it's impossible to focus on it, with her sitting so close to me.

Her sweet vanilla scent wafts into my nostrils, hardening my dick. All I can think about is how much softer her skin is now, and how well we would fit together, my cock snug inside her virgin pussy. I bite my fist to stop the groan from escaping my lips. Neither she or Seb seem to notice, thank fuck.

As I sit there uncomfortable as fuck, enjoying her presence, I start to notice how heavy her eyes seem to be. I should be watching the movie, but like a creeper, I'm watching her. It doesn't take long for her to nod off, her body slumping over, her head gently pressing against my shoulder.

Her lips are parted, soft breaths escape through them and it takes everything in me not to kiss her. When it comes to Jules, I'm not in control. She owns me, she fucking owns me. The movie finishes and Seb gets up from the couch and goes into the kitchen.

"Take her to your room. I'll bet she hasn't had a good night's sleep in weeks." He pauses briefly, his tone deepening. "Then come back out here. I want to have a talk with you."

Looking to Jules, she's completely out, and I bet he's right. Between the shit storm I brought down on her and the loss of her brother and father, I'm sure she hasn't been sleeping well. I give him a nod and gently pick her up, tucking her close to my chest.

She whimpers, burrowing deeper if that's even possible. When I reach my bedroom, I exhale. It's been three years since we were both inside this room together. Three long years since we laid in that bed together.

With shaking hands, I place her down on the bed, allowing myself to stare at her for a second longer than necessary. God, I've missed this, simply admiring her beauty. Her soft blonde curls circle her head like a halo, her hands are tucked beneath her rosy red cheek, and her face is at peace. She's beautiful, so beautiful and I never thought something like this would ever occur again, having her in my room, in my bed.

*She belongs here. She's yours.*

My heart says with every gush of blood. She sighs in her sleep, and I have the urge to touch her all over, to kiss every inch of her, to worship, and protect her. I want to make her mine. Before I do either of those things, I walk out of the bedroom, closing the door quietly behind me. We aren't like that anymore. She's not mine, she doesn't want me.

Each step I take away from the bedroom hurts, like I'm physically stabbing myself in the heart. Running a hand through my hair in frustration, I try to figure out what the fuck I'm doing.

"Grab a couple beers, son. We need to have a talk."

My brow furrows in confusion, but I do as he says. Giving him one and cracking one open for myself. I don't even get to take a sip before he's talking.

"You hurt her?" he asks. I've never lied to my father, but I want to right now. I want to so fucking badly because I know what's going to happen when I admit to him what I did.

"Yes," I answer shamefully. His hand tightens on his beer bottle giving away his anger.

"You hit her?"

His question catches me off guard.

"Fuck no. I wouldn't hit her. Not ever." I can almost see the relief flood his features. I might be lost, broken, angry, but I couldn't ever intentionally hurt her, not with a slap, or punch and I would kill any bastard that did try and touch her like that.

"Good. I didn't know in which way you hurt her, and I know I raised you right not to lay a hand on a woman, even if she hits you first, but lately, I've been worried if my good-natured son is still inside you."

His words sadden me further. I've let him down. Disappointed him.

"I'm still here, Dad. Just lost, really fucking lost."

"I know, but you've been found. She's back, Rem. She's back and I can tell she still cares about you."

I swallow, the saliva thick in my throat.

"I don't know, Dad. She might still care, but I've hurt her pretty badly, did some really fucked up shit." I don't elaborate and I definitely won't mention the audio I shared with my buddies. My dad would murder me if he knew I did something like that.

That's my burden to bear, my own pain.

"But you won't do that shit anymore...right? You won't try and get even with her for breaking your heart? Which, by the way, wasn't her fault."

The muscle in my jaw ticks. Of course he would say that. He's been taking her side since the day she left, and I know she wasn't really to blame for my pain, she was someone I could put the blame on. My mother left, and then she did too.

It was hard...too hard to fucking face alone.

"No. I won't hurt her anymore, I swear," I admit.

I decided before I even came here today that I wasn't going to fuck with her anymore, but now that I promised my dad, it's like it's been set in stone.

She'll always own a piece of my heart, that will never change, no matter how much I try and take it back. And I know now that hurting her only hurt me more. Now I can only hope that it's not too late for her to forgive me.

"Good, 'cause I'm not too old to kick your ass, don't you forget that," he snickers.

"Funny, old man," I joke, and finish the beer in my hand before heading back up to my room. I have this overwhelming urge to be close to her. It's like I need her in my arms to feel whole again. Staring at my bedroom door, I wonder if I can do this again. If I can subject myself to possibly losing her all over again.

I guess that's just a risk I'm going to have to take.

Sighing, I open the door to my room quietly, hoping not to wake her, but when I step over the threshold, I find her sitting up on my bed. Alarm bells go off inside my head.

She's breathing hard, each breath labored while her hands are pressed to her chest, her big blues wide and full of fear when she notices me standing there staring at her.

"What's wrong?" I scan the room for something, anything that would explain her outburst of fear, but there's nothing to be found, it's just us in here.

"Just a bad dream." She blinks herself out of what seems to be a trance, her voice shaky and weak. I close the door behind me and cross the room until I'm standing next to the bed. I turn on the bedside lamp and watch as she scoots up to the headboard, pulling her knees to her chest in the process.

"Are you coming to tell me our truce is over? That you're back to hating me?" Her voice is trembling, and I can't stand to see her in such an anxious state.

"I'm not going to torment you anymore. I'm done fighting, Jules. I'm done. I don't care anymore. You're here and you aren't going anywhere, and I've come to the conclusion that there is nothing I can do to change that. So please, don't worry anymore. I can't stand to see you so anxious, so worried. I won't hurt you anymore...I'll stop trying to break your heart like you broke mine."

Her big blue eyes fill with tears, but her relaxed facial expression tells me she's thankful for my words, for my apology.

"I didn't...I mean... I wasn't trying to break your heart."

"Just..." My tongue feels heavy and I scrub a hand down my face, trying to gather the strength I need to talk to her about this.

"Let me finish and then you can say whatever you want."

"Okay," she mumbles, playing with a string on her t-shirt.

"I've never hated you. I know I said I did, and I know I treated you like I did, but I don't think I've ever really hated you. I hated that you left, and I had no one to blame but you, but I didn't hate you. I couldn't."

I lick my lips, and continue, "The truth is I hated myself for a long time for letting you go like I did. For not trying. The day my mother left, it killed me, but I had you. You were there to hold me up, keep me together, and then suddenly you were gone too, and I had no one. It felt like my entire world was crumbling."

My voice cracks and I feel every single emotion I've tried to swallow down over the last three years rising to the surface. My gaze stays trained to the floor. I can't look at her right now. I just fucking can't.

"I didn't know...I mean...I knew but..." There's a rustling of sheets, and then a second later her hand is cupping my cheek, forcing my head up and my eyes to meet hers.

"You didn't know?" I question, my voice deeper, my eyes bleeding into hers, searching for the answer to my question, an answer I know that lies deep inside her.

How couldn't she know? I didn't go on any dates with girls that asked me out...I never even had sex with someone, not until after she left. I was saving myself for her, waiting until she was ready, and I would've waited an entire fucking lifetime if I had to.

The look on her face is doleful. "I didn't realize you wanted more until it was too late."

There it is the proverbial slap. The confession.

"That's bullshit, Jules," I growl bitterly.

"No, it's not. I was afraid, Remington. Afraid that I would lose you, my best friend. I was afraid if we crossed that line, if we jumped off the edge and it didn't work out, that you would be gone forever. I was afraid of losing you...and then I lost you anyway so I guess it wouldn't have mattered."

*She was afraid...fucking afraid.*

I can't even grasp onto the words that she just said.

"I loved you, Jules. I fucking loved you. Every single piece of you was embedded into my skin, and when you left a part of me died. I became bitter, angry, so fucking angry, and I'm still angry, but I've come to realize that the reason I'm this way has everything to do with me and nothing to do with you."

"I'm sorry," she apologizes tearfully, and I retreat a step, watching as her hand falls into the air.

"Me too," I mutter, feeling like I might break down. I keep walking backward until my back hits the wall, and then I slide down it, holding my head in my hands.

*I fucked up. I fucked up so bad.*

## 14

## JULES

*I* don't know if I should go to him or stay seated on the bed. He looks as devastated as I feel. And yet all I can think about is wrapping him up in my arms and asking him if he still loves me. I want him to still love me. The need to go to him is so overwhelming I find my body moving toward his as if it's on autopilot and something I'm meant to do.

I move to where he's sitting against the wall and slide down it, pressing my side against his. I can hear how heavy he's breathing, his hands are gripping angrily at the long strands of glossy brown hair.

"Rem?" I whisper, turning toward him. He doesn't say anything. His body seeping with tension. When I came here today, I didn't expect for this to happen. I was certain I would leave here with tears in my eyes, and I think I still might. I don't know if Remington is okay, if he's mad at me, at himself, at us.

He's not speaking and I'm starting to freak out a little.

I don't know how to fix this.

How to fix him.

"I...I can go if you want me to?" My words must shake something inside of him, because he lifts his head, and turns to look at me.

I can't contain the gasp that escapes my lips when I see the tears glistening in his eyes.

"Don't leave, Jules. Not tonight. Stay with me. Let me hold you. Let me pretend that I didn't fuck everything up. That I didn't ruin us."

"We aren't ruined, Rem." *Are we?* I don't know if things could ever go back to being the way they were before, if we could ever be friends like we used to be, not with all the carnage, all the heartache, but ruined? We aren't ruined.

"Let's go lie down on the bed. We can talk more whenever you want, but for now, I just want you to hold me." I tug on his arm, but he doesn't move right away, and for a moment I wonder if he's changed his mind.

Then as if he can feel the doubt creeping in around me, he gets up. I notice his eyes are swollen and bloodshot as he pulls me to my feet, and I stare up at him, completely consumed by the man before me.

Instead of walking to the bed like I expect him to do, he goes over to the dresser and opens a drawer or two, rummaging through them as if he's looking for something. A moment later he pulls out some sweatpants and a t-shirt I'm sure he's worn a million times.

"Will you be good sleeping in this?" he asks, handing me the shirt.

"It isn't my Mickey one, but it'll do." I grin, taking the shirt from his outstretched hand.

He smiles back at me and then I watch him as he flicks the button on his jeans and pushes them down his muscled thighs. I all but swallow my tongue at the image before me. I know we were just like this the other night, but I was drugged then and had no honor or morality.

Tonight is different though...tonight I'm me, and Remmy is, well him, and we're normal, or as normal as we can be.

"Are you going to change or are you just going to stand there and watch me?"

"I...I don't know, maybe I should change in the bathroom," I say nervously.

"You know I pretty much saw you naked the other night, right?"

My cheeks heat in embarrassment, of course he did. *Stupid Jules. Stupid.* I must be showing every emotion that I'm feeling right at that moment because Rem cringes as if he realizes he said something wrong.

"I'm sorry Cole hurt you... If I would have known what he was planning, I wouldn't have left you alone with him. I swear I had no idea that he put something in your drink and I thought you wanted to be with him since you went on a bunch of dates together. I was trying to let you go, let you be happy."

"Dates? *What?* I never went on a date with him!" I nearly yell.

That fucking asshole.

Rem gives me a disbelieving look. "I saw you, Jules... at the diner, with Thomas and his girl. You all looked *cozy.*" There's a jealousness that lingers in his voice.

"That wasn't a date, Rem. I was there to pick up some chocolate cake and he talked me into sitting down with them while I was waiting. I was there for like five minutes and as soon as the waitress came back with my order, I jumped up and left. It wasn't a date, Rem, believe me. I've been doing everything I can to avoid him. The last thing I would do is subject myself to an hour long date with the guy."

"Fuck!" he curses, clearly angry with himself that he believed Cole's pathetic story.

"Yeah, we weren't dating and as for the other night, I just want to forget it ever happened. It's one of the biggest mistakes I've ever made."

"Well, I want you to know I wouldn't ever do that to you...to anyone..."

"I already know that. You're a pure gentleman." I roll my eyes, and he lifts a questioning brow at me.

"I wouldn't go that far. I'm definitely an asshole, but I wouldn't do that. I can't believe I was friends with him, that I didn't see his douchebagness from a mile away. He never did end up coming back to the frat house and even if he tried, I wouldn't have let him in. I won't live with a fucking rapist. He's pathetic and if I ever see him again, I'll do more than rearrange his face. His family will need to make funeral arrangements."

"He's not worth it," I respond, pulling my shirt off, and then unbuttoning my pants. As I push them down my legs, I catch Remington's eyes wandering over my naked body. There's a hunger in them, a primal need that's directed right at me and it only gets worse when I reach around and unhook my bra. The need inside of me mounts when his pink tongue darts out over his full bottom lip. I want to kiss him, taste him.

My pussy clenches, but there's nothing there to sedate the ache forming inside of it. I want Remington, almost as badly as I wanted him three years ago.

I slide the bra off and pull the shirt on that he gave me, trying my best not to react to him, and the heat in my core. When my head pops through the head hole, I find he's still staring at me, but the look in his eyes has diminished a bit, almost like he's suppressing the need.

"You want to wear the sweatpants too?" he asks, his voice deep, thicker than normal.

I shake my head without thinking, turn around, and walk over to the bed. He pulls off his shirt, discarding it on the floor before he follows me to the bed in nothing but a pair of boxers.

My mouth goes dry, and I chew on my bottom lip. I try not to let my gaze linger on his muscular chest and well-defined abs, but it's so damn hard. It's so unfair how good the last three years have been to his body. All deliciously firm muscle, each ab carved out like stone.

Gah, I have to stop.

He smirks when he catches me staring and I quickly crawl into bed, pulling the blanket up to my chin. I involuntarily shiver, my pulse quickening when he slides into bed and under the same sheet as me.

*Bad. This is so bad.*

"You're just as shy now as you were back then."

"Am not," I lie.

"Shh, you don't have to lie to me, Jules. I won't judge you, or tease you." There's a teasing tone to his voice and I roll over to face him. I probably shouldn't, but I've spent the last three years wondering if I should've told him I wanted him more than a friend. I think I can handle being this close to him now.

But as soon as I face him, I clam up. He's so intimidating, not in a sense of being scary, but in a sense that he's been with a whole lot of girls, and is far more experienced than I ever could imagine being.

"Jules?" he whispers my name, his voice caressing something deep inside of me. He moves to face me, his body rubbing against mine as he does so, and I can feel the heat of his skin rolling off of him and crashing into me, blanketing me with warmth.

"Yeah?" I croak.

"Do you feel it? The connection between us?"

I consider telling him no. We don't even know if we're friends yet, doing anything else would complicate things, and then my brain, my stupid brain reminds me of what it felt like before, when he fingered me. Yeah, he was doing it out of anger, but he was gentle, and his touch brought immense pleasure.

"Yes..." I answer him breathlessly.

"Do you..." He pauses, and I feel my heart threatening to beat out of my chest. "Do you want me to touch you?"

I stare into his eyes with a thousand different reasons to say no, all while knowing none of them matter right now.

"Yes," I whisper so quietly I'm not even sure that he heard me until he reaches his hand out to touch the side of my face. He traces the contours of my face with his finger, his eyes moving to my lips, and like a crack addict, I'm addicted to his touch.

"Please?" I lick my lips impatiently and when all he does is smile, I move, pushing him onto his back so I can straddle him.

It's so unlike me to be this possessive, in control, but it's always been this way with him. I've always felt the need to touch him, to let him touch me. I just never understood why. I move, then he moves, and then we move together as one.

Tossing my leg over his middle, I press my panty-covered center against his bare stomach before he can move. Peering down into his almost black eyes, I gasp. I can feel his hardened cock against my ass. The temptation to press my bottom down against him is too great and as soon as I do, he's reacting.

"Shit, Jules," he growls, and his hands circle my hips, his hold possessive as he moves them just enough to send a shiver of pleasure up my spine.

"I want you." The words come out breathless. "I want you to touch me like you did before." I can't believe I'm admitting this, especially out loud.

"You do?" he asks as if he has a hard time believing me.

I nod my head and a big grin spreads across his face.

"Okay...but you have to do something in return for me."

"W-what?" I'm nervous to hear the answer, not because I don't want to do it but because I'm worried he's not going to appreciate my clumsy and inexperienced moves.

"I want you to kiss me."

*A kiss?* Not what I was expecting but something I can do. Lowering my head, I slant my lips over his and press them firmly against his full ones. Fire fills my belly, and something inside my soul ignites at the contact of our lips touching.

This time, there is no hesitation between us.

As soon as our lips touch, he pulls me even closer, my chest flush against his, the thin fabric of my t-shirt being the only thing keeping us from fully touching, and I hate it.

I want the fabric gone. One of his hands moves from my hip and threads into the silky strands of my hair, pulling me closer, deepening the kiss until my whole body is consumed with flames of pleasure.

Consumed by him.

My nipples harden at the contact of his hard chest, and I rub them against him, small jolts of pleasure rippling across my skin as I do.

"Fuck, you're so beautiful." He pulls away just enough to speak, and I grind my center against his hard abs, every little movement making my blood sing, my body, my pussy hungry for more.

"I want you...please?" I mewl, nipping at his bottom lip. I'm unsure of what I really want or need, all I know is that whatever it is, it lives inside of the man under me, the man looking into my eyes with so much love, so much passion.

"You have me..." he whispers, his fingers tracing my face as if he'll never get another chance to.

"No, I mean..." I kiss him again, feeling like I have to make up for lost time. "I want you to make me..." I'm still slightly ashamed to say it out loud.

"Come?" he asks, a twinkle of amusement in his hooded eyes. "You want me to make you come?"

I nod my head furiously, not even worrying how eager I must look.

"With what? My tongue, or my fingers?"

Oh god, I didn't think it would get this far. Swallowing, I wonder for a moment why he didn't say cock, then again, I'm sure he knows I'm not ready for that.

"Your fingers," I croak. As soon as the words pass my lips, he's flipping us, my back lands against the mattress where he was just laying moments ago.

Goosebumps break out over my body, watching as he lets go of whatever was holding him back from devouring me. His hands shake as he pushes my shirt up, peppering my belly with wet kisses. I can't help myself, the sensations rushing through me are unlike anything I've felt before and I start to squirm against the bed sheets. As if he knows my body better than even I do, his deft fingers start to pluck gently at one of my hardened nipples.

My teeth sink into my bottom lip to suppress the moan that wants to rip from my throat. He continues his assault against my breasts until I'm nothing but a withering mess, my thighs spread, and my center burning hot with need.

"Shit. I bet I could make you come just from playing with your tits," he says, giving me a cheeky grin, and I wouldn't bet against that, cause I'm pretty sure he could too.

When he pulls away, I whimper, wanting more of him and damn near sigh when I feel him sliding my lace panties to the side with nimble fingers. His touch is gentle, a caress against the silky smooth skin.

"If you want me to stop, you need to say so now."

The tension in his body and deepness of his voice tells me he's barely restrained, close to the edge, but I don't care I'm so consumed with need, my body burning up, that I couldn't ever imagine telling him to stop.

"If you stop, I might explode. So don't you dare stop," I warn with a smile.

My response causes his gaze to darken, and before I can say or think anything else, he starts his assault on my pussy, rubbing small circles over my swollen clit.

*Oh god.*

I can't hold in the moan of pleasure any longer, and it releases from deep inside me, vibrating through my core.

"Ahhhh..." It's loud, louder than I intended it to be and my cheeks pinken.

"Shhh, my dad is down the hall," Rem snickers before shutting me up with his lips on mine. He kisses me deeply, his tongue entering my mouth as soon as I part my lips, all the while he continues to dance over my center with his fingers.

My folds are slick with arousal, and I can feel how easily his thick fingers move over me and it only makes me crave him more.

His finger slides down my slit once again, the friction against my clit almost too much, as he finds my entrance. He slides into my slippery channel with ease, his thick finger coated with my arousal. He doesn't move, giving me a moment to adjust to his finger. This is how I've always imagined it would be.

No rush, no hate or anger.

Just need, pure need.

"So tight, so ready for me."

"Yes," I answer, my chest heaving, one of my hands gripping onto his arm just to feel him. I watch him through hooded eyes as he watches his finger as he starts to move in and out of me with deep, steady thrusts.

"You going to come for me? Squeeze my finger like I know you want to squeeze my cock."

Is that even a question right now? All I can feel is him, his body, his soul, owning every part of me. My legs spread wider, giving him more room to claim me and his heated gaze lifts to my face.

I lift my hips out of reflex, needing more, just a tiny bit more, that's all I want.

All I need.

"Rem..." I moan, and as if he knows just what I need, he adds a second finger, scissoring them deep inside me. He does this a few more times, his fingers finding this sweet spot at the top of my pussy, a spot that sends me crashing over the edge and into straight oblivion.

"Fuck me, Jules...my cock's so envious of my fingers right now. I want to be inside you, feeling your pussy tighten around me, milking my cock." I can barely hear him over the blood rushing in my ears and then everything falls apart. I start to clench around his fingers, my body suspended in time as waves of pleasure caress every inch of me.

"Mmm..." is all I can muster up as he gently withdraws his fingers and brings them to his lips. My arousal, my release coating his thick digits.

"I've fingered you, and next I'll feast on you, dipping my tongue in and out of your tightness until you fall apart, then I'll make you mine in every way just as I imagined I always would. There won't be an inch of you that I haven't tasted, touched, or caressed."

His confession terrifies me a little, okay, maybe a lot. He can't possibly mean that, can he? He doesn't want me. *Does he?* The question I just asked myself gets lost somewhere in my mind when he places those two thick digits into his mouth and sucks my release right off of them.

*Holy hell.*

His eyes close briefly and a deep moan rumbles from within his chest.

"You know we can't be friends, Jules."

I blink, hurt and confused. "What? Why?"

A grin spreads across his lips and he leans forward, his taut body pressing me farther into the mattress. He's all man, owning me, possessing me.

"Because we were never just friends. It was always something more, even if you didn't want to see it, even if you were afraid it was always going to be more than friendship. We were never meant to be friends. We were always meant to be lovers."

I nod, unable to form a response, because I know he's right and I'm still a little scared to face that fact.

"Do you?" My eyes move to the excessively large tent in his boxers. "You want me to return the favor?" I briefly felt his cock before, against my ass the first time he fingered me. He felt huge, but I never got the chance to really look, to see how beautiful it really is.

"I won't deny a hand job, but I cannot handle your mouth on me right now. I want you too badly."

"So, is that a yes?" I question, my lip between my teeth.

"It's not a yes, but a fuck yes." He lowers himself to the mattress beside me. I pull my shirt down and push up onto my knees, licking my lips nervously, feeling a flush creep over my cheeks. My inexperience is getting the best of me.

"Will you...you know...show me how?"

Rem's eyes go wide, and he tips his head back against the pillows.

"You're going to kill me, Jules. You've never given a hand job before?"

I shake my head. "Is that bad? Do you not want one now? I know I'm inexperienced, but it can't be that hard, can it?" I panic, afraid he might pull away, tell me he doesn't want me to do it.

I'm nothing like the girls he's been with, I know this, but I want to please him, pleasure him like he did me.

"Do I not want one?" He shakes his head. Unhinged need

flickers in his eyes and he pushes down his boxers, exposing his cock to me.

His very large, very angry looking cock.

"You have no idea how much I want your hands wrapped around my dick. Knowing that you haven't done this with anyone else...it's a huge fucking turn on. I don't need you to be like the other girls I've been with. When it comes to you, there is no comparison."

He reaches for my hand and I give it to him, letting him guide me to his shaft. I wrap my fingers around his thickness, my hand trembling.

He's so soft, so warm.

Why is such a small act so intimidating? When he places his hand over mine, I shiver, and look away from his cock and back up to his face to gauge his expression.

There's a seductiveness to him and for once I wish I wasn't so inexperienced. He starts to move my hand up and down his shaft, and I'm surprised by how soft the flesh feels. My gaze is fixated on his cock, on my hand as it moves up and down.

Remington's head tips back against the pillows, his eyes close, and his features draw tight like he's in pain.

"Am I doing okay? Are you in pain? I can stop if you want me to."

He blinks his eyes open. "No...no pain...it just feels so fucking good, so good. You have no idea how long I've waited to feel your hands on my cock. I've envisioned you doing this since I was fourteen beating off in the shower to the image."

His confession makes me feel powerful, it gives me this strange courage and I smirk, continuing to move my hand with his, I pull his hand off of mine, and stroke him all on my own wanting to finish the job myself. A glistening drop of cum beads the tip of his penis, and I lean down and swipe it up.

At the contact of my tongue on his cock, a deep rumble fills the room. A surge of endorphins rips through me, as I do it again. He rewards me with another moan, and I keep doing it. His biceps strain and his hands fist the bed sheets.

He's at my mercy, completely, and I love it, I love it so much. I suck on the head of his cock while continuing to stroke him. It doesn't take long for him to start bucking his hips, his cock slipping farther and farther into my mouth. I know he said he didn't want me to give him a blow job, but he doesn't seem to be objecting now.

"I'm close...if you don't want me to come in your pretty little mouth then pull away now," he whispers gruffly, his chest rising and falling rapidly, and while I want to do that sometime, tonight isn't the night.

Releasing him with a pop, I watch as he falls apart, tremors of pleasure ripple through his body and his cock twitches in my hand a moment before sticky hot cum jets from his cock, landing on my hands and his lower stomach. His whole body tenses before he relaxes back into the mattress and only then do I pull my hand away.

"Was it good?" I gulp.

He came yeah, but was it enjoyable? Maybe that's what I should have asked?

"Jules, it was amazing, *good* isn't even close to the word I would use to describe what that was. I've never even.... It was hot as fuck, incredible."

I'm stupid proud myself, I get up and go to the bathroom to

wash my hands and Remmy follows close behind, cleaning himself up.

When he is done, we get back into bed and he pulls me into his side so I'm lying half on top of him. My body relaxes into his and it doesn't take me long before I feel like drifting off to sleep. I want this to be real, I want to trust him, to go back to the way it used to be between us, but I don't know if I'm ready for that yet.

## 15

## REMINGTON

Yawning, I open my eyes, wondering if last night was a dream. Then I look down and see Jules is still in bed with me, her body molded into my side. My arm is stiff from holding onto her all night, but I don't care. I just didn't want to wake up without her.

I watch her sleep for a few minutes, my eyes lingering on her soft lips, adorable little nose, and tight body. She let me touch her last night, let me bring her pleasure. It was incredible, and soul-searing even if it was only fingering. As the thoughts linger, my cock hardens... fuck no. Grabbing my phone from the nightstand to distract myself, I realize we've overslept.

*Fuck*, it's ten, English class is in an hour.

Nothing could get me out of this bed for one of my classes right now, but this is the one and only class I share with Jules and I know her well enough to know that she will be freaking out if we miss a class.

"Jules," I whisper while giving her a gentle shake.

"Mmhhh." She cuddles deeper into my side, and I seriously consider calling Seb and asking him to somehow have English class canceled. Staying here in bed with her would be worth it but knowing how upset she would be to miss class has me deciding against it.

"Jules, it's ten in the morning," I whisper and that seems to get her attention because her eyes fly open and she sits up, rubbing them furiously with her hands.

"What?! Ten? It's ten?" She blinks a couple of times, giving me a disbelieving look. "We have class in an hour!"

There's a permanent grin on my face. She hops off the bed and starts running around the room like a chicken with her head cut off while I remain sitting on the bed, enjoying the view.

"Get up, you need to drop me off at my place. I still have to get my bag, and clothes, and brush my teeth." She's almost yelling at me, all while tugging on the corner of the blanket. A feeble attempt to get me out of bed, but one that works.

"Okay, okay, I'm up," I mumble, shoving from the bed. I pull on a pair of jeans a t-shirt and grab my phone and keys. When we get in the car and I pull out onto the road, I notice Jules nervously playing with the hem of her shirt and I can't be one hundred percent sure but I don't think that it's her worrying about being late for class.

"You okay?" I ask but she averts her gaze out the window and I wish she would let me see her face so I could figure out what's going on inside her head.

"I don't know," she finally whispers and an ache forms deep in my belly, the feeling similar to being punched in the stomach. She seemed so happy last night, so sure. I should have known that she'd come to her senses in the morning.

*We were just pretending...*

"Are we okay? I mean, I know what you said last night, but did you really mean it?"

My knuckles turn white against the steering wheel. "Yes, of course, I meant everything I said last night. I'm a man of my word, Jules."

"You said we can't be friends. But...I don't know if I can be more right now. I want to...but I want to be with the guy you were last night, the Remmy I know...but there is this other side of you, and now that I've seen it. While I don't think I can forget that part of you exists. I don't know if I can trust you to not turn into that person again?"

She doesn't trust me and of course she is right not to, God knows I've broken her trust in ways I'm not ready to tell her.

"So where does that leave us?" she asks before I can muster up a response to her previous question. Sucking in a deep breath, I let her sweet vanilla scent waft into my nose while I think of what to say to her.

*Where does that leave us?*

I feel like my brain has just been run through a blender. What can I say or do to make her understand how serious I am about fixing this?

I wish I could guarantee that the person she's seen the last few weeks won't reappear ever again, but how could I possibly promise that? It's not like I can flip a switch and turn that part of me off. I've lived this way for three years and as much as I want everything to just go back to the way it was...the way we were, I know it's an unrealistic thought.

Still, I'm not going to give up on her, on us. We've both

changed, but that doesn't mean the feelings between us have, last night being evidence of that.

By the time I park in front of her place, I still haven't come up with anything to say.

"I'll see you at class, okay?" There's a dismal look in her eyes as she opens the passenger side door and gets out. I want to give her all the answers she seeks, but I just... I can't.

I don't know what to do yet.

"Jules...wait, can we talk after class?"

She pokes her head back into the car for a moment. "Sure," she tells me with a little smile on her lips, before closing the car door and jogging up to her front door. I watch her ass sway in her tight jeans as she walks away from me.

*Friends?*

I don't know if I can be *just* her friend and hold on to my sanity.

I want her...all of her.

Making a pit stop at the frat house to get my own books for class, I climb up the stairs, grab my shit and walk out, I'm nearing the door when Thomas stops me in the kitchen.

"Hey Rem, have you seen Cole?" Just hearing his name makes me murderous.

"No, man, no clue what's going on with him." I try to keep my voice even. Hiding the anger within me. I've got a pretty good idea where he is and I definitely know why he hasn't shown his face around here, but I don't want to share that information for a plethora of reasons.

"I've got to get to class, catch up with you later?"

Thomas gives me a nod, and I rush out before he can ask me any other questions that I don't want to answer. I start my walk across campus and to English class. When I pass the coffee shop on the corner, I check my phone for the time and decide it'd be worth arriving late to class for. I order my usual and before I even realize what I'm doing, I'm ordering something for Jules too. When I walk into the classroom, most of the other students are already in their seats, even though class hasn't started yet.

*Overachievers.*

Walking to the back of the class where Jules is already writing who knows what in her notebook. She's still a total nerd and if I had to guess I'd say she has her schoolwork color-coded and alphabetized. My eyes roam over the rest of the room and right behind her sits Layla, smiling seductively while batting her eyelashes at me. Her gaze drops to the two coffee cups in my hand, her smile widening.

She probably thinks one of them is for her. Tough shit, like I would buy her coffee. Walking over to Jules' row, I stop at the seat beside her. There's a guy sitting next to her, a guy I don't know, nor do I care to know.

"Hey, find somewhere else to sit," I order him.

He looks up at me in shock, ready to complain or maybe even tell me off, but after a few seconds he just gets up, mumbling something under his breath.

*That's what I thought.*

Plopping down into the seat next to her, I look over to find her staring at me. Her nose snarled upward in distaste. *Cute.* Cute as fuck.

"What are you doing? You can't just make people move, Remmy."

"Looks like I just did." I chuckle.

Jules stares at me expressionless and I decide to change the subject.

"I brought you a drink." I grin, holding the hot paper cup out to her. She glances at the cup and then back up to my face.

"I don't like coffee," she announces like I don't already know that.

"I know." I roll my eyes at her. As if I didn't know that she hates coffee. Best friends since we were five and she thinks I could just forget the simplest things about her.

"It's hot chocolate."

"Oh, well... thank you." She beams, taking the cup from my hand, bringing it to her lips. She takes a small sip, and a cheesy smile starts to form on her lips, her eyes twinkling with joy.

A moment later she says, "You had them add cinnamon...I can't believe you remember that."

*This girl. I swear.*

"You think I would ever forget ten-year-old you stomping your foot and yelling at your mom for not putting cinnamon in your hot chocolate?"

"I think you just remember that everyone was laughing because I was pronouncing it *cimmanin*."

"That too, but it wasn't like I was trying to make fun of you," I lie, because I totally was trying to make fun of her.

She gives me a disbelieving look, "You're still bad at lying, Remmy."

"Is that so?" I lift a brow, enjoying the light banter between us. This I miss. The conversations, the memories, always having that someone to lean on when you need them most.

"Rem," Layla calls behind us, and just like that, the perfect balloon sheltering us from the rest of the world pops. The smile on Jules' face falls, and she turns so she's facing forward and away from me.

*Fuck you, Layla.* For once in my damn life, I wish I wasn't such a fucking manwhore. I know Jules is uncomfortable sitting beside me with Layla behind us, probably because she knows we've fucked, and she's more than likely comparing herself to her when there is no comparing her to anyone.

Jules is Jules. Layla's just another chick I used to try and rid the memory of the one and only person I ever loved.

"Layla," I greet her coldly.

"Why don't you come sit beside me?" she whines.

"I'm talking to Jules."

"Whatever..." she huffs, tossing her blonde hair over her shoulder. Thankfully she doesn't say anything else to me. Class seems to drone on for what seems like hours. Jules remains facing forward, not even looking at me once.

Gritting my teeth in frustration, I try to figure out how to make this easier for her. I've fucked a lot of girls, and the last thing I want is to upset her, but I can't change the things I've done in my past. I was hurting and using my body to get over that pain was the easiest thing I could do.

When the professor finally excuses us, all I want to do is drag Jules somewhere where we can be alone and talk. I feel jittery, my knee bouncing up and down before I jump up from my seat. I wait patiently while Jules gathers her stuff. I'm about to ask her to come home with me when Layla positions herself in front of us with her hands on her hips.

Saying a silent prayer, I hope like hell she keeps her fucking mouth shut...but of course, as soon as I think it, her mouth opens.

"I see you found yourself a new lay for this week, Rem." Her tone tells me she's jealous, and if she was a guy, I would slug her right in the fucking face, but she's not, so I just stand there watching the train wreck in slow motion. When she turns cattiness on Jules, I almost lose it. My fists clenched so tightly I might pull a muscle.

"Layla..." I warn, but she ignores me, her eyes bleeding into Jules. What the fuck was I thinking letting this bitch touch me?

"Don't get too attached, he'll come back to me when he needs his dick sucked good, you don't look like the kind who knows what he likes." Layla slaps her glossy lips together.

Before I even realize it, Jules is pushing past Layla. Reaching for her, I try and grab onto her arm to stop her, but like always, she slips through my fingers.

"You fucking bitch," I spit in Layla's face. "If you know what's good for you, you won't talk to her again. Unlike you, she's a permanent fixture in my life." I don't waste any more words on Layla and instead, take off running after Jules.

Jogging out the door, my heart thumps loudly in my chest. The thought of losing Jules because of someone like Layla takes root in my mind. I can't lose her, not when I just got her back. I spot her up ahead, her booted feet pounding against the pavement angrily.

"Jules," I call out to her, running a little faster to catch up.

"No...don't..." I can see her shaking her head, but I don't care if she doesn't want to see me or talk to me. I belong to her...and she belongs to me, we don't have to admit it to each other, but we both know it's true. Once close enough, I reach out and grab onto her shoulder, turning her around, and pulling her into my chest so she can't escape me. My chest heaves, my lungs burning from chasing her, and the simmering of my building temper over Layla's remarks.

"Just go back to her...go let her suck your..." She trails off and I smile, almost chuckle because she can't even say it.

"She's nothing, Jules, nothing." She struggles in my arms. "And I'm not letting you go just so you can walk away from me thinking something ridiculous."

"I can't do this, Rem. You've been with a lot of women, and most of them are here at this school. I've never even kissed anyone besides you." She's scared. Afraid. The sadness in her voice makes me wish I had the strength to punch myself in the junk. Why did I think with nothing more than my dick for so long?

"Look, I didn't know you would come back to me. Had I known, I'd still be a virgin too, and you would be my first. I know I can't take back the things I've done, but I won't skip out on you. I don't want anyone but you, you're all that I want. Your inexperience doesn't mean shit to me. In fact, it makes me want you more."

Her hands grip onto my t-shirt, pulling me closer instead of pushing me away.

"You don't mean that..." She's mumbling and I won't have it. I won't let her think that she's less than any of the girls here not when the truth is the opposite. She is so much more. Tipping her chin up, I force her to look at me.

"I only want you, Jules. Only you. I don't want Layla or any other person in the entire fucking world. I. Want. You."

Tears swim in her gaze, and she nods her head as if she accepts what I'm saying, but I'm not stupid. It won't be that easy for her to move on from this. I've got a reputation and there is bound to be more issues like the one that occurred with Layla today.

"I've got to go," she whispers, trying to pull away.

"Come home with me," I beg with my eyes.

"No. You can't be just friends, and I can't be in a relationship with you, so until we figure out what we are, we should probably keep some distance between us." Her response isn't what I want to hear, but I understand. Releasing her even though it kills me, I take a step backward.

"Whatever you want, Jules. I'll give you whatever you want, but you can't leave me. I won't make it through losing you again."

Dropping her arms down to her sides, she looks up at me one last time. "I'll see you later, Remmy." And then she turns and walks away, leaving me standing there with my heart in my hands, wondering how I'm going to make the only person that I ever really loved trust me again.

# 16

## JULES

"Whatever you want, Jules. I'll give you whatever you want, but you can't leave me. I won't make it through losing you again." Remington's words haunt me, whispering in my ear, making me feel a rush of feelings I never thought I would feel toward him again. I won't hurt him again, but I also won't allow myself to get swept up in all the emotions I'm feeling.

Remington still hurt me, he still said horrible things, and though he apologized, and I understand why he did and said the things he did...I can't just shut off those feelings. I can't just act like he wasn't a complete asshole to me.

Forgiving is easy, forgetting is something I can't do. I think about this all day, how Layla talked to me after class, how Remington's reputation will always be what it is. How people will always look at me when they see me with him.

*How can we be whole again?*

Last night was amazing, waking up in his arms, even more amazing, but losing myself inside him, that's a fear only I can truly feel. I walk to my last class of the day, secretly wanting to skip it but knowing I shouldn't. As soon as I enter the room, I realize that this is the same class I share with Cole.

*Fuck.* My gaze sweeps around the room for him. He's nowhere in sight, but that doesn't mean he won't show up soon, class doesn't start for another five minutes.

A shiver of fear makes its way up my spine as I force myself to take my usual seat. Maybe he won't show up? I was so caught up in my own thoughts, in my thoughts about Remmy, that I failed to remember my one class with Cole. Remmy said that Cole doesn't live at the frat house anymore, but that doesn't mean he's going to stop coming to classes.

There's a sticky sick feeling that coats my insides as I watch the door like a hawk. I'm waiting for the moment he shows his face so that I can bolt. I don't want to be in the same room with him ever again. When the professor comes in and starts class, the dreadful feeling in my gut lessens. Maybe he just left school altogether. The more we get into the class, the calmer I start to feel and the more convinced I become that he's not coming back.

After class, I gather my stuff and head outside. I should call Cally and ask her to grab some dinner with me. It's been awhile since we talked and I want to catch up. I'm completely lost in thought as I walk outside and down the small path behind the building.

I don't come back to the current reality until I crash into another body. I go to mutter a sorry but lift my gaze just in time to see who it is. My lungs cease to work as my heart kicks into overdrive. The fear that's been simmering within me the last few days rises to the surface. I'm frozen, suspended in time like a deer seconds away from being hit by a car.

"Hey Jules," Cole says casually, like he didn't try and rape me the other night. Taking in his features, I see that Remington got him good. His face is covered in big purple bruises, one eye is swollen closed and his nose is crooked.

Taking a step back, I try to put some distance between us, but he just takes another step forward. My stomach churns. The next step I try to take, he stops me, his hand grabbing onto my wrist, his touch rough, searing into my skin like fire.

"Let go of me," I order, my voice much weaker sounding than I want it to. I want to be strong, I want to be able to kick and hit him and get away, but his hands are wrapped around my wrists like iron shackles. I still try to escape though. I try to kick him, but he shoves me against the wall of the building, knocking the little bit of air that was left inside my lungs out of me.

"Don't be like that, we both know you want this." He grins through his busted lip.

*No, I don't!* I don't want any of this, I never wanted him.

"Let go, or I'll scream and this time you won't get away with hurting me," I whimper, unsure if I would even be able to muster up a scream. I'm terrified. It feels like I'm reliving the nightmare that appears in my dreams each night.

"Scream... please scream, I like it when they scream. It makes my cock hard."

He leans into me, and I'm seconds away from puking, bile rising in my throat. I glance around, praying for someone to walk around the corner. But there's no one to save me, no Remington. It's just me and the sick bastard in front of me and I know I have to do something.

His fingers dig into my skin with bruising force and a small cry passes my lips.

"You feel that, the pain? That's how my face feels but a hundred times worse, and all because of stupid fucking Remington," he seethes. "You're a fucking cock tease, crying wolf, after you pawed at me all night, you practically begged me to fuck you, and then when it came time to follow through, you fucking tried to run...because of you, I had to move to the dorms...a fucking junior in the dorms." His tone grows darker and darker, his hold on my wrists beyond painful now. My lungs burn as I forget to breathe.

"Please...I didn't mean to..." Another cry of pain passes my lips when he twists my wrists, shoving them against my chest, making it hard for me to breathe, hard for me to do anything but feel paralyzing fear.

"You think I'm so bad? You should hear about the things your white knight has done? The girls he's fucked, the people he's hurt. He's no better than me." He curls his lips, rage burning in his eyes.

"Please, I don't care about him...." Tears sting my eyes, and I feel so weak, so fucking weak, and I hate it. I don't want to be helpless. I want to be strong. I want to save myself from the monster in front of me.

"I liked you, Jules. I really fucking did," he sneers, leaning into my face, his lips graze mine, and I press them together refusing to kiss him.

"I'd rather die than kiss you," I growl, somehow finding the courage to speak.

He smiles and it's downright frightening, I feel light headed, sick to my stomach. I let out a sigh when he releases my wrists, but my relief is short-lived because he grabs me by the chin in the next instant, slamming my head back against the wall. Pain lances across the back of my head and I choke on a sob.

"You're going to make this right. Tell him it was nothing more than a miscommunication. Do you understand me? Tell him that you wanted it."

When I don't say anything, he let's go of my chin and grabs me by the shoulders, giving me a hard shake. My head bounces off the brick wall.

"Tell me you'll do it, Jules, tell me you'll tell him it was a lie." The air is thick, making it hard to breathe. He shakes me again and I'm afraid I might pass out.

Gulping air into my lungs like a fish out of water, I nod my head. As soon as I do this, he slams his lips down onto mine. *No.* Shaking my head, I claw at his face and open my mouth, sinking my teeth into his bottom lip.

He finally pushes off of me and I don't miss my chance, my body springing into motion before my brain does. I run past him as far and fast as I can. The coppery tang of his blood is on my lips and in my mouth only making the sick feeling in my stomach worse.

I've never been a great runner, but today I could run a marathon. My lungs burn, my muscles ache, but I don't stop, and I don't dare look back. I don't even slow down until I reach the door of my house. Frantically I unlock the door and hurry inside, slamming it closed behind me, I turn the lock into place. But even the sound of the lock turning doesn't make me feel safe, not really.

Slumping down to the floor next to the door, I wish Cally and Bridget were here while just as equally being glad that they are not. I don't want to talk about this...not about any of it. All I want is to forget about what happened and for Cole to leave me alone.

After a few minutes, I force myself to get up and go into my room. I take a hot shower hoping I can wash away the feeling of his touch on my skin. Unfortunately, no amount of soap or water could do that. The memory of that night is ingrained in my mind, no matter how hard I try and forget it. Unable to hold myself together, I sob quietly into the spray of water.

I never should've come here...first everything with Remington, and now Cole. I should have known better. I swipe at the tears, willing myself to stop crying. I'm stronger than this. When I'm finished, I dry off and lock myself in my room. What the hell am I supposed to do now? I think about calling Seb, but when I imagine telling him what happened, I can't bring myself to pick up the phone. I don't want to relive this, I just want it to stop.

I want Cole to go away, his memory to disappear. I think about calling Remmy, but I don't even have his number and even if I had it, I'm not sure I could bring myself to tell him either. Seeing how he reacted that night, I'm afraid to see what he would do now.

How far would he go? I can't have that on my conscience. The easiest thing is to just leave it alone. Maybe I can see about switching classes? I take a couple calming breaths to stop myself from having a full-on panic attack then I get dressed and sit down at my little desk, gazing down at all my homework.

Only after I've been staring at it for what feels like an hour, do I admit to myself that I can't do any of it right now. My mind is too full to concentrate on math and bio.

I let my head fall onto the desk and close my eyes trying to clear my mind, I think about anything else that will come to mind, chocolate cake, my brother, Remington, but nothing helps.

All I see is Cole above me, his lust filled gaze piercing mine. All I feel are his hands on my skin...his finger biting into my flesh. It feels like I'm suffocating, the fear of the unknown crippling me. For hours, I sit on my bed, crying, wishing I could turn back time and change what happened. I hear Cally and Bridget walking around the house, talking to each other but I don't go out to see them.

There's no way I could handle seeing them right now, not without breaking down and telling them what happened. So instead I stay barricaded in my room...attempting to ignore their presence altogether.

It grows harder and harder to do and I almost break down when Cally knocks on my bedroom door to ask if I'm hungry. I bite my tongue and ignore her while silent tears slip down my cheeks.

After a while, I hear them going into their rooms and only then do I check the time. It's a little past ten and I wish I could close my eyes and go to sleep, but I don't even try. Cole's image haunts me every time I close my eyes. Another hour passes, and I can't take it anymore, the walls of my room are closing in around me. The dread and loneliness in my gut becoming too much to handle. I need someone...someone who understands me, and makes me feel safe, someone who was there that night. *Remington.* I pull on a sweatshirt over my flannel pajamas and put on my sneakers before unlocking my door.

I walk out into the hall, and then the living room. The house is quiet and dark, but I try not to get hung up on it. I just move quicker than normal. With nothing but my keys and my phone, I run across campus just as I did earlier today, without stopping for anything until I'm standing in front of Remmy's place, my heart in my throat, and my lungs burning.

I knock on the door with a shaky hand, almost regretting my decision to come here. I hear footsteps approaching the door and I pray that it's Remmy behind that door, but when it swings open, I see it's Thomas on the other side.

"Oh, hey Jules…"

I don't even answer him. I just duck under his arm and push into the house, running straight for Remmy's room. When I reach the door, I turn the knob to open it, but it doesn't open. *Why is it locked?* Panic claws at my insides. What if he isn't here, or doesn't want to see me? What if Layla is here?

I keep wiggling the knob as if it will magically unlock while slamming my palm against the wood. I can feel the stinging of tears in my eyes, and like a total loser, I stand there continuing to beat against the door.

Several seconds later the door opens and an angry looking Remmy appears before me. The moment he sees me, his features soften, worry creasing his forehead.

"What's wrong, Jules?" I fall into his room and into his arms without answering him.

I'm only partially aware of him closing the door and half carrying me to the bed. I'm too consumed by him, how I'm finally in his arms, my face buried in his chest, just like I wished to be all day. He wraps his arms around me, holding me tighter and for the first time today, I feel safe. Inhaling his scent calms me further and my eyes drift closed, suddenly feeling heavy with exhaustion.

"Jules, you need to tell me what's wrong. I'm kind of freaking out here. Did something happen?" He gently rubs small circles against my back. I'm close to breaking down and telling him about Cole cornering me, but I just can't get the words out, my tongue too heavy, my throat clogged with too much emotion. I feel weak and disgusted with myself even though I know it's Cole that I should be disgusted with and not myself.

"I… I just had a bad dream," I lie. "I got scared and I wanted to see you. Is that okay?" At least that part isn't a lie.

"How did you get here?"

"I walked," I admit and at my confession, Remmy's pulling away, holding me at arm's length, his eyes roaming over my face, inspecting me from head to toe. His chest rises and falls angrily, and I don't understand what his problem is.

"You can't be doing that again. It's dangerous to walk places in the middle of the night, even on campus, and especially alone. Next time, call me, text me, whatever, but do not walk over here by yourself again," he scolds harshly, and I nod my head in agreement. Then as if nothing happened, he's pulling me back into his arms, placing my head against his chest, while cradling the back of it.

The warmth of his body seeps into mine, and I wish I could crawl inside him. I wish I could be his, and he be mine. He could make me forget about Cole.

"You're shaking, Jules, are you sure it was just a dream? Did something happen while you were walking here?"

I bite the inside of my cheek, bile rising in my throat, while I hold my confession deeper inside, letting it eat away at me.

"It was nothing, just a bad dream. I'm okay now."

"Was it...?" His voice trails off, and I know what he's asking without even asking him to elaborate and this time I don't lie.

"Yes," I sigh, feeling some type of relief at saying it out loud. "Every time I close my eyes, I see him. I see myself lying there beneath him, begging him to stop, but he never does...he never stops, Remmy." The tears start to fall without permission, and I hope this is a one-time thing, Cole's presence simply bringing all my fears to the forefront tonight.

Remmy's hold on me tightens. "He will never touch you again, Jules, never. I will fucking kill him if he tries to hurt you again. I don't care if I go to prison for the rest of my life. He will never do to you what he did again."

And that is yet another reminder of why I have to lie to him tonight, why I keep the truth hidden beneath the sleeves of my sweatshirt.

"I know." I exhale a ragged breath. "I just wanted to be somewhere safe, somewhere I know that the nightmares can't reach me."

Remmy's lips graze my forehead, and then he's pulling us backward, positioning us on the bed with my body draped across his. He doesn't say anything, and it's like he knows what I need, like he knows I need his heartbeat beneath my ear.

He soothes me, his hand moving up and down my back with gentle strokes.

"I'll do this every single night if I have to. If you need me, I'll be here. I told you earlier...I'll be whatever you need me to be. I'll do whatever you need me to do. If all you need is someone to hold you at night, then I'll be that someone. If you want me only as a friend, I'll be that for you."

My chest shakes as I force oxygen into it. I want that...I want all of it, him with me each night, him as mine, and mine alone.

"Would you really?" I whisper, hoping he doesn't hear me.

"Yes, Jules. I would do anything to make you mine again, and I will, make you mine again. As long as it takes, I'll wait. I'll climb whatever mountain I have to, be whoever you need me to be. I'll do it because you're worth it Jules, you're fucking worth it."

And just like that, I feel whole again. The nightmares will take time to fade, the memory of Cole will always be there, but with Remington's promise in my heart and wrapped around my soul, I'll never be alone again.

"I love you." I'm pretty sure I say inside my head...my eyelids growing heavier and heavier with exhaustion...and just as I'm about to drift off to sleep, I swear I hear him say the words back to me.

*"I love you too."*

## 17

## REMINGTON

*R*emington

TELLING her I loved her was easy, letting the emotions wrap around me even easier. Being with Jules was natural. She owns me, since day one of kindergarten she had carved out a piece of my heart, stealing it and carrying it with her everywhere she went. She lives inside me, just as I live inside of her.

The last two days have been bittersweet. I know what happened with Cole is eating away at her. She's scared, the nightmares plaguing her at night, hell, even during the day she seems jumpy and on edge. And even though I hate that she feels like this, there's a selfish part of me that revels in how she is leaning on me to be her everything.

Physically and emotionally, she is leaning on me in every way she can and that's all I've ever wanted in the last three years, was for her to need me like I need her.

She's slept at my place for the last three nights, the first when she ran over by herself but the last two, she's called me, and I picked her up. If it were up to me, she would never leave, and I would hold her in my arms every night for the rest of my life, but it's not up to me and I won't push her until she's ready.

"Are you okay?" I ask her, causing her to jump a foot off the bed.

"Oh, yeah...I'm fine." Her body trembles and I know she's lying. She's been lying this whole time, and I've just been too big of a pussy to confront her but watching her jump at something as simple as a question angers me.

I can't bear to see her lie to me anymore. I need to know what's going on, to know if it's just the dreams plaguing her or if there is something deeper going on.

"Really? You jumped a foot off the bed because I asked you if you were okay?" I keep my voice gentle and sit down next to her.

She scrunches up her nose. "It's just the nightmares, that's all."

"And what are they about?"

Panic fills her eyes, and when she blinks, it's gone. "I don't want to talk about it, okay? I just want to forget about my bad dreams," she tells me, twisting her body toward mine and slinging her leg over mine so she is straddling me. I know she's trying to distract me and fuck, it's working.

The last three nights, I did nothing but hold her in my arms. I told my dick over and over again to calm the fuck down which has worked so far but now she's straddling me, grinding her hips, pressing her center into my lap, making her pussy rub against my steel hard cock, making all rational thinking fly out the window.

"Jules...we should really—"

She cuts me off, her lips crashing into mine, making me forget everything I just wanted to say. Fuck, she knows exactly what she is doing. She snakes her arms around my neck, pulling me closer. And fuck, I'd be lying if I said I didn't want to rip off her clothes and fuck her senseless.

I can feel the heat of her pussy through the denim of my jeans, so close, but yet so far away. I've wanted her body more than anything the last couple of days, but I can't do this right now. Whatever she's attempting to cover up is bigger than I thought.

"Fuck," I hiss, pulling away, her teeth sinking into my bottom lip to stop me. If I don't stop her now, then I'll forget all about asking her what her problem is, and though that's her intention, it's not what I want. Unwinding her arms from my neck, I push her back a bit, noting the frown forming on her lips.

"You don't want me?" she murmurs, and the look in her eyes kills me.

"I do. I want you so bad, my cock is literally begging me to sink inside you, but I want to make sure you're okay above all else."

She shakes her head, sending a tumble of blonde curls across her face. When she tries to pull away, I grab her by the wrists and she winces, actually winces as if I've hurt her when I know for sure that I didn't.

I wasn't even grabbing her that hard.

"Jules?" She tries to pull away again, tears in her eyes, her bottom lip quivering, and I know something is seriously fucking wrong. I release her wrists but grab her hand and pull up her sleeve. Worry gives way to blinding fury.

"What the fuck?" Tears are now running down her cheeks and

her lip shaking has turned into whole body shaking. Panic claws at my insides, what the hell happened? I don't let go of her hand, I just stare at the bruises around her delicate wrists.

Blue, black and already yellow in some places tell me this happened recently.

"Who did this?" I question, my voice a whisper of disbelief. When she doesn't answer me, I curse under my breath.

"Jules, you need to tell me what happened." I look up, her lips are pressed into a hard line and she keeps shaking her head. It's like she's shutting down and I can't fucking have that. Why is she so scared of telling me? Then it clicks... like a puzzle piece finding its home.

"Did Cole do this? Is your other wrist bruised like this too?"

Before she can answer me, I snatch her other hand and pull up that sleeve as well, finding the same marks on that side. My imagination takes over, her silence only fueling the horrible scenarios running through it.

"Jules, if you don't tell me what happened...I will assume the worst and then I will go and find Cole right now and break his fucking neck. He touched you and that's a worthy enough cause." My response gets her attention and suddenly she's reeling.

"No, no, no, this is exactly why I didn't want you to know!"

My brow furrows. "What the hell? Why? Because I would protect you? Kill him? Destroy him?" Fury burns deep in my veins...he's going to pay for hurting her. I swear he hasn't seen the last of me yet.

"Yes! Because I knew you would go and do something stupid. I knew you would want to go and kill him or at the least beat the crap out of him."

"And what's the problem with that? He touched you, he left fucking bruises, Jules, he literally squeezed your wrists so hard he left bruises and you expect me to just let him be, to not fucking kill him? You're insane if you think I'll let him get away with this."

"The problem is that you'll end up in jail or worse, get yourself killed," she whispers, and I shake my head at her response feeling too many emotions all at once.

"I don't give a fuck. I'll go to prison for the rest of my life if I have to. He shouldn't have fucking touched you." I didn't know what Cole's obsession was with her, but I wasn't going to wait to find out. In my eyes, he was as good as dead.

"And what about me? What's going to happen to me if you go to jail? You would just leave me like that?" Her words hit me like a bullet to the chest, searing through the tissue and muscle, leaving behind a gaping wound.

It hadn't really occurred to me that she's just as scared of losing me as I'm scared of losing her and somehow that realization has me crashing back down to Earth. I can't do something that's going to cost me, her, not when I just got her back, but I also can't just let Cole get away with putting his hands on her.

"Did you go to the police or at the least campus security?"

She shakes her head. "No, I just want to forget about it. I don't want to have to tell them what happened over and over again. I just... I just want to forget...forget it all."

"And what exactly did happen?" My whole body is vibrating with anger and it takes everything inside of me not to jump up and go find him, but I need to know what he did to her. I need to be here for her now. She needs me.

"He just told me to tell you that I lied. That I wanted it..." Her eyes lift to mine the blue in them bluer than I've ever seen. "But I didn't want it Remmy, you know that, don't you? I didn't want him. I still don't. I just want to forget him, forget that he didn't stop when I told him to, forget what his body feels like, his lips..." Anguish clogs her throat as she speaks and she grabs onto my shirt, clinging to me, her face mere inches from my own.

"Make me forget, Rem, replace every memory...take me, make me yours..."

And fuck if I hadn't always wanted to hear her say those words, just not like this, not under these circumstances.

With a soothing hand, I rub up and down her back. "You don't need this right now... I want you, Jules, so badly it's killing me, but I don't want you to regret it. I don't want you to wake up tomorrow and wonder if you made the right choice."

And I don't. I don't want our first time together to be something she regrets for the rest of her life.

"I love you, Rem. I've loved you since we were kids, and nothing will ever change that. You should know that...but I can't keep living like this. All I feel is him...his hands on me and I want it to be you. Make me forget, give me new memories. Please?" More tears slip from her eyes, and she's breaking my fucking heart. She knows I can't deny her, not when the need is pulsing inside me.

"Jules," I groan, knowing damn well I can make her forget that shitty memory.

"Please, I'm begging you..."

And just like that, I snap. I can't deny her something I want just as badly as she does. Slamming my mouth against hers, I claim her with unyielding need. I'll ingrain this moment into her mind, wash away the memories that bastard left behind. I'll hold her, kiss her, sear our souls together so she never forgets this moment.

Jules' moan of pleasure fills my mouth and I swallow it, my tongue gaining entry past her lips. I stroke her tongue with my own, until I feel her clawing at my shirt, a primal need to undress me consuming her.

Pulling away, I let her pull my shirt off. I do the same, pulling her shirt off and tossing it to the floor. My gaze roams over her, and I gulp, my body shaking, my cock hardening to a damn near painful state. She looks so innocent, her chest heaving, her breasts swelling out the top of her soft pink bra. With a gentleness I wasn't aware I even had, I press her back against the mattress, reaching for the button on her jeans.

My eyes lift to hers, and I need to know she still wants this, that she hasn't changed her mind.

"If you want me to stop...you need to say so now. I want you, so fucking bad, but I can wait, Jules. I've waited my whole fucking life, what's another month, or year?"

She shakes her head, her white teeth sinking into her pink bottom lip seductively, and I wonder if she even knows she's doing it. God, she's so beautiful, so perfect, so fucking mine. I'll destroy Cole for touching her, and any other son of a bitch that thinks he can have her.

"No. I want this. I want you. I'm yours, and nothing will ever change that, no amount of time will change that. Take me."

My heart soars out of my chest, and I flick the button on her jeans and move my hands to her hips, grabbing the denim. I peel the skin tight fabric down her legs, admiring her creamy white flesh. So delicate, soft, and pure...fuck, she's everything I don't deserve, but I'll be damned if I'm going to give her up. I toss the jeans to the floor, reveling in her tiny little nails that sink into the tender flesh of my arm.

"I'm going to taste you...taste this pretty little pussy, do you want that?" I murmur, brushing my lips against her smooth tummy. My eyes lift to hers, seeking approval. Her long lashes fan against her cheeks, cheeks that are now a rosy pink, like nothing I've seen before.

"Yes..." she answers breathlessly, and I smile against her skin, loving that she reacts to me the way she does. I pepper her skin with kisses, making my way down her body and knead one of her perky tits through the lace of her bra, finding her nipple already hardened for me.

"You're so fucking perfect. It's like your body was made for me...mine to fuck, to eat, to worship," I mumble, pulling my hand away from her tit so I can rid her of her matching pink panties. I slide them down her legs and fling them over my shoulder. Then with a gentle hand, I push her legs apart, my eyes moving straight to her heat.

"Fuck me," I groan, licking my lips. Her folds are glistening, hiding her tiny little clit inside. The selfish part of me is thankful as hell that I'll be the one and only man to feast on her, to feel her tightness squeeze around my cock. While the other part of me feels like I don't deserve this gift that she's giving me.

"Please?" She grins down at me, her soft voice dripping with need. With a chuckle, I slide both my hands under her ass cheeks, and lift her, my lips pressing over her slit. She wiggles, lifting her hips to bring my lips right where she wants them.

"Patience, love, we've got all night and yes, I do plan on devouring you, then fucking you, and then devouring you all over again."

"Remmy." She lets out a frustrated sigh as I skim over her slit, one last time, before slipping the tip of my tongue between her folds.

As soon as my tongue flicks against her diamond hard clit, she gasps, her hands flying into my hair. She tugs at the soft strands urging me to give her more and as badly as I want her, to taste her release on my tongue, I give in.

I circle her clit, flicking against the nub, alternating between flicks and sucking on it, till I feel her thighs quake. She's so wet, so fucking warm. My hands move on their own, one to her hip to hold her in place, while I take the other and swirl a finger through her arousal. I coat the thick digit in her sweet syrup, before moving it to her entrance.

I'm panting, burning with need when I slip inside, watching as her face morphs into pure angelic fucking pleasure. I've never seen something so intoxicating, so perfect in my life.

"God... oh...." she pants and I pump that finger in and out of her while keeping pressure against her clit. Her hips buck, and I feel her pussy tightening, her core squeezing my finger so tight, my chest heaves, my eyes close for a brief second. Fuck, she's so tight, I worry for a moment that I might not fit. I don't want to fucking hurt her, but there is no way in hell I'm not claiming that part of her. Her virginity is mine, all fucking mine.

"Come, Jules, come on my fucking hand," I order, my voice rumbling against her core as I flick my tongue against the hard bud while continuing to finger fuck her. Two more soft thrusts inside her and she's coming, her body shaking, tremors of pleasure washing over her.

Her forehead is sweaty and her chest heaves as she tries to catch her breath. A beautiful flush creeps up her neck and onto her cheeks and I continue to pump in and out of her, extending her pleasure until her body stops trembling and she sinks back down into the mattress.

"That was..." she gasps.

"Amazing? Earth shattering?" I grin, and move off the bed, undoing my jeans and shoving them and my boxers down in one swoop. My cock juts out, standing proud and when I lift my gaze to Jules, I see both fear and excitement reflecting back at me.

"What's with the look? It's not like you haven't seen it before." She visibly gulps, her eyes still on my cock.

"I know, but it wasn't going inside me last time." She's got me there, but I've prepared her body, she'll be okay, plus I'm not going to fuck her. I'm going to make love to her, and there's a difference.

"It's okay, Jules," I whisper, leaning in, pressing a soft kiss against her lips to ease some of the fear out of her. Her tiny nails dig into my biceps as I situate myself above her, holding most of my weight on my forearms. This close, I can feel how nervous she is, her body trembles as I hitch up one of her legs, spreading her wider. My cock grazes her heat, and a shiver of unbridled pleasure ripples through me.

"I want to take you bareback." My hot breath fans against her face, and with one hand, I tip her chin upward to look at me.

"Without a condom?" she questions, her adorable nose wrinkling.

"Yes. I've never fucked anyone without a condom, and I want you to be my first. I can't give you my virginity, but I can give you this."

She licks her lips and then nods her head, and I swear to god I don't fucking deserve her.

"I'm not on birth control," she admits as I pull back.

"I'll pull out and after this we'll go and get you on birth

control," I tell her, feeling the need to be inside her consume me. "If that's what you want."

The thought of getting her pregnant doesn't change a fucking thing. In my mind, I always knew if I ever had kids, it would be with her. It would just tie her to me in another way, but as much as I want to keep her tied to me in every way possible, I don't want to do that to her right now. We'll have children when she is ready. Taking my cock into my hand, I stroke it a few times, staring down at her before I guide the velvety head to her drenched entrance.

She grabs onto me like I might run away, and I press into her heat, my eyes rolling to the back of my fucking head as I stretch her tight little hole.

"Remmy," Jules whines and I grit my teeth, forcing myself to focus on her, and not just thrust deep inside her channel with all my fucking might. I open my eyes and look down at her. Pain contours her features, and I lift a hand, cupping her by the cheek, my touch gentle.

"Just breathe, baby, it'll only hurt this time," I growl, barely breathing myself. Fuck me, all I've got is the tip in and I'm losing my mind. What happens when I'm eight inches deep? How will I stop myself from fucking her with her tightness squeezing the life out of me? My body shakes, and a bead of sweat forms against my brow as I push in another inch.

Jules gasps, her grip tightening. "You're so big...I don't know if it's going to fit."

I grin down at her, my thumb gently caressing her cheek.

"Oh, it's going to fit. Your pretty pussy was made for me. Every inch of you was made for me." Refusing to prolong the pain, I swoop down and press a heated kiss to her already swollen lips, as

I thrust forward at the same time, pushing through her barrier and deep into her virgin channel.

Tears spring from her eyes, sliding down her cheeks and I pull away, though I keep my lips just a breath away from hers. She feels like heaven, so soft, warm, and wet. She fits around me like a glove, my cock twitches, my hips and muscles burning as I remain deathly still deep inside her.

"I'm sorry," I whisper over and over again, wiping her tears away while peppering kisses to her face. After a short time, I start to move again, watching her intently. Her grip on me is still hard, but I love it. I love having her hold on to me like she's afraid I might disappear.

As I move more and more the discomfort in her eyes seems to diminish and soon I find myself moving in and out of her at a torturously slow pace. I don't go as hard as I normally would, but with Jules, I don't need to. My body's already burning up, pleasure searing through my bones with each shallow thrust. My muscles burn, my body begging for me to thrust deeper, to go harder, to have her like I've always wanted.

"More, I want more," she urges, lifting one of her legs, pressing her heel into my ass to pull me closer.

"I don't want to hurt you," I hiss out, even though I really, really want to fucking do as she's asking.

"You aren't," she pants, her big blues pleading, and I feel her pussy flutter around my cock. Fuck, she's going to come. I didn't know if it was possible the first time. I thought there would only be pain, but like always, Jules is perfect in every way.

"You want to come all over my cock, baby?" I purr in her ear, going a little harder, relishing in the moan of pleasure that escapes her lips.

"Ohhhh..." she mewls.

"Milk my cock...with your pretty pussy," I growl into her flesh, pressing kisses to her throat before hanging my head in the crook of her neck, inhaling our mixed scents. I could lose myself completely in her, in every way possible and that terrifies me, it scares the shit out of me.

"Remmy..." She digs her nails into my shoulders, and I thrust even harder, hitting the back of her channel. "Sooo...good...want more..."

Her words give me the final push over the edge. The last shred of self-control I have rips straight down the middle and I start thrusting into her deeper and faster than before, listening to her moans and pants in my ear as they act as fuel pushing me closer to the finish line.

Sex has never felt like this before, so raw, emotional and all-consuming. I didn't even know what the term love making meant until today. The connection between us has grown, we're now tethered body and soul.

It's like we are becoming one in this moment, and I don't have a fucking clue where my body ends and hers begins. Our limbs are tangled, our skin fused together as we slide across one another, molded ourselves, my hard pieces pressing into her soft pieces. We are two complex shapes that somehow fit together perfectly.

"I'm close...so close..." she pants.

"Fuck...yes, baby, come, please come..." I growl, thrusting deeper. I swivel my hips and move one of my hands between our bodies to find her clit. When I do, I press my fingers right on the small bundle of nerves. Her body jerks against mine and as soon as I touch it, she falls apart, her body arching off the bed, her nails raking down my back.

I want to look at her face and take in every second of this, but with her pussy clenching around my cock, I can't hold off my own climax much longer. Keeping my fingers on her clit, I maneuver into a kneeling position, easing out of her slowly so I can find my own release. I fist my cock with my free-hand and stroke it while watching the aftershocks of Jules' orgasms run through her body.

Her clit throbs on my fingers just like my cock throbs in my hand and without even thinking about it, I explode. Jets of sticky cum spurt from my cock and land on Jules' lower belly, and a groan I'm sure the entire house can hear escapes my lips. Stroking my cock, I watch the ropes claim her delicate skin, until there's nothing left inside me.

When I fall back down to Earth, I catch sight of the mess I've made, and then look up to Jules' face. She gives me a sleepy grin, and I'm overcome with emotions. She looks satisfied, in more than just a physical sense... as if she feels whole, happy, and content.

Whatever it takes, I'll do it, just to keep her in my arms, to keep her as mine.

"Are you okay?" I ask, wanting to comfort her, needing to make certain I didn't hurt her. "Do you want to take a shower? Or do you just want me to get a washcloth and clean you up?"

"I'm great. I just don't want to move," she murmurs, looking like she's about to go to sleep, her eyes heavily lidded.

"Hold on," I tell her before going into the bathroom to grab a washcloth. I wet it with a little warm water and then apply a small amount of soap and lather it. Jules is still laying with her legs spread apart, making it easier to clean her up. Using care and a gentleness that I've seemed to master, I clean her up. By the time I'm done, she can barely keep her eyes open.

Once I'm done with her, I clean myself off and slip into bed next to her, pulling her into my arms, and immediately regretting that I didn't put some boxers on. Even though I just had her, I'm already thinking about taking her again.

*Tomorrow*, I tell myself...and then the day after that...and the day after the next...and forever, because there is no way in hell now that I've finally made her mine again, that I'm letting another man touch her, that I'm letting her go.

## JULES

"I want you," Remington purrs in my ear, sucking on the skin right below it. He knows exactly what to say and do to get me out of my panties, but that isn't happening right now, maybe later tonight but not right now.

"Homework." I barely get the word out, a moan escaping just after it.

Remmy pulls away, chuckling like the evil man he is. "Are you sure you want to do homework? That moan sounds a lot like something else."

Rolling my eyes, I slug him playfully in the arm. "Remington," I scold. "I need to do homework, so less trying to get my panties off of me, and more helping me study."

He gives me a frown but pulls away, putting some space between us. It's easier now than ever to get caught up in him. We're not officially an item yet, but I know he isn't going to step out on me and not just because he tells me fifty times a day.

He told me that I make him want to be a better man, a better man than he has been in the last three years. I told him to prove it to me, and boy has he been trying. I can see how much he wants this...see how much he wants us.

I'd be lying if I didn't say I want the same. I want this part of him so much. Day by day, I believe him that the person he became while I was gone is not here anymore and won't ever return. I haven't told him yet, but I'm ready.

I'm ready to give us another chance, to forget about the past. I want to focus on the future and stop dwelling on the things that neither of us can change. I want to make up for lost time and give us the chance we never got, the chance we deserve.

Remmy makes me feel whole, he fills the missing pieces in my heart. My nightmares are gone with him and I feel better overall, less scared and more content than I have in years...three years to be exact.

"What are you studying for anyway? You don't need to study."

Of course he would say that.

"Yes, I do. I can't just wave a dollar bill and pass a class."

"What's that supposed to mean?" he questions, almost seeming as if he is hurt.

"That I need to study to actually pass my classes, which basically means you need to shut up." I grin.

"You're implying that I use money to get good grades?" He narrows his gaze.

"Of course not. You totally study and go to class every single day," I tease.

A second later, my phone chimes on the nightstand interrupting our conversation.

*What the hell?* No one ever texts me, not unless it's Rem or Cally.

Remington's phone goes off in his pocket a second later and my brow furrows in confusion as I pick up my phone to glance down at the screen. It's a text from a number I don't recognize. Out of the corner of my eye, I catch Remington pulling his phone out as well.

I click on the text and realize it's a voice recording which leaves me even more confused. Why would someone send me a voice recording? Whoever it is must have the wrong number, still, curiosity gets the better of me and I use my thumb to press play.

"*Should I fuck your pussy or your ass?...Maybe I'll fuck both. Tell everyone you were a whore that begged me to take both of your holes...*"

"*Remington...*"

My heart beats out of my chest, my pulse seeming to race faster and faster with each word that meets my ears. I grip my phone so tightly in my hands that I can feel the metal digging into my flesh.

"What-what is this?" I turn to Remington who is looking down at his phone, pure fear and horror taking over his features. Oh...oh my god... I remember this day, the first time he touched me... but I didn't know he was recording what happened. Was this... had he planned this all along?

"You recorded us?" I push from the bed, refusing to be anywhere near him.

"Jules..." He looks up at me like he knows he's lost me for good.

"What did you do?" I stammer. "Who sent this?" I yell, still not getting the response I want. When he moves off the bed and takes a step toward me, I shake my head, feeling the tears sting my eyes. Betrayal cuts through me, slicing so deep I can hardly breathe, hardly think.

Why did he do this? Is he still trying to hurt me? Is this part of his game?

"I didn't..." he starts. "It's not what you think. I don't know who sent it, but I can assure you that this wasn't my intention. I would never... I'd never..."

When he reaches for me, I slap his hand. My entire body starts to shake, my mind reeling. Who has this recording? Who sent it? Why did he do this to us? There are a thousand questions coursing through my mind and no answers in sight.

"Did you even love me? Did you even care? You took my virginity...was that what this was? A game for you to see if you could get in my panties? Was I just another conquest? Another notch on your bedpost?" The downcast look he gives me confirms my assumption, and the room seems to grow smaller around me.

"I can't believe you." My stomach churns, knotting and twisting so painfully it feels like someone is stabbing me with a knife. "Actually, I can. This is who you are, who you've always been." The words come out bitter, angry, and the voice emitting the words doesn't even sound like it belongs to me.

"Wait, just let me explain, Jules." Remington's voice cuts through the fog encasing my mind. He reaches for me again and this time I let the fury burning inside me out.

"You did this!" I grit my teeth, my hand rearing back to slap him. I slap him so hard my hand stings, the pain a welcoming feeling beside the sadness clinging to my heart. His head swings to the side with the blow and I shove him toward the door.

"I can't believe you did this. Was it all just a game? A sick fucking joke? Huh? Tell me! Tell me right now!" I scream, uncaring who hears me.

"No." His head hangs in shame and I refuse to let him act like he is the victim in this.

"No... No... you don't get to act like you're the one hurt here. You fucking did this. Was it revenge? Was everything you told me a lie?" I don't know why I'm asking these questions, they don't matter anymore. My heart shattered in two the moment I heard the first word of that voice recording.

"It's not like that. I didn't send this."

"You're a liar. A fucking liar." I shake my head, unable to believe anything he says. I thought we had found love again, but it was just a joke. A knock sounds on my bedroom door, and a moment later, Cally walks in with a horrific look in her eyes.

"Did you get the text?" she whispers and that's when something inside me snaps. Losing Remington the first time hurt, but this time...I feel nothing...he shared our very first moment together with everyone, every single fucking person.

"Jules, please...let me try and make this right..."

I'm shutting down. I no longer hear his words or see his face. There is no friendship, no love, everything was a lie, built on lies, and spread as a joke by him.

"Leave," I whisper.

He looks at me like I've slapped him. "Please, Jules don't..."

"Leave!!!!" I scream, pointing toward the door. I can feel the tears in my eyes, my chest heaves, and my heart slams against my ribcage so painfully it might as well be beating on the outside of my body.

"Let me explain this to you first...It isn't..."

"Leave, or I'm calling the cops," I scream, shoving him in the chest, and he lets me, he lets me shove him. "I hate you, I can't believe I let you do this. I trusted you and you...I hate you so much. You're dead to me...I never ever want to see you again. We're done, all of this, it never existed. To me, you never existed..." I hit him over and over again, and then just like I asked, he turns around and walks out of the bedroom. My hands fall to my sides and I stare coldly at the spot he was just standing in.

As soon as I hear the front door close, I sink down to the floor. I'm distinctly aware of my knees slamming into the carpet, my stomach clenching into a tight knot, pain searing every single cell in my body. It feels like my heart is being ripped out of my chest.

*This is what he wanted. This was his revenge.*

He used me, and I played right into his fucking hand like a stupid girl. Stupid. I was so fucking stupid to believe he wanted me. He warned me when I first got here, he told me what he was going to do, and I let him...I let him do this to me.

"Jules." Cally's voice registers in my ears, but I don't react. I'm too far gone, too broken to feel anything. Through tears, I watch as she sinks to the floor in front of me, her arms wrapping around me. I can feel her holding me tightly, but nothing will fuse me back together again. I thought I was hurt before, shattered beyond repair, but nothing compares to now.

"I... I... need to leave." I push to my knees abruptly, and then onto my shaky legs.

"What? You can't leave, Jules, not in this state."

Ignoring her, I grab a bag out of my closet and start stuffing clothing into it, not even paying attention to the items I'm grabbing.

*Where will I go? Who can save me from him?*

I pause, thinking to myself. Only one word comes to mind: Sebastian.

He'll protect me. He'll make sure his brother doesn't come for me.

"Jules, you can't leave, where will you go?" Cally's voice is filled with fear, with worry, but it doesn't register in my mind. I search the room for my phone, pick it up, ignoring every single message that lights up the screen. Scrolling to Sebastian's number, I hit the green call button. It doesn't even ring once and his deep voice is filtering into the speaker.

"Jules?"

"Can you pick me up, please?" My voice is numb, no emotion to it whatsoever.

*He did this to you. He used you. Stole from you.*

"Of course, where are you?" I can hear him moving around, the sound of keys jingling in the background.

"My house," I respond.

"Okay, I'll be there in a few."

I hang up the phone, power it off and shove it into the bag with the rest of my stuff.

"Jules, please, just talk...you need to talk about this. I can help you fix this, we can report it to administration. They'll make him pay for hurting you."

*Pay? He'll never pay for hurting me, and if I stay here, I'll just get hurt more.*

I shake my head, my throat burns, bile rising from my stomach and into my throat. I feel sick, and the last thing I want to do at all is feel, because feeling means pain, and pain is a reminder of what he did to me. He ruined me. He made me love him deeper than I ever loved him before, and then he ripped me to pieces, ripped the love right out from under me.

"No," I croak. "I'm leaving. If he comes back here, tell him to leave. Do not tell him where I went..." I sling my backpack over my shoulder. The frown on Cally's face deepens, but she nods her head in agreement and I leave the room, heading for the front door.

I'm numb, broken, the lies and betrayal cut through me so deep that the pain doesn't even register in my mind anymore. The wound in my chest bleeds with every beat of my heart and I hope for the day when my heart stops beating for a man that never loved me, that merely used me as revenge. When Sebastian's SUV pulls up in front of the house, I slip through the door, hoping I never have to return to this place again.

There's nothing here for me anymore...nothing.

## 19

## REMINGTON

It's so hard for me to focus on my steps, my eyes blurring with tears. My heart beats so furiously it feels like I'm on the verge of a heart attack. I've lost her...in the same week I got her back, I lost her. The hate I have for myself rivals any anger, any revenge, I ever wanted.

She didn't deserve this. My head hangs low, I'm ashamed. I know I've lost Jules, I know it deep in my heart...but that doesn't mean I can't make the person who sent out that text pay. Without Jules, I have nothing to live for, which means it won't matter if I get thrown in prison for killing the fucker that I know did this.

Every muscle in my body burns with an urge to act out in violence, and I curb it by clenching my hand into a fist, my nails biting into my palm. I jog back to the house, even though it's the last place I want to go. Blood pounds in my ears, the hole in my chest burns, as Jules words play on repeat inside my head.

*You hurt her...you got your revenge...*

The words fuel my burning rage, my hate for myself and everyone around me. I'll destroy them all, everyone, including myself. When I finally reach the frat house, I open the door, sending it flying into the wall. Thomas is the first to notice me, our eyes clash, and I know he got the message with the recording too. I can tell even without asking, the look on his face one of complete horror.

"It wasn't me," he says, his voice laced with sympathy.

I haven't told him how I feel about Jules, but he isn't stupid, he knows she means more to me than anyone else. I'm not worried about Thomas though. I know exactly who it was, and still, I have no way of finding him right now, which only makes me more irrational. I can't hold the burning rage in any longer and slam my fist into the nearest wall. Pain radiates up my arm, but it doesn't hinder me, instead, it's a welcoming feeling. Uncurling my fist, rivulets of blood drip down over my knuckles.

*You did that to her heart. You broke it. You made it bleed.*

"Dude, are you okay?" Alan's voice cuts through the air and I turn around, swinging my fist at him. It connects with his cheek, and he falls back against the couch from the blow. He raises a hand to his face, shock appearing before anger and I dare him to stand up to me, to try and fight me. I want it. I want his fists…I want to feel pain. I want someone to hurt me…because fuck do I deserve it.

"Don't fucking talk to me. None of you. I hate you all…each of you will pay for this." My lip curls, the need to make all of them bleed burning deep in my veins, but even in my irrational state, I know this isn't their fault. This is mine, all fucking mine.

I ruined us. I hurt Jules. They didn't. I fucking did.

Knowing I have to get out of here before I do something

stupid, I stomp up the stairs and into my room. Once I'm alone, I lose my damn mind. Tears sting my eyes, slipping down my face, my entire body shakes as I break and destroy every single thing inside the room. I hate this place. I hate the person I've become. I hate it all. I pummel the wall with my fists until all I feel is the warmth of blood coating my skin.

It drips down onto the floor, and I stare down at it. Jules' words haunt me. She thought it was a joke, she thought it was revenge. Curling my hand into a fist, I beat it against my head.

Why was I so stupid...why did I let my feelings rule my actions? All I can do is ask myself why? Why? Why did I do this?

*I hate you...I trusted you...I hate you so much. You're dead to me...*

I'll never be able to forget the look in her eyes as she said those words. I had lost her all over again, and because of such a childish fucking thing. A bet... something I had played, had done since freshman year. No one had ever gotten hurt before, not until now.

My fingers slice through my hair, grabbing two fistfuls, I pull on it so hard I think I might pull it straight from my scalp. The sting of pain runs ripples across my scalp, but it's not enough. I want to feel the physical pain. I've never craved pain so much in my life.

My hands are already bloody, my knuckles aching, but it's not enough. It will never be enough... no amount of pain can rival what Jules is going through right now. Not only did I break her with this, but I shattered her... I tried to reason with myself, but she wouldn't forgive me, not ever. Fuck, I wouldn't forgive me. I didn't deserve her forgiveness...her love. Plain and simple, I didn't deserve her, but I couldn't stop loving her.

Tears fall from my eyes. I can't stop punching the wall, over and over again, the drywall sticking to my bloody fists, but I don't stop.

I want to hit something else and nothing's quite as appealing as one person's face.

*Cole.* I need to find him, he did this. He hurt her, threatened her... he sent that fucking recording. I'm fucking sure of it.

Nothing else matters to me. I told Jules I wouldn't go after him, but that was before, before my entire world exploded. Now he would pay, just as I was. He would suffer.

Before I realize it, my feet are moving on their own, carrying me out of my room and down the stairs. All the guys have congregated in the kitchen, their heads snap up when they see me coming. I don't pay them much attention...my focus on one thing, and one thing only.

Which is probably why I don't see that one of the guys standing among my roommates is my brother Sebastian. Confusion... What the hell is he doing here?

I was ready to throw a punch at any of these fuckers, but Seb? I open my mouth to say something, but I don't even get a word out before he's on me. His face is a mask of barely controlled fury, and I know he knows.

His fist slams into my face once, twice, three times...the impact of his punch jarring. Then he releases me with a shove, making me stagger backward. My knees almost buckle, and I have to lean against the wall to keep myself upright.

I deserve this... I deserve it so much.

"What the fuck is wrong with you? How could you do this to her? I can't even believe you are my fucking brother." He shakes his head in disbelief, and I want to tell him I can't believe it either, but I keep my mouth shut.

"I'm so fucking ashamed of you."

Every single one of his words slices through me like a hunting knife carving through my chest. The words are bad, but they are nothing compared to the tone of his voice. I've never heard him sound like this. The agony in his voice. He means everything he's saying...and he should. I'm a disgrace to my family, to the male race.

My father didn't raise me like this. He raised my brothers and me to be good people, not pieces of shit and immature bastards. I can barely look into Sebastian's eyes, the shame, the guilt it owns me. I think of my father... I doubt I'll ever be able to look him in the eyes again, because I know that it will never be the same, he'll never see me as just his son.

I'll always be a reminder of the pain I inflicted on Jules and though my family has forgiven me for some fucked up shit... they will never forgive me for doing this.

"I would have been pissed and disappointed if you did this to another girl...but Jules? I can't even find the words to tell you how I feel right now. Jesus fuck Rem, we've known Jules our whole fucking life. She is like a sister to me, like a daughter to our father..."

The air is sucked from my lungs, and my thoughts start to swim, my head spinning.

"Fucking say something!" Sebastian spits in my face before pulling his fist back and punching me in the stomach so hard I double over and slide to the floor. My knees hit the floor first, the impact vibrating up my body.

*Say something.* What could I possibly say? There is nothing I could say that would make this any better. I can't defend myself, because there is nothing to defend. Everything he has said is true. I did this...to Jules.

*I. Fucking. Did. This.*

I don't even care. I want to forget...to live in pain, to let it own me. But Sebastian isn't like everyone else, and he cares for Jules like her brother did, and so I know he won't let me forget hurting her. He'll protect her...make things right. He will do everything I should be doing right now.

"Why? Just fucking tell me why?" he growls, and I gaze up at him, tears leaking from my eyes.

"I was angry with her. I felt betrayed," I croak. I know it's a shitty reason, now looking back on it, my pain was nothing more than heartache, but it felt deeper like losing her was losing a piece of my soul. I had already lost my mother, so when Jules left, there was nothing left. I thought I was heartbroken back then, but the pain I'm feeling now is so much worse.

"Angry for what, Rem? Because her father got a job somewhere else and moved away? That's your big fucking reason for doing all of this? She was fifteen, Rem, what the fuck was she supposed to do?"

A spark of fury ignites inside me, and somehow, I find my voice again.

"She wasn't supposed to leave me!" I scream back at him. My skin heats, and my stomach rolls, bile rising into my throat. I'm disgusted with myself. And my emotions are out of fucking control. I didn't even mean to yell at him, then again maybe I did. I want him to punch me again. I want him to hurt me for what I did to Jules. I don't deserve anything else but the pain. I don't even deserve to live. I don't deserve shit...just pain, heartache, and death.

"You are the most selfish, self-absorbed person I have ever met in my entire life. You never deserved her, never. She loved you, and you destroyed her. You literally could've ripped her heart out of her chest, and it would have hurt less."

He is right, I could've, and once again there is nothing for me to say. There are no words that can be said to take back what's happened. A loud knock on the front door startles all of us.

My head snaps up and I realize that Thomas, Alan, and Kia are still standing only a few feet away from us all looking at my brother and me with the same expressions on their faces.

Guilt, shame, and complete shock. Their faces mirror how I'm feeling only I'm feeling it a million times more than them. They didn't just lose the love of their life, their family, and their fucking life. To them it was a game, to me it was the biggest mistake.

Thomas turns away from all of us and walks over to the front door. As soon as he opens the door, two guys from campus security walk in. Their eyes scan the room until they find me bloodied and beaten on the floor. They don't even look shocked to see me like this, neither do they look concerned or sorry for me.

"Remington Miller, we need you to come with us."

Sebastian drags me off the floor and into a standing position. I don't even need to ask why they're here. I'm sure the audio has made its way around campus by now, and into God knows whose hands. Walking on unsteady legs toward them, I try and shrug off my brother's hand that's digging into my arm, as if he thinks I would fucking run or something.

"I'm sure you know why we're here," one of the men speaks. Sebastian gives me a little shake and I lift my head, staring at him right in the eyes.

"Yes, I know why you're here," I answer, my vocal cords shattered.

"Good. You're being brought in for questioning at this time. You're not being detained or accused of any crimes," the other man states and we walk out the front door. Sebastian practically dragging me down the walkway.

"I'll drive him in since I have to be there during questioning anyway," Sebastian announces, and they give him a curt nod. He releases me and we walk to his SUV. I open the door and force myself to get in. I don't even have the door closed and he starts the car, pulling away from the curb while following the campus security officers.

"I can't get you out of this mess, not that I would if I could. You've dug yourself a deep hole, deeper than money can buy."

"I know." I stare out the window.

"You know?" Disgust coats his words. "You don't fucking know. You have no idea what this is going to do to Jules. She will never want to show her face here again. Once again, she has to find another school, another place to live."

Everything starts to sink in...his confession slashes against my skin. She won't come back to school here, in fact, she'll leave, all over again, and this time it will be my fault, my fucking fault.

"Why don't you say anything? Does this affect you at all?"

A spurt of anger rushes through me. "Of course it fucking affects me, but what do I do, Seb? What the fuck do I say, or do to change what has happened?"

He shakes his head, gripping the steering wheel until his knuckles turn white and all I can envision in that moment is me wrapping my hands around Cole's neck, strangling the filthy fucking life right out of him.

"I didn't send the fucking audio. It wasn't meant to be heard by anyone but the guys."

Sebastian laughs bitterly. "Oh, so that makes it better because it was only meant to be heard by you and your dumbass friends. Well, it shouldn't have been recorded at all." I can tell he's barely restraining himself and I don't even care that he's taking her side, he should, and I'm glad she has him. She needs someone to protect her, because that's not me. I'm a failure, a pathetic bastard.

"No, it doesn't. It was a fucking mistake, and one I will regret for the rest of my life. But aside from that, I didn't send it out. I just want you to know that."

"Then who the fuck did?" He gives me a disbelieving look as he pulls into the administration building parking lot.

"Cole Robson." Simply saying his name out loud angers me. He shakes his head and I know he doesn't believe me. Why should he? Everything I've done, the bet, the recording, the way I've treated her. All of the horrible things point right at me.

"It doesn't look good for you, Rem, not at all. You've got a history with women at this school, and you've done some bad shit in the past. I can tell you now that you had better prepare yourself for what's to come, because it's going to be bad."

I shrug. "I don't care what they're going to do to me."

Nothing could be as bad as watching the one woman you love more than life tell you that she hates you, and never wants to see you again. Nothing...and I mean nothing can hurt worse than that. So I'll take whatever they give me, because God fucking knows I deserve it.

Sebastian doesn't say anything and instead parks and kills the engine. When he opens his door, I suck in a calming breath and climb out of the car, walking around to the front of it.

They can do their worst...say whatever they want, punish me however they please, but nothing will touch the pain I already feel, the guilt and shame that coats my insides like sludge.

I did this.

I broke her.

I ruined us.

## 20

## JULES

I've been standing under the spray of the shower for so long that the water has turned completely cold. Oddly, I don't feel cold. I don't shiver or crave warmth. I don't feel much of anything right now. I'm only in the shower because Sebastian made me. I had no desire of being here. If it were up to me, I would still be in bed staring at the ceiling, which is all I've wanted to do the last two days.

"Jules?" Sebastian's muffled voice comes through the bathroom door. "You okay?"

*No.* I'm not okay. I don't know what I am right now but okay is not the word I would use to describe me right now. Numb. Broken. Those would be much better words, but I don't tell him that either. I don't have the strength to use words, and I'm sure I don't need to use them either. Sebastian knows everything already.

"You've been in there forever. Come on out, I made us some lunch."

I turn off the water and step out of the shower, my movements almost mechanical, just like the way I've been feeling. Like a machine, a robot with basic functions without feelings.

Drying off, I get dressed, picking clothes from the pile of folded clothing on the vanity that Sebastian had laid out for me. I open the door and find Seb still standing in the hallway waiting for me. He gives me a soft smile and I know I should smile back. It's the polite thing to do, it's what normal people do. Yet, I can't get my lips to curl up even the slightest bit.

*Will I be like this forever?* The thought doesn't really bother me, not like I know it should. We sit down at the kitchen table where two plates with little sandwiches are waiting for us. Turkey, muenster cheese, on rye bread with apple slices. It's my favorite which is exactly the reason Seb made it. Unfortunately, I still don't have an appetite, so I just stare at it for I don't know how long until Seb pushes the plate even closer to me and orders me to eat. Picking up the sandwich, I take a small bite.

"Jules, I really think you should talk to someone," Sebastian starts, his voice soft. "You know you can talk to me, but if you don't feel comfortable, you can talk to someone else. I can have someone come here, you wouldn't even have to go out."

I continue chewing the food in my mouth without even looking at him. I don't want to talk to him or anyone else. I just want to forget and be left alone. All I wanted when I came back here was a normal life. I had already lost so much, and then I lost it all, all over again.

"I'm sorry I made you come to family dinner, Jules. I was stupid not to see it then. I didn't understand why you were freaking out over seeing him. I had no idea how bad it actually was. Fuck, Rem has done some fucked up shit...but what he did to you...I never in a million years would have thought he was capable of something like that."

His name elicits an emotion, anger, or maybe sadness? I don't know...but what I do know is that I don't want to hear his name, not now, maybe not ever.

"He's going to pay for hurting you, Jules. He's my brother and I love him, but he had no right to do what he did. He had no fucking right." Seb slams a clenched fist down on the wooden table, but I don't even flinch at the action.

"Please..." My throat is raw, making it hard for the word to come out. "Please stop, Seb." I stare at him blankly, and he nods, holding his anger in, swallowing it down. In all the years I've known him, I've never seen him this mad before.

"I'm sorry..." He blows out a harsh breath. "I'm just trying to understand it all and I'm pissed because I can't. I don't understand." I don't tell him that I am too, that I'm so shattered inside it hurts to breathe, to feel the stupid organ inside my chest beat. Heartache shouldn't hurt this bad, but this isn't just heartache, this is betrayal too.

I can live like this if it means I never have to face him again, if it means I never have to think about what happened. If I don't think about it, then it never happened in the first place.

Grabbing my plate, I get up and dump it into the trash, then I place it in the dishwasher and walk back toward the hall.

"Jules."

I blink, registering that he's saying my name, but I ignore it. I don't want to talk. I don't want to think, or even feel. Life is better without those emotions...it's better without the pain.

ANOTHER THREE DAYS PASS, each day consisting of the same thing. Wake up, shower, eat, lay in bed, eat, rinse and repeat. Seb doesn't try and talk to me about *him* again and I'm thankful for it. Today, I sit in the living room instead of the bedroom, which I suppose is a small step forward. I don't really know. I have no ambition to be anything. All I'm doing is living my life as a shell of the person I was once before.

I look out the window, staring into the back yard, staring into the nothingness. I can hear Seb in his office, moving things around. His phone rings and a second later he answers it.

"Yeah, I know." His voice is monotone, much like my life now. "Well, he did this himself. Suspension is the least of his worries, right now." I should feel something, anything hearing Seb talk about *him* being suspended, but I don't care. I have no emotion toward the things I'm hearing.

Anger, sadness, hate, those feelings are long gone, left behind with the old Jules.

"She's doing as good as someone who went through what she did is going to." Seb sounds frustrated, but I can't bring myself to feel sorry for involving him. I needed somewhere to go, somewhere I know no one would be able to touch me, talk to me.

"Yeah, I'll let you know if anything changes." Silence settles over the house once again. Seb's chair scrapes against the wood floor and a moment later, I feel his presence in the room. He doesn't say anything, and I wonder if maybe he walked away.

Then his throat clears. "Dad wants to see you...talk to you..."

I swallow thickly at his words but don't respond. I have nothing to say, and him coming here and talking to me will change nothing.

Seb comes around the couch to face me, his features are tight, worry creases his forehead, and I wonder why I ever came here. Looking at Seb is like staring at an older version of *him*. The nightmare, my ruin. Seb sits down beside me, his hand grabbing onto mine.

His touch is warm, and my body reacts to it with a shiver.

"I can't hold him off forever, Jules. I want to help you and you know I'll do whatever I can, but I need you to find your way out of this. I need you to find your way back."

I blink and look from his hand that's holding my own, before looking back up at his face. Sharp jaw, piercing green eyes, a dimple in the corner of his mouth. Every time I look at Sebastian, I see *him*.

He squeezes my hand gently, bringing me back to the present. "Will you try, Jules? You don't have to leave the house or go anywhere, but I need you to try and talk to someone, even if it's just me, even if it's a conversation about nothing at all."

The smile he gives me is one that used to melt all my worries away, but I have no worries anymore. There is nothing that can hurt me, because to hurt me, would mean I would have to feel, and that's what Seb is asking me to do...to feel, and I'm not there yet.

I pull my hand from his and get up walking back toward the bedroom, without a single word spoken.

"Come on, Jules, please," Seb croaks, emotions I refuse to acknowledge clogging his throat. "I'm begging you..."

I halt mid-step, but only because Seb doesn't beg, it's not like him, and hearing him like this, well I won't lie and say it doesn't reach my heart, because it does, but if hurting him protects me then I guess that's just a choice that has to be made.

I continue walking until I reach my bedroom, then I slip

inside, closing the door softly behind me. Another day without pain...another day without *him*.

~

"I'm sorry, Jules. I'm so damn sorry." *I want to believe him. I want to believe him so badly that I tell myself I can, but should I? He's hurt me...he's broken me. I'm a shell of the woman I was before. My bottom lip quivers and tears slip down onto my cheeks.*

"How could you do this to us? I thought you loved me?" *Remington's face morphs into something else, and he almost looks pained.*

"I do love you. I fucked up, Jules, I fucked up, and I'll never be able to prove to you how much it hurts me to know that I did this to you. How stupid and foolish I was." *I shake my head, because in my heart, I know I want to forgive him. I want to let go of the pain wrapping around my heart, eating away at my insides, but I'm not ready.*

"Come back to me, Jules, please, I am begging you. I will be everything you need me to be and more. I will never hurt you again." *His green eyes plead with me, his voice is like a soothing balm to my aching heart....*

Waking up, I clutch a hand to my chest, my heart beating out of my chest. Even in my mind, in my dreams, I cannot escape him, and deep down, I know I probably never will. The heart wants what it wants, but sometimes the heart is fucking stupid and needs to shut up. I blink away the sleep from my eyes and sit up in bed right as a noise outside my door filters into my ears.

"She's not ready." Sebastian's voice is right outside my door, and I wonder who he is talking to. And for a moment, one single moment panic creeps up on me, but before it can actually hit me, I pull back. I fortify my walls because I know if I let any feeling in, even the smallest bit, everything is going to come crashing down. I hear another voice, and every remanence of any oncoming emotions have completely faded away.

"I don't really care, son, now move or I'll move you. That girl is like a daughter to me and I'll be damned if I'm going to let her sit in that room all alone, numbing herself of all feeling."

Sebastian must take what his father says seriously because a second later, my bedroom door opens, Papa Miller's big frame is entering through it.

He smiles the moment he sees me, but I don't return the smile.

"How is my girl?"

I shrug as he walks deeper into the room. Sebastian gives me an apologetic look from the doorway as if to say he's sorry, but he doesn't have to be sorry, none of this is his fault.

Papa Miller settles down on the bed beside me, his big body eats up most of the space, making the room feel smaller then it is.

"I talked to your mom. She planned on coming home, but she's buried deep in work. I told her I would come in her place instead, since I know how much you love me." He grins down at me, his smile reminding me of memories and a certain person I can't stomach to think about right now. I drop my gaze down to my hands that are sitting in my lap to protect myself. I can't think about him.

For the first time, I'm actually glad my mom cares more about her work than me. I'm glad she isn't here, and I don't want her to come in the future either. She's always been like this, work above everything else, even her own children. I remember being resentful about that growing up but now I can't even remember what that feels like.

"I know you're hurting, Jules. I've never seen you so broken before, but I can't let you keep living this way. I miss your light, your smile..." He trails off and I block out the rest of whatever he is saying. If I listen, then I'll start to feel something, and I can't bear to feel anything but nothingness.

"I'm worried about you," he admits, his voice soft, somehow that one single statement caresses a response out of me.

"Don't be. I'm fine."

"You are not fine, Jules, you need to talk to someone, that's the only way you will pull through this. The longer you hold this in, the harder it's going to get. Every day that passes, you only inflict more pain on yourself."

I tell myself he doesn't understand, he doesn't understand that if I let myself feel anything at all, it will just get worse. I can't open my eyes to reality...I can't say the things I need to say. I can't let my damn heart feel the emotions swirling deep inside me because if I do, everything I've been holding back will rush out of me. It will drown me, sweeping me under the current, pulling me down, invading every pore of my body until there is nothing left.

"I'm very close to losing it, Jules. You're like a daughter to me, but I can only help you if you let me. Sebastian has been keeping me in the loop about everything. I'm managing Remington's break down, and he's managing yours, but we're all suffering here."

The mere mention of his name makes me shudder. *No.* I clench my teeth. I will not feel anything. I will not let him break down my walls. I will protect myself.

"I want to take a shower," I say, already pushing up and off the bed. I can't stay here, I can't listen to him and risk him saying something that will open up the floodgates of hell.

"If it helps any, he's hurting too. He asks me to put him out of his misery every night and I tell him he dug his own hole, that he did this to himself."

I don't care. I don't care. I tell myself as I stomp to the shower and lock the door behind me, refusing to let his words affect me. I turn on the shower, but I don't get in. I just sit on the toilet hoping that he'll leave and won't want to talk to me again. The sound of the water drowns out the noises inside my head, and after awhile I hear nothing, nothing but the steady beat of my heart, and the inhaling of air into my lungs.

Don't want to feel, think, I don't want anything. I sit until I forget that he was even here at all and I'm back to being a ghost…a ghost, that's how I feel. I'm in this world, with people carrying on with their lives around me. I can see them smiling and laughing, but the emotions can't reach me, nothing can. I'm so cut off from reality that it's like I'm here, but I'm not. Not completely anyway.

Part of me is just gone, floating in space, or maybe I'm just broken, so broken that there isn't any fixing me, and strangely I like myself like this. I don't know which one is true, maybe I'm a little bit of both, but all I know is that I can't imagine ever being whole again.

Time will never heal my wounds.

## 21

## REMINGTON

Walking into the same office they questioned me in the last time, I feel a sliver of anxiety. When I enter the room and look up, I realize that there is a big change. There are actual police officers in here this time instead of just the campus security. They're not wearing uniforms, but I can see the badge and gun attached to the belt from where I'm standing.

Most would be shitting their pants right now, but the constant guilt, grief, and anger consuming me leave little room for anything else. I don't have the energy for any other feeling, and I don't really care what's going to happen to me anyway.

I deserve whatever punishment is served.

"Mr. Miller, please have a seat," one of them greets me. "I'm Detective Garcia and this is my partner, Detective Stevens." His voice is monotone and his face emotionless, unlike his partner who looks like he's about to jump me. I take a seat in the hard metal chair and Detective Garcia starts talking again.

"I want to inform you that we have just opened up an investigation on you, Mr. Miller. Campus security contacted us this morning with some disturbing information and since there is overwhelming evidence compiled against you, we are taking this very seriously…"

My jaw flexes with tension. I fucked up, but I didn't physically hurt Jules, surely they know that.

Before I can say anything, we are interrupted by a loud knock on the door. I look over my shoulder just as Sebastian enters the room, a confused look on his face.

"Why is he being questioned again? We've already discussed this at length, and why are you talking to him without a lawyer present?" He points at the two police officers, anger now seeping into his face.

*This is your fault, Remington.* All the frustration, my father's anger toward me, Sebastian's disappointment, the police being here, Jules hurting, it's all on me.

"Mr. Miller has the right to an attorney, but he has not requested one and we are not arresting him at this moment, so legally I do not have to read him his rights. Now, may I ask who you are?"

"I'm his legal counsel for right now," Seb growls and takes the seat beside me. A part of me wants to tell him to leave, to tell him that there is no point in trying to save me, but I know that the police wouldn't be here if something hadn't changed and I'm not dumb enough to make him leave me alone in here just to end up saying the wrong fucking thing.

"Well, let's get straight to the point then," Detective Garcia announces. He opens a folder, and takes out the first page, sliding it across the table, and all but shoves it into my face. My gut clenches as I glance over it. I don't have to read every word to know it's a manuscript of the recording. I'll be reminded of my mistake for the rest of my life.

"Do you acknowledge that the male voice in this recording belongs to you?"

"Yes," I answer. What's the point in lying? I already admitted to campus security that it was me, plus I deserve whatever they plan to slap me with.

"Do you admit to being the one who recorded the interaction that took place between yourself and Ms. Peterson?"

"Yes," I respond once again.

Both detectives nod and take the paper back. Then they pull out another paper from the folder and slide it over just like they did with the first. As soon as my eyes land on the photo, I freeze, time seems to stand still. My blood stops pumping through my veins and every ounce of oxygen in my lungs evaporates. I'm only vaguely aware that one of the two cops is asking me a question, but my brain just isn't digesting what I'm seeing.

"Jesus fuck, Remmy!" Seb's voice brings me back to reality. I look at him, his face holds nothing but disgust and hate for me. He stands up and turns away from the table, unable to look at the pictures any longer. I turn my attention back to what's laying on the table in front of me. I can't believe what I'm seeing, and I have to stop myself from lashing out, from getting up to break something. The pictures show Jules passed out on a bed in nothing but her panties. I remember that night... I remember saving her, from him. *Cole.*

I'm going to kill him. I will fucking kill him even if it's the last thing I ever do.

"Mr. Miller, do you admit to taking these pictures?"

"Fuck no! I didn't take these!" I jump from my chair, causing it to slam back against the wall. A snort comes from Detective Stevens, who hasn't said anything until now.

"You think we are going to fucking believe you? We know you were at this party and we know you left with her, and we know you brought her back to your place and made her stay the night. We have witnesses and proof, you pervert, so do us all a favor and just admit to it so we can get this wrapped up."

Dread hangs thickly in the air, making it hard for me to think, breathe, function. They want me to admit to a crime I didn't commit. They want to put the blame on me because it's easier than looking at the big fucking picture.

"The recording, yes that was me. I'll admit to it, because I did it. And yes, I was at that party, but she was not there with me and I didn't take the pictures."

I take a deep breath, trying to figure out what I should say next. If I tell them the whole story, they will go straight to Jules and ask for her statement. She didn't want to tell anyone for this exact reason, she doesn't want to relive what happened and I more than respect that. If I tell them now, then I will betray her trust again. She will suffer because of me...just so I can clear my name, and I'll be damned if I do that.

*I can't tell them, no matter the consequences.*

"Look, this will go over with a judge way better if you just admit to taking the pictures."

"I already told you I didn't take those photos. I wouldn't fucking do that to her." I slam my fist down on the metal table, over and over again, willing them to fucking listen to me. Every time I see one of the photos my stomach churns and I have to hold back the need to vomit.

*Cole. He's the one who did this. He fucking did it, and still, I'm paying for it. I'm reaping the repercussions.*

"This isn't looking good for you, Mr. Miller, so I really advise you to come clean, it would be a better option for you."

My lips pull into a thin line, and I cross my arms over my chest.

"I didn't do it, and I won't tell you that again."

The questioning goes on for another twenty minutes with the same results. Each time they ask me a question I get angrier, the dread, the guilt, the fucking shame, pales in comparison to the hate I have for Cole, and myself. With a look between them, the detectives get up, one of them closing the folder and placing it under his arm.

"Am I under arrest?" I question.

Detective Stevens answers, "Not at this moment, but mark my words, I will find enough evidence to nail your ass to the wall. There are far enough assholes like you in this world, believe me when I say you won't be missed. We'll be in touch, Mr. Miller."

They leave the room, leaving me and Seb to our own devices.

"Seb, I didn't take the pictures." I don't know if he believes me or not and I can't muster up the courage to look him in his eyes. I'm so angry at myself, so fucking pissed that I brought Jules into all of this.

He leaves the room, just as the detectives did, slamming the door shut behind him. I let my head fall into my hands, wishing this was all just a bad dream, one that I would be waking up from any minute now. I imagine I would roll over and she would be there, tucked into my side, but she's not and she never will be again, because I did this to us, turned this nightmare into a reality. Tears sting my eyes. I miss her so much, her touch, her smell, her fucking smile.

Closing my eyes, I remember her face, her blue eyes, soft blonde curls, adorable button nose, the way she whimpers and moans when she falls apart, her pink lips. A thousand memories rush through me flickering right before my eyes like an old style movie.

I sit there for a long moment, letting myself relive those things before I push the emotions aside and get up and walk back to my house like a robot. By the time I get home, my mind is still in disarray. I need to clear my head first, then I need to find Cole, but I don't know how, or even where to fucking start. I decide to go on a run, maybe that will help calm down the ever-growing storm inside of me.

When I reach my dresser, I pull open the top drawer and freeze. My knees buckle and I almost fall to the ground. I pick up the shirt that's neatly folded on top and clutch it to my chest for a few minutes before returning it to the drawer. I get out my own stuff, but I leave the worn out cotton shirt with a faded Mickey Mouse logo laying on top.

I don't think there is a chance that she will ever come back to me, but I can't bring myself to think that she wouldn't. I can't let myself believe that there is no chance at all of her being mine again. We're two pieces of the same soul, each other's forevers and if I lose her, I might as well be dead.

*Hope always dies last.*

~

THE DAYS MOVE SLOWLY without Jules. I force myself to run every night just to stop myself from going to her. Sebastian hasn't admitted it, but I know she's staying with him, and it takes everything in me to give her time, space. Each day without her feels like an eternity. My reason to breathe starts and ends with her.

Gritting my teeth, I push harder, my lungs burn, a delicious ache forming in my muscles, as I round the block and sprint the rest of the way up to the house. As I get closer, I notice Sebastian and my father standing outside. They look as if they're in a heated conversation, one that I don't want to involve myself in. I've got enough going on inside my head. I don't need to add more to it, that is unless it has something to do with Jules.

"Rem, you need to come with me," Sebastian orders as soon as I reach the driveway. His jaw is clenched, and he looks pissed off.

"What's going on?" I ask between breaths, sweat dripping down my forehead and chest, soaking my t-shirt. My father has a strange look in his eyes, one I've never seen before.

"The police are looking for you. They want you to come in right now."

I roll my eyes. Fuck them, there is nothing to investigate or question. I didn't do shit, not yet. They would have something to investigate if I could get my fucking hands on Cole, but thus far, I have no leads on where he is.

I lift my shirt, wiping at my brow with the fabric.

"Do I have time to change and shower?"

Seb shakes his head, and that only frustrates me more.

"Well, I guess let's fucking go then," I grumble, heading toward the SUV.

"Let them ask you their questions, son. You fucked up yes, but I know you didn't hurt Jules like they're saying you did."

I don't even care, there is nothing I can do to make them believe me, not without revealing what happened that night and I won't do that to Jules. I'll never hurt her again, ever.

Sebastian and my father get into the SUV, and we start off toward the police station I itch to ask him how she's doing, if she still isn't talking or eating, if she's still having nightmares, but I worry that he wouldn't tell me the truth, even if I did ask.

Dad's the only one who's told me of her current state. Sebastian is cold and aloof and doesn't often mention Jules, if ever, when I see him.

"I know you think I did it, but I didn't. I love her too much to do something so foolish."

"You think because you tell me you love her that I'll believe you?"

The tone of his voice catches me off guard, and before I can respond, he's talking again.

"She refuses to eat, talk, shower, and sometimes I have to go into her bedroom at night because I worry that she might stop breathing... that she might just give up, might stop trying."

There are no words, no response to what he just said. My heart literally fucking aches.

"You're my brother Rem, and I love you, but you hurt her, you hurt her so badly, and I know you're sorry, and that you didn't mean for it to get this out of hand, but it did. It fucking did and now there are consequences for your actions."

"I didn't do it, Seb. I took the recording, but I didn't take the photos. I saved her that night, from him..." The confession slips from my lips with ease.

"What? Who is him?"

"I can't say. I don't want Jules to have to relive that night. If I say something, they'll ask more questions, they'll go to her, they'll bring her into all of this, and I don't want to hurt her any more than I already have. I can't fucking bear it."

Sebastian sighs. "So you'll take the downfall for the photos, to what? Protect her? They're going to end up questioning her anyway."

I shrug. "Then she can tell them whatever she wants. If she wants to tell them the truth, of what really happened that night, then she can. If she doesn't, then I'll take the fall."

We pull up to the police station and park in the small parking lot out front. I open the door, but my dad grabs my arm and stops me from stepping out.

"Maybe we should get a lawyer before we talk to them."

"Dad, I didn't take the pictures," I growl. I'm seriously getting tired of having to tell people that. I might have been fucking stupid enough to share that recording with the guys, but if I had photos of Jules, I wouldn't be sharing them with the entire campus.

Those would be mine, all fucking mine.

"You heard what the lawyer you talked to said. There is nothing they can charge me with. The recording was fucked up but not illegal and I didn't take those fucking pictures. I've denied it a million times and I'll continue to deny it, because it wasn't me."

He sighs and lets go of my arm. I'm sure he thinks I'm being stubborn, but I won't tell these assholes something just because they want to hear me say it. I get out of the car with my father following behind me.

"I'm going back to my place," Seb announces. "Call me when you're done, and I'll come and get you. I don't have the patience to sit through another session of *questioning*."

We walk inside, all eyes snap up and land on me, like I'm some deranged criminal or something. It's a small police department and it seems like everybody knows why I'm here. Detective Garcia comes around the corner and greets me in his usual emotionless way.

"Mr. Miller, would you please follow me." He motions to the back and I start walking, my dad hot on my heels. "I'm sorry, sir, you will not be able to come with us into questioning today."

"And why is that? Is my son under arrest?" My father's voice bounces off the walls, filling the small space.

"Not at this moment, but I do, however, have a warrant to collect a DNA sample, which I will be doing."

"DNA sample? For what? He didn't fucking rape her." My father expels anger coating his words.

"We have someone that's come forward stating this isn't the first time you've done something of this nature. The second girl has come out and said you sexually assaulted her. She went to a hospital for a rape kit which came back positive."

My pulse quickens, my stomach twisting into a tight knot. I'm being set up...there is no other way to explain why this is all being put on me. I've never had sex with a woman more than once, and I never take from someone who isn't willing. *Never.* I might have hurt Jules, but there is a fine fucking line between raping someone who doesn't want you and recording something without their knowledge.

"What?" I growl. "That's ridiculous. Why would you even accuse me of something so disgusting? I would never do that."

The detective stares me straight in the eyes as he speaks, "Because the girl specifically named you. Miss Layla Hart, does her name happen to ring any bells, Mr. Miller?"

My lip curls, my veins fill with ice. "You've gotta be fucking kidding me."

For the next few hours, I'm questioned by the same two detectives that questioned me the first time. Someone comes in and swabs the inside of my cheek for DNA halfway through. I don't know how many times they ask me the same questions over and over again. They want to break me down, get me to confess but there isn't shit to confess to.

After a while, I just try to drown them out. I think about my father's face when they accused me of rape. I know he didn't want to believe it, but when I looked into his eyes, I could see the doubt plaguing him. I want to be mad at him for not believing in me, but how can he after all of the things I've done. After the ways I've disappointed him. All evidence is pointing toward me so I can't really blame him for doubting me. If I didn't know for a fact that I wasn't that kind of man, I would doubt myself.

I refused a lawyer hours ago. I didn't see the point. They can't make me confess to something I didn't do and there is no evidence that I did anything, because it didn't happen.

"Okay, Mr. Miller, that's all the questions we have, *for now*. You'll be hearing from us soon though," the detective says, clearly unhappy about the outcome.

I don't care about his fucking feelings. I'm out of the room and down the hall before they can change their minds and lock me up in one of these cells. When I get to the little waiting area in the front of the station, I realize that my dad is no longer here.

I walk out of the station, hoping he might be outside, but after looking everywhere possible, I don't see him. It shouldn't come as a surprise to me that he left, still, it stings. People have a tendency of leaving me and this is just another reminder of that. Anytime you need someone they aren't there, or at least that's how it is with my family.

I take out my phone to dial my dad's number, but I can't make myself push the call button. I decide to run back to campus, it doesn't really matter since I'm still in my workout clothes anyway. It's only about five miles give or take, so I should be there in less than an hour. I start jogging, but it quickly turns into a full-blown run, and I pick up speed with every stride. My lungs burn, but it's a good burn, one that makes me feel like I can finally breathe. At least I can still control my body, because fuck if I don't have control over anything else right now, most of all my emotions, my life. And as I run, running like I'm trying to outrun all the misfortunes that are taking place in my life right now, I ask myself how we got to this point...

*How did my life get so fucked up?*

## 22

## JULES

As soon as Sebastian enters my room, I know something is up.

He has a nervous look on his face, a look that's borderline terrified. Without even knowing it, I can tell he's about to tell me something that I'm really not going to like.

"Jules, someone is here to talk to you."

I close my eyes and shake my head. My chest starts to heave with uneven breaths. I can feel the panic creeping in.

"No, no, I don't want to talk to anyone."

"I know...but I'm afraid there is no way around this. I'm sorry, Jules, but it's the police and they really want to talk to you. I think it would be good for you."

"What would be good for me is if everyone left me alone," I grit out, feeling a pang of anger for the first time in weeks.

"They are in the living room waiting for you. Do you want to go out there or do you want me to let them come in here?"

I find myself shaking my head. There is no way I want them in here, this has been my safe space for weeks, and I'm not letting them invade it. Pushing myself off the bed. Sebastian sighs loudly, running a hand through his hair and I know he is relieved.

"I'll be in my room if you need me, okay? Unless you want me to come out there with you."

"No, I'll do this alone," I tell him, there is no need to involve him any further in this mess. I walk out into the living room and find a man and a woman sitting on the couch, both smile at me the moment they see me.

"Miss Peterson, it is very nice to meet you," the woman greets me. Her voice is soft and comforting, much like how a favorite blanket might feel, and I know without a doubt she's a shrink. I've seen shrinks before, my dad made me go and see one when I had a hard time coping with the move.

"I'm Susan, would it be alright if I call you Jules?"

I nod slightly and take a seat on the recliner. Pieces of me want to run back to the bedroom and hide in the bed, while other pieces of me know it's time to talk, even if it's just a little.

"Jules, this is the detective who is leading the investigation we are here for today. He will only be here listening and taking notes. I will be the one asking you questions, is that okay with you?" I nod again and she continues. "I know this is going to be hard for you to talk about, but it is very vital that we get some information from you."

I suck in a shallow breath, but the air doesn't even fill my lungs.

"Okay, just ask so this can be over with quick," I tell her and even though I know I sound rude, she only smiles at me, not paying any attention to my harsh tone. Susan looks to the detective for a moment and then clears her throat.

"Jules, did Remington Miller sexually assault you?"

My heart aches hearing his name, the scabbed wound over my heart now pulsing with fresh blood. It hurts so badly that it takes me a second to realize what she just asked me.

"No, he didn't," I divulge and watch as the detective scribbles something down on his notepad. I want to ask him what he's writing down, and why but don't. I don't want to subject myself to anything more than I have to.

"The recording that was sent to students at your school, do you know when and where that was taken?" I try to keep my walls up and not let any emotion in, but this is getting harder and harder by the second with them asking questions that all but force me to remember the man that broke my heart in two.

"It was taken in my room, a few days after I started school here, maybe the fourth of April."

"Are you certain? We have reason to believe that it was taken at a party you attended a few days after that."

I shift in my seat suddenly having the urge to get up and run away. Why would they ask about the party? Aside from trying to forget him, I've tried my best to forget that night.

"Jules, are you aware that pictures were sent to the school shortly after the recording was sent out?"

I give her a confused look, not understanding what she is saying. "Pictures? What kind of pictures?"

"Pictures of you. Pictures that appear to have been taken at that party you and Remington attended." A sudden feeling of impending doom drenches over me like acid falling from the sky.

"What kind of pictures," I repeat.

"You weren't fully dressed in these pictures and it looked like you were passed out. It looks as though the pictures were taken without your consent."

"I want to see them," I demand, every muscle in my abdomen clenches and as if she was expecting me to ask to see them, she pulls a black folder out sitting beside her. She hands it to me, and my heart starts to race inside my chest, the sound filling my ears. Something feels like it's wrapping around my throat, making it hard to breathe, to swallow.

I open the folder and... the world falls away. What I find is exactly what she stated, but a part of me hoped maybe she was lying. As I stare down at the photos, I see that it's me, half naked in a bed, it's from the night Cole drugged me. The memories come rushing back to me and it's hard to think about anything else. I close the folder and throw it on the table, my hands sinking into my hair. Why won't the memories go away?

*Him.* The man who broke my heart, he sent the memories away, but without him, I am subjected to their memory, but with him, I am subjected to the memory of his heartache.

"Do you know who took these photos of you, Jules?"

"Yes," I grit out, but don't elaborate further. "I don't want to talk about that night. Are we done?"

"Jules, we know this is hard for you, but there is another girl that has come forward." She pauses briefly, her eyes moving between the detective and me. "You are not alone anymore, and your statement may just help other girls in the future."

"Other girls?"

"Yes, someone has come forward, and accused Remington of raping her."

Her accusation sends me reeling.

A rush of anger breaks through my barriers like a wave crashing against a cliff's edge.

"You're wrong. Remington would never do that. You're wrongfully accusing him." He disappointed and betrayed me in so many ways, but I know...I know in my heart that he wouldn't do something like that.

Both Susan and the detective look at me with puzzled looks.

"Jules, I heard the tape and I've seen the pictures..."

"Remington didn't take those and what exactly do you think happened on that tape?" I try to think back to that night, another memory I have to dig out of my brain because I tried to bury every single memory, thought, and feeling when it comes to him. I know he said some crude things to me that night, but would it have sounded like he was raping me?

"It's not really clear what happened from just the sound. Was the sex in it consensual? Don't feel like you need to protect him, Jules."

My nostrils flare, and I clench my fists. Why are they trying to get me to admit to something that never happened?

"There was no sex. He just..." I pause, not wanting to say it what really happened, but then I realize they've already heard the tape and the only way to clear this up is tell them the truth. "We didn't have sex, he...he just made me come...with his finger and then he left." My cheeks heat at my confession.

Susan nods without judgment, encouraging me to keep talking. "But what about that party? People saw you leave with Remington that night."

I jump up from my seat, unable to stay in a sitting position any longer.

"I don't want to talk about that night, okay?" I yell, unable to control the volume of my voice.

Susan gets up as well and takes a step toward me. Showing me her hands, palms up like she is trying to calm a wild animal. "

"Jules, you can tell us what happened. I know it's hard, trust me I know, but this information might be crucial to the investigation into Remington. Whatever he did to you, he could've done to this other woman. Don't you want to help us?"

Help them? Help them hurt him? I know the answer without even thinking.

"He didn't do anything to hurt me, he saved me that night. I was being such an idiot, I had a bad feeling, but I pushed it away."

After I say the first few words, the rest follow with ease, the word vomit just keeps coming, and I don't even care to stop it.

"I didn't know there was anything in the drink. I didn't taste anything, and suddenly I felt so weird. Hot and cold all at once. I didn't want to go with him, but he brought me to the bedroom, and then he started to take my clothes off. I asked him to stop, but he didn't...I begged him to stop and when that didn't work, I tried to push him off, but he was too strong." My voice cracks at the end, my broken soul shattering a little bit more and I don't even realize I'm crying until Susan hands me a tissue.

I swipe at my eyes and continue. "Remington came into the room and pulled Cole off of me, then he punched him." I don't think I should tell the cops that I thought he was going to kill him, so I leave that part out. The last thing Remington clearly needs right now is to find himself with an assault charge.

"Then he helped me get dressed and got me out of there. That's all that happened that night."

"Who is Cole?" Susan asks, and I cringe just hearing his vile name. I don't think I can talk or think about him for another second, but then I remember what Susan said in the beginning. This might help other girls in the future. If I don't speak up now, then Cole will walk away a free man, giving him the chance to do this to another woman and that in itself is enough to keep me talking.

"Cole was Remington's roommate. He had this strange obsession with me. He's the one who drugged me and tried to..." I can't even say the word out loud, because then it feels like it's real, like it happened, and though I know it almost did, it's easier to swallow if I don't say it.

"Then a few days after that, he cornered me. We shared a class together, he didn't show up, so I thought I was safe, but after class, he got me alone and tried to force me to tell Remington that I wanted it. He made an idle threat about how I would pay if I didn't. I was scared, but I wasn't going to tell Remington because it was a lie, I didn't want it." Tears stain my cheeks.

"I didn't want him," I whisper more to myself than anyone else in the room.

"I know, Jules, I know you didn't." Susan comes up beside me, reaching out for me. She places her hand on my upper arm, her touch is gentle and comforting as she rubs her thumb over my skin. It reminds me of how my mother comforted me as a child, how Remington comforted me the night that all of this happened, and I miss that comfort...I miss him.

"It was never Remington. It was Cole. Remington saved me, and I only didn't say anything until now because I just wanted to forget."

"You don't have to explain yourself, this is completely normal," Susan assures me and somehow that makes me feel better.

I don't know why but I was sure people would judge me for what happened but now looking at her, seeing that there is no judgment at all in her gaze, and only understanding, I know I was wrong.

A throat clears behind us making me turn to face the noise, it's then that I notice the detective is now standing, and that Seb has entered the room.

"We have all the information we need now. I just have one question, Miss Peterson." The detective's gaze softens as soon as he sees my face.

"Yes?" I croak, blinking through the tears.

"When was the last time you've seen or heard from Cole?"

"That day he cornered me after class. I can look at my call schedule and tell you the exact date, but I can't remember it off the top of my head."

"That would be great, Miss Peterson. Just email me the information as soon as you can and thank you again. I'm sorry to have had to put you through this again." He gives me a sympathetic smile and hands me a card. I take it, holding it in my clammy hand.

"While we are handing out cards, here is mine." Susan hands me a card as well. "If you need to talk again, or simply vent, that's my office number on the top and my cell on the bottom. You can call me any time, day or night."

If you would have asked me two hours ago if I would ever call her, my answer would have been hell no, but now that I've actually talked to her, I do consider it. I will definitely keep her card close to me.

"Thank you," I tell both of them and watch as Seb sees them out. As soon as I hear the front door close, I sag onto the couch.

Talking about that night lifted a weight off my chest, but it also made me confirm that it happened and that was almost more terrifying than remembering it.

Sebastian walks back into the room, a sad look on his face. "I didn't mean to eavesdrop, but I did hear a bunch of the stuff you said, mostly because you were yelling, which I'm glad you did. You have no fucking idea how glad I am to see you be angry and yelling."

I give him a sad smile. "I owe you Seb. I owe you lots."

He grins, walking over to where I'm lying on the couch. Without warning, he's pulling me to his chest, his arms wrapped tightly around me.

"Never do that to me again, never. I understand why you did it, that you were hurting, but I was afraid, Jules, so damn afraid."

Hurting Sebastian was never my intention, but I can see now that I had.

"I'm sorry," I admit, feeling his arms tighten around me.

"Don't be. The only person that needs to be sorry is that fucker for hurting you, and I swear, Jules…the police better find him before I do, because if I find him first, he's a dead man. He is never going to pull this shit again."

His words reassure me further that I made the right choice when it came to telling them what I knew. Not only did it clear Remmy's name but also point the police in the right direction to find the real criminal. I couldn't stand by and let them accuse Remington of doing something I know in my heart he wouldn't do.

"What do you think happens now?" I ask, feeling a coldness sweep through me as he releases me.

His eyes twinkle with darkness. "Now we find the bastard."

Now that everything is on the table, I need to come to terms with what happened. First, I need to digest what Cole did to me. Then I need to work through what Remmy's done and either I find a way to forgive him or find a way to move on with my life.

Neither way will be easy, but then again, life never is.

## 23

## REMINGTON

*I* almost slam the door in Detective Garcia's face when I see him standing on the other side of it. The only thing that stops me from doing so is that he's actually showing some emotion on his face today. His dark eyes hold an apology, and I grasp onto that look.

"You better be here to apologize or tell me that there has been a change in the case." My fingers bite into the wooden door frame as I speak.

"Do you mind if I come in, Mr. Miller?"

*Do I mind...?*

"By all means, come in," I mutter and take a step back so that he can come in. He walks through the door and into the foyer and I slam the door closed behind him. I stroll past him and into the living room. He looks around the room, at the kitchen that opens up into the living room. The place is pretty clean for a frat house, if I do say so myself.

"Do you want to sit down?"

"Sure, thank you." He takes a seat on the couch and I take one on the loveseat waiting for him to spill. "First of all, even though it turns out that you didn't rape Layla Hart nor took the pictures of Miss Peterson, I will not apologize to you. For one, you did take the recording and showed it to your friends, which may not be illegal in this state, but is still an asshole thing to do. Furthermore, I was just doing my job and all evidence did point to you, so that is why I will not apologize."

"Fair enough." He does have a point, even if I don't like it. "So why are you here then?"

"Why didn't you tell us about what really happened that night of the party?"

"Jules asked me not to tell anyone. I knew if I told you, you would go question her and she didn't want to talk about it."

Garcia gives me a somber nod. "Jules told us everything herself. We let her know that someone else accused you of rape and she told us that you would never do that. Then she told us about Cole and the threat he made. We also questioned Miss Hart again, and she admitted that it wasn't you who raped her, but Cole. He threatened her and convinced her to place the blame on you."

"That piece of fucking shit." I might have been on the rocks with Layla, but fuck I wouldn't wish that on anyone. She was just trying to protect herself, like I was just trying to protect Jules by not saying shit. Detective Garcia's face hardens as he opens his mouth to speak again.

"Do you know where Cole is? We've looked everywhere that we're told he frequents, but no one has seen him, not since the recording was released."

"Trust me, if I had a single clue where he was, I would be there in a heartbeat to smash in his face."

Garcia gave me a small smile. "As a father of two girls, I appreciate your enthusiasm, but as a detective, I advise you against doing that. Let the law do its job. If you can think of anything that could help us find him, please call us right away before doing something on your own."

If I find him first, then he'll be praying that the police get there before I'm finished with him. Against the law or not, there isn't anyone that's going to stop me from smashing that fucker's face in. For Jules, for Layla, he will pay for preying on innocent women.

"I can't promise you that I won't do anything, Detective, and I'm sure you understand why. As for more information on him, you are more than welcome to check out his old room and ask any of my other roommates if they know about his whereabouts. As far as I know, none of them have heard or seen him."

"Let's start with his bedroom, and I'll see about contacting your roommates." He gives me a look of relief as if he didn't expect me to help him in any way, but that's not me. I'm angry for being wrongfully accused, but I'm angrier that, that sick son of a bitch is out there somewhere doing God knows what.

Getting up, I show him to Cole's old room, most all of Cole's stuff is still inside it. Garcia spends close to twenty minutes going through the room before he walks out of the bedroom shaking his head.

He leaves shortly after that, handing me his card, all while leaving me to wallow in my own sorrows once more. I want to thank Jules for talking about what happened, but it seems like such a stupid thing to do. It's not like she did it to save my ass. All she did is to tell the truth...a truth that probably hurt like hell to tell.

*Fuck, she's so strong, so perfect.*

I'm seconds away from going back upstairs and into my room to take a shower and head to bed when a loud knock resonates through the room. *Who the hell could that be?* I walk back over to the door, pulling it open, half expecting it to be Garcia again, maybe with some more questions, but instead, I find Seb standing there, his hands shoved into his pockets.

"Hey," he murmurs.

"Hey." He doesn't wait for me to invite him in. He just brushes past me, strolling into the living room like he owns the damn place. I close the door behind us and follow him like a lost puppy. When he shoves down onto one of the couches, I do the same.

"I'm sorry I didn't believe you. It's not like I didn't want to believe you, but the evidence against you was pretty staggering, and without Jules talking, it just made everything that much more difficult to figure out."

I understand...and I don't blame him at all. He's my brother, and at the end of the day, nothing could ever change that.

"I'm not mad at you. I gave you plenty of reasons to doubt me and honestly, in some way I was glad you didn't believe me. I fucked up big time when it came to Jules. I let her down, let my emotions rule my actions." I pause briefly, wanting to ask if she is okay, how she is feeling, but I don't.

"I'm just glad she was able to tell them what happened, and that no one else had to do it for her. That was her story to tell and no one else's."

Sebastian grins. "She still loves you. Even through all the stupid bullshit that you did, through the mistakes you made, that girl still fucking loves you." He shakes his head in disbelief, and my pulse quickens at the thought of her being mine again.

"Is she...is she okay?"

"She's doing okay, smiling and talking, which is much better than how she was before." That makes me smile, knowing she's getting back to being her old self. One month. One whole fucking month I've gone without her. In the big scheme of things, it's not long, not when I went three years without her, but it was long enough, after just having got her back.

"I want to go to her, to talk to her, to apologize, to fucking plead, and beg," I admit.

"I would wait, at least until tomorrow. Give her tonight to breathe, to think about everything that happened today."

I nod, agreeing. As much as I don't want to wait, I know Sebastian is right.

"Now we just need to find Cole, make him pay for what he did."

Seb nods, a darkness flickering in his eyes. "I want him to pay as much as you do. For hurting her, for putting the blame on you. I mean that recording was a dick move, but Cole coming after Jules, trying to..." His jaw flexes, and I know he doesn't want to say it. Neither of us do, neither of us wants to think about what he almost did.

"He will pay, Sebastian. I might go to prison, but he will pay."

"Don't do something that's going to get you put behind bars. You have Jules, if something happens to you, then who does she have?"

I grin. "You know she said the same thing to me before."

He rolls his eyes. "I believe it. She's the smart one out of all of us, how she ended up with you, I'll never understand."

I slug him in the arm. "Dude, seriously?"

"What? Even you admitted you don't deserve her."

"So, that doesn't mean I'll give her up. She's mine and as long as she'll have me, then I'll be hers." I was going to marry her, put babies inside her, and make her mine for as long as we both shall live, but first I had to prove myself to her, gain her trust back.

I need to show that I'm worthy of her love.

"Alright, enough. I don't want to hear about your epic love story anymore. I need to get back to the house to check on Jules, and then get to bed. I've been pulling all-nighters lately, and they're seriously starting to wear on me."

I nod. "Same, between the investigation, looking for Cole, and trying to stop myself from going to her, I've been losing my mind. Maybe I'll be able to get some sleep tonight." I grin. One can only hope, right?

As Seb and I get up off the couches and he starts to head toward the door, his phone chimes in his pocket.

He pulls it out and glances down at the screen. I don't even have to get a full look at his face to see the ashen fear in his eyes.

"What's going on?"

"We need to go. I just got a notification that someone broke in through the sliding glass door at the house."

I don't even think. I just start moving. If something happens to her again, if he touches her again, I'll kill him.

## 24

## JULES

*J*take a long hot shower, and then make myself some hot chocolate. It's not as good as the one I typically get down on the corner next to campus but it still tastes good, and plus it's chocolate. Who passes up on chocolate?

It's not until the cup is half empty that I realize my taste has returned to normal. Sebastian left about thirty minutes ago, letting me know he would be back soon. He didn't tell me where he was going or what he was doing, and though it's none of my business, I feel a little guilty for scaring him the way I did over the last month.

I crawl into bed with a book and try to enjoy the story while I sip on my hot chocolate and skim the pages of the paperback in my hands. It's the first time I've picked up a book in weeks, the first time I could focus on something besides my thoughts.

I had lost complete interest in any kind of entertainment but opening up to that therapist earlier this morning, lifted a huge weight off my chest and now when I take a breath, I can actually breathe. I can actually feel the air filling my lungs.

I know I'm far from being back to my former cheery self, but at least I've taken steps toward it. At least now I can see the light at the end of the tunnel when this morning I was still in complete darkness. Hearing them talk about Remmy like they did, accusing him of such horrible things just cracked the walls holding back my emotions and talking about what happened broke them down even more.

No matter how angry, hurt, and devastated I am over what he did to me, I can't live in a world where Remmy is in jail for something he didn't do and all because I didn't speak up. Thinking about him now feels different. Before talking to Susan, I felt almost nothing for him and the slithers of feeling that came through were not pleasant.

Now that I've allowed myself to feel again, I remember all the good times we shared and I wonder if maybe I can forgive him, eventually. I try to imagine my life going forward, I try to think of a life that would make me happy, a future that I would like to live in.

I put the book down beside me, unable to concentrate on it any longer. My head starts to throb as I rack my brain running through a hand full of scenarios in my head.

I think about my friends, school, what I want to study, and where I want to live. After a few minutes, I realize that every single scenario has Remmy in it. There is not a single future I can imagine without him and that scares me a little.

I don't know if we can go back to being together again, still, I know I need him in my life somehow. Even if it's just as a friend. I love him and I can't deny myself that. I've always loved him even though it wasn't always the same kinds of love, it was love nevertheless.

I rub at my temples. I doubt that I will ever be whole without him close to me. I feel like he holds parts of my soul inside him and that without him, I will always be missing a part of myself. I could never be fully happy without him by my side. Now the question is, can we find a way back to each other? I mean, does he even want to find a way back to me?

A loud noise from the living room pulls me from my wallowing. I kick the blanket off of my legs and leave the confines of my bedroom, tiptoeing out into the living room. In all the time I had lived here with Sebastian, he has never brought anyone home.

Surely he would tell me if he was going to, right? I tell myself that I'm overreacting and being skittish after the whole Cole thing. I know it's normal to feel the way I do, even more so after all I've experienced since moving back here.

However, I realize that is not the case as soon as I step out into the foyer. My eyes take a moment to adjust to the darkness, but when they do, I see a figure standing in the living room, the sliding glass door behind them broken, glass peppering the floor. A scream catches in my throat and for one single second, the entire world freezes around me.

*Cole.*

My body screams for me to run, but my muscles refuse to move, my feet cemented into the floor. The organ inside my chest beats furiously and all I can hear is the swooshing of blood in my ears. This is it, this is when he gets me.

"I didn't think it would be this easy to get to you, to find you." His voice feels like razor blades slicing through my skin. There is no one to save me this time, no one to protect me from him. I swallow around the lump of fear that's formed in my throat in the last second. My entire body shakes with fear and without thought,

I start back the way I came, my bare feet slipping against the floor as I put all my strength into putting as much distance between us as possible. In the process, my body collides with the wall, my chest heaving, spots forming in my vision.

*He's come for me.*

"Oh no you don't," he hisses loudly.

I hear his heavy footfalls directly behind me, and as soon as his hand grips onto my arm, I scream. I scream so loudly the sound rings in my ears. His grip on me tightens and his hand feels like fire against my flesh.

"No," I scream, thrashing my body against the wall in an effort to get him to release me.

"Yes, so much fucking yes. I waited an entire fucking month to get to you. Over thirty days, Jules, we have some making up to do."

This can't be happening again.

Grabbing me by both arms, he shakes me harshly, my head slams against the wall, my brain rattling inside it as stars appear before my eyes. My knees buckle, and I almost slump down to the floor, but the feeling of Cole tugging on my clothes, trying to get my shirt off sends a surge of anger through me.

*No. I won't let him hurt me.*

With that anger comes clarity and strength. I still my flailing arms and just let them hang down at my sides. I stop fighting him and instead play possum, the tactic works almost instantly, confusing him, and just long enough for him to not see my knee flying up toward his groin, not until it's too late that is.

A painful grunt rips from his throat as he doubles over, pressing his hand to his balls.

"I'm going to kill you," he snarls, hate like I've never seen before in his dark eyes. As soon as he loses his hold on me, I run back up the stairs, making it into my bedroom just as he reaches the bottom stair.

I close the door and lock it behind me, but I'm not dumb, I know that flimsy little door isn't going to stop him and there isn't any way in hell I'm letting him get in here with me. I look around the room, thinking of what I could put in front of that door to hinder his entry.

When my eyes connect on the dresser across the room, I know there is no way he'll make it through that thing. I jog over to it and start moving the heavy six drawer dresser toward the door. I grunt, my movements slow at first. I'm pretty sure this thing weighs more than me, and it shows as my muscles scream at the sudden exercise. With adrenaline coursing through my veins, I find I'm able to move it as if I'm a weightlifter who does this daily.

I don't hear anything from the hallway and hope that maybe he just left. He might have, right? It's merely wishful thinking, I tell myself. He wouldn't come all this way just to attack and leave. I stare at the door, dread coating my insides. I run to the nightstand and grab my phone, it's slippery in my sweaty hands and I almost drop the damn thing several times. The icon on the screen shows five missed calls. I unlock it and dial the first number that comes to my mind.

Remington answers after the first ring. "Jules?"

"He is here, Cole is here." The words come out so fast I don't know if he can even understand me. "He broke in and I didn't know. I got away and I'm hiding in my room. I locked the door, but I think he is still here."

"I know, baby, we're coming. We are on our way. Five minutes, we'll be there in five minutes."

I can hear the car engine rev up in the background.

"I'm scared," I whisper, my eyes trained on the door. The fact that there is no noise coming from the other side only heightens my fear. What is he doing? Where did he go? Why isn't he attacking? I try and calm my breathing, my heartbeat, but I can't calm down. I can't let go of the fear, because he is here...he came for me again.

"It's okay, just stay put, Jules. I will not let him hurt you again. Four more minutes, that's all. Hide in the closet if you have to." Remmy's voice comes through the phone and even though I can hear the edge and fear in his voice, the mere sound of his voice has calmed me enough to stop the impending panic attack.

That little bit of calmness evaporates when I hear someone walking up the stairs, and down the hallway. I hear something scraping against the wall...

"Come out, Jules." Cole's muffled voice comes through the closed door, and my body starts to shake, my teeth rattling inside my head.

"Remmy... he is...he is right outside the door," I whisper into the phone.

"Three minutes Jules, just...stay calm baby..." The fear in Rem's voice terrifies me further.

*Bang.* Cole kicks the door and the loud noise startles me so much so that I drop the phone onto the floor. I scramble, picking it back up with my shaking hand.

"Jules?!" Rem's panicked voice fills my ears as soon as I press the cell phone back against my ear.

"I'm here, he is trying to kick in the door."

*Bang.* Another kick echoes through the room. *Bang.* The sound is so loud and violent, I feel it in my bones. I feel the anger, the energy he's exerting with every single kick.

"Two minutes, Jules, two minutes," Remmy assures me.

"I don't know if the door will hold that long," I rasp, watching wide-eyed as the dresser moves with every kick.

*Bang.* The last kick has the dresser moving away from the door an inch and the next one after that has the door handle coming off. Each kick eats away at the only thing protecting me from him. My heart races so fast I don't even feel it beating anymore. I just feel like my whole body is vibrating with fear.

"Jules, are you there?" I don't answer, the words are lodged in my throat when I see Cole pushing the door open. I jump up, dropping the phone where I am and run over to the dresser, trying to push it back against the door.

I'm pushing from one side while he pushes from the other, almost like we are in a reversed tug of war. I use every ounce of strength I have, but I can feel him gaining on me inch by inch. I dig my heels into the floor, but I keep sliding, the dresser skidding away from the door with each shove.

"I'm going to really enjoy making you bleed, bitch." Cole's voice is much closer now and when I look up and crane my head around the dresser, I find that he is halfway into the room. Squeezing his body through the small opening, he gains entry.

*I'm trapped...trapped, with nowhere to go.*

"Was that really needed?" His eyes gleam with rage as he lurches toward me. His hand wraps around my throat, and within seconds, I'm slammed against the nearest wall. If there were air in my lungs, it would be gone, but there isn't any air...because Cole's grip is so tight it feels like I'm breathing through a straw.

"Now instead of just fucking you...I'm going to fuck you and then slit your throat. I'm sure your precious Remmy will enjoy finding you with my cum dripping out of your cunt, all while you're lying helplessly on the ground choking on your own blood."

His meaty hands start to rip at my clothes, tearing the fabric with one hand while keeping the other tightly around my throat. It's getting harder to breathe, harder to keep my eyes open, but that doesn't stop me from fighting him.

I'll fight him until my last breath if I have to. I scratch, hit, slap, and kick at him like I'm a wild animal. I do anything, and everything I can to keep him from touching me. I claw his face and get him in the eye, making him hiss out in pain and tighten his grip on my throat. He adds his second hand and squeezes until my vision blurs.

No! I dig my nails into his skin, feeling them pierce through the flesh but he doesn't budge, not until he hears the loud bang of something hitting the door. He turns to the now moving door, his eyes going wide.

Cole releases me the moment Rem and Seb appear in the room. Cole swings his closed fist at Rem, but he's too fast. Rem's closed fist smashes into Cole's face half a second later. The impact sends Cole staggering backward and the next thing I know, Seb is on him, tackling him to the ground. Sebastian starts raining punches down on Cole's face too.

My body is shaking, the entire room spinning around me, and then Remmy appears in front of me, kneeling on the ground.

"Are you okay?" His eyes roam over me as if he is scanning me for injuries. He lifts his hands to touch my shoulders, but I don't let him, instead I lunge at him, throwing my arms around him. I close my eyes and bury my face into the crook of his neck, inhaling deeply.

"You're okay now, I'm here," he whispers into my hair and waves of relief wash over me.

I know what he's saying is true.

*He is here now and I'm safe.*

I can hear police sirens approaching in the distance, and I cling tighter to Remmy. He holds me in his arms, shielding me from Cole, from the blood I know that mars Sebastian's fists, from the chaos going on around us.

He holds me together as I fall apart all over again. And still, as the world comes crashing down on me, I find he's the only person I want holding me up.

"D-Did you call the police?" I ask him.

"Yes, didn't you call the police before you called me?"

"No." That fact only now occurs to me.

"It's okay. They're here now, that's all that matters."

The police fill the room, making it seem smaller and smaller, but Rem never lets me go. They handcuff Cole and drag him out of the room all the while I'm clinging to Remmy with a death grip.

"I'm sorry...I'm so sorry," Remmy keeps repeating quietly and that's when I realize I already know the answer to my earlier question.

*Could I ever forgive him? Yes.*

"I love you. I have always loved you and I don't think that will ever change." At my words, his arms tighten to almost pain around me.

"I love you too, Jules. So fucking much. I don't know what's wrong with me. I don't know why I keep fucking up, but I do know that I love you and that I will do anything that I can to prove it to you if you let me."

"I don't want to be apart anymore," I say. "I want to be with you...always."

"And you will be. From this day on, it's you and me, Jules. You and me."

## 25

## REMINGTON

*Two Weeks Later*

LIFE WENT BACK TO NORMAL, or as normal as it could be. All that matters to me really is that Jules is mine again. I vowed to work toward being a better man, to making better choices.

I had plans, plans that involved me making up for lost time, that involved putting a ring on her finger and giving her my last name. I won't ask her today, or even tomorrow, but soon.

Soon I'll make her completely mine, as she was always meant to be. But before that, it's important to me that she heal from the wounds I've created and the assault that Cole inflicted on her. She tells me often she feels safe with me, that she doesn't want me to go anywhere without her, and I never will, never.

"Jules." My father's voice fills my ears, ripping me from my thoughts.

"Papa Miller," Jules greets my father with a smile and releases my hand to give him a hug. Today is our first Sunday dinner together in well over a month and I'm basking in the glow of it. I'm still running daily, mainly to deal with the anger rushing through my veins over Cole, over being so stupid and immature. Plus, it helps me clear my head.

"How are you feeling, pretty girl?" my father asks her while I go into the kitchen to help Sebastian finish up dinner.

"Good. Feeling more and more like myself every single day." Her confession warms my soul. I could only wish for the day when she was back to her normal cheerful self. I miss that side of Jules.

Sebastian nudges me in the shoulder, and I look over at him. He's been wearing a permanent look of shame on his face over how he treated me for the last month and every time I see him, I want to wipe the look off his face. He's my brother yes, and family, but just because we are family didn't mean he had to believe me. I can't blame him for reacting as he did, especially with all the evidence pointing at me, and him wanting to protect Jules.

"How are you doing?" he asks.

"Well, I would be doing better if you would stop looking at me like you're sorry all the time. You want me to punch that look off your face?" I grin.

Sebastian smirks. "You could try." The smirk slips a smidge. "I just feel like an asshole. I'm your brother I should've believed you."

"Stop feeling bad. I was partially guilty anyway. I hurt Jules, maybe not as bad as Cole did, but I still hurt her. You had every right to believe what you did. I'm just thankful you were there for Jules when I couldn't be. If it weren't for you..." I trail off, a distinct ache forming in my chest. I don't want to think about what it would be like for Jules if she didn't have somewhere to go.

Sebastian places his hand on my shoulder, stopping the thought from taking root. "All that matters is that you have her back, she's healing, and that you won't make the same mistakes again. She loves you, and I know you love her, so don't do anything stupid to ruin it."

"Oh, I fucking won't. I'm never giving her up, ever."

Sebastian smiles. "Good, because if you do, I will seriously kick your fucking ass."

"Don't worry, you won't have to. I'll kick my own ass."

We both laugh and I help Jules set the table for dinner while Sebastian finishes up the salad and breadsticks.

"I love you," I whisper against Jules' lips as I pull her into my chest. She wraps her slim arms around me, and I relish in the feeling of her wound around me. It's been two weeks, two weeks of holding her, and still, I can't get enough of having her in my arms. Once upon a time, I wanted revenge...I wanted her to feel my pain, but now all I want is to take away her pain, take away the nightmares that still plague her.

Love, the deep unruly kind that claims every ounce of your soul has a way of changing things, and it changed me, completely. The sound of Jules' belly rumbling makes me pull back.

"Hungry?" I smirk.

"Starved."

"Hurry it up in there, Seb. Jules is going to eat the house down."

Jules elbows me in the stomach and shakes her head, a tiny little smile on her pink lips. At that same moment, a loud pounding on the front door startles all of us. After spending nights at the police station, I wouldn't be surprised if it was Detective Garcia dropping by to check in on us. I release Jules and walk to the door, pulling it open without even looking through the glass window off to the side.

As soon as I open the door, my mouth pops open. Shock and excitement paint my features when I see no one other than my oldest brother, Alexander, standing there with a knowing grin on his face. He's bigger, taller even, and I have to blink a couple times to actually be sure that it's him standing in front of me.

"You going to let me in, Rem, or do I have to stand outside?" He snickers, his russet brown eyes twinkling with amusement. I move out of the way, giving him room to walk in.

"What's going on? Who's..." Sebastian's words cut off when he sees Lex.

"Holy fucking shit," he mumbles under his breath. "Dad, you've got to see this."

Lex rolls his eyes, acting as if we're being dramatic or something, but in reality, it's been over a year since we've seen him, so having him walk in here without warning is going to take a little bit of getting used to.

"What the hell, son, the game's on, and Jules and I are..."

Lex's gaze sweeps over me. "Hey, Dad. Jules."

Dad and Jules come walking around the corner a moment later.

"Well, I'll be damned. I've got all my boys back at home again." Our father wraps Lex in a tight hug. "You're staying this time, right? Please tell me you didn't re-enlist."

"No, I'm home for good now," Lex responds, the emotions are cut off from his face, almost like he's hiding them, or he isn't letting himself feel anything just like Jules did and if that's the case then I feel incredibly sad for Lex.

"Thank goodness. I've missed you, son, how are you? How was your flight in? If you had let us know you were coming home, we would've had a party or something."

Lex shakes his head. "And that's exactly why I didn't tell you. Sunday dinner with my family is all that I could ever ask for."

Humble, kind, determined, and stubborn, those were just a few words to describe my brother. Joining the Marines was all he ever wanted, and I think it was good for him, gave him discipline. But now I wonder what seeing the dark parts of the world had done to him.

"Jules." Lex winks at her, and she shakes her head, walking up to him. She wraps her arms around him, and he squeezes her tight to his chest.

"I presume that Seb and Rem are still driving you up a wall?" he asks.

"You have no idea," she squeaks as he gives her a final squeeze.

"Are you hungry?" Seb asks.

"Do you even know me?" Lex laughs and it's deep, hearty, something that will take me time to get used to hearing. I love my brother, but he also left when we needed him. Like always, I had grown accustomed to those I needed in my life, leaving.

"Well, let's eat." My father slaps a hand to Lex's back, and we all head into the dining room. I grab an extra set of silverware, plate, and cup and place them on the table in Lex's usual spot. He settles into his seat, we chat and eat. Lex tells us what he's been doing for the last two years or at least the parts he can share with us. Followed by how he is going to use his GI bill to attend classes here at the university.

"If you need help with anything, let Rem or I know. I'll be in the admin building and Rem, well, he's a student so he can help, I guess. Oh, and Jules too," Sebastian offers while Lex takes a drink of his water.

"I've already got an apartment. I've just got to register for classes," he announces. Obviously, he's been planning this for some time, the question is, why didn't he call to tell us he was coming home? There were a lot of question about Alexander's reappearance in our lives, and not a lot of answers.

∽

"ARE you happy to have Lex back home?" Jules asks later that evening after we're back at her house. I strip down to my boxers, and she's wearing her Mickey Mouse t-shirt.

Seeing her in that thing makes my dick hard. We haven't done anything more than kiss, and I'm fine with that, but I wouldn't be a man if I didn't say holding her in my arms, feeling her soft curves against my hard planes, and listening to her soft whimpers while she sleeps didn't leave me wanting her on a deeper level. A level that includes putting my dick inside her.

"Of course I'm happy to have him home. But unlike Seb and my father, I know that he's not the same."

"What do you mean?" She leans into me, giving me a puzzled look, her tiny hands skimming over my chiseled abs. Fuck. If she keeps touching me like that, I'm going to come. Come like a teenage fucking boy.

"I mean, he's got a look in his eyes. I don't know if I can pinpoint it. All I know is that he didn't have that before he left. I'm used to people leaving and I know when, and if, someone wants to come back. I just know Lex is hiding something." I meant to say the last part more to myself than to her. I don't want her worrying about anything but herself right now.

She's going to therapy to deal with the nightmares and all the trauma that happened in the last couple of months. I want her to get healthy and be happy before she starts worrying about me or anyone else.

"Kiss me," Jules whispers, nibbling on her bottom lip with a seductiveness I haven't seen in what seems like forever. As if I could deny her such an easy request, I kiss her, cupping her by the cheeks and pulling her into my lap. Her heated core presses against my stomach and I feel the dampness of her panties against my skin.

She wants me...she fucking wants me, and I feel like the luckiest bastard in the universe because I get to keep her.

I pull away, breaking the kiss, leaving us both panting. "We don't have to do this yet. We have all the time in the world, Jules," I assure her, brushing a few strands of her blonde hair behind her ear. She's angelic, absolute perfection and God was more than looking out for me when he put her in my path.

"I know we don't *have* to, but I want to, Remmy. I want to feel close to you again. I want to feel you inside me. My body craves yours. You're the healing balm, the one thing that grounds me to this world, that keeps me sane when all I want to do is block everything out."

Her confession is all I need to hear for me to take the lead on worshipping her body. I have both of us undressed in seconds, her pink nipples hardened even before I take one into my mouth, sucking on it. A whimper escapes her mouth as she clings to me, her lips moving over my throbbing pulse.

"I want you," she purrs like a kitten.

"I know, baby, but I want you drenched. It's only your second time and I don't want to hurt you." I really don't, the thought of hurting her ever again, physically or emotionally, makes me sick to my stomach.

"You won't." She grinds her center against my steel cock, making it hard for me to breathe, hard for me to think about anything but sinking deep inside her channel.

"Jules," I groan, my hips flexing forward, the head of my cock bumping against her entrance.

"Please, Rem? Please, just take me. Show me how much you love me, how much you've missed this."

"You're going to kill me," I growl, lifting her by the hips, my cock slipping just inside her tight hole. Her blue eyes stay on mine as I slowly, ever so fucking slowly, sink her down onto my cock. Once she's seated fully, she squeezes my length so painfully that I'm sure I might actually die. I move a hand into her curls and ravage her neck, sucking at the tender flesh, branding her in a way that only I can.

Then we start moving as one, her hips lifting with each thrust, her pink lips singing a song only I can hear. Her nails sink into my shoulders and our foreheads touch. All I feel is her...all I need is her.

"Are you close?" I groan, feeling the pleasure zing through me, and down my cock with each stroke.

"Yes," she moans, her eyes drifting closed.

"Open those pretty eyes, baby...I want to see your face when you come. I want to see you," I order, and she does as I ask, her eyes flickering open once more.

A few more strokes and a swivel of my hips grazing that sweet spot deep inside of her and she falls apart, her mouth forming a perfect O, her chest rising and falling rapidly. Her heart beats furiously against her rib cage, as if it was trying to escape and find me.

"Remmy...Oh..." she whimpers, falling against my chest. That's when I take over, my control snapping, and I fuck her like a savage beast. Holding her tightly against my chest, I refuse to let even an inch of space separate our bodies. Fire fills my veins as I bottom out inside her, my balls slapping against her ass, pushing me closer and closer to the edge.

"Come for me, Rem. Come for me," she whispers against my lips and just like that, I do. It's like she has complete fucking control over my body. I come so hard black spots appear over my vision...so hard I swear I can feel our souls molding into one. Ropes of sticky hot cum fill her womb, my cock jerking with aftershocks of pleasure while I remain seated so deep inside her I can feel her heart beating in unison with my own.

"I love you," I croak. I've gone from a man broken to a man healed, and all because of love, because I let go of the pain, let go of the anger and anguish.

"I love you too, so much, so damn much." Her words sink deep into my skin, branding me, branding us, and I hold her in my arms just like I vowed to do every single night.

Jules isn't just a memory, or a bet, she's everything, the air, the light, the fucking very thing needed for me to live, and without her, I'm nothing.

There is no Remington Miller without Jules.

## EPILOGUE
### REMINGTON

*E*very new school year comes with a new set of douchebags. This year's douchebags will be no different than the previous years. My old frat house is holding an end of school bash of the year and as badly as I don't want to go, I promised Thomas that I would come, at the very least make an appearance.

"If you don't want to go, we could go back to the apartment," Jules exclaimed.

"Don't tempt me. I'd love nothing more than to take you back to the apartment, spread those creamy thighs, and—"

"Dude, you made it!" Alan's voice calls out, interrupting me before I can finish what I wanted to say. He's standing at the front door, busty blonde in his arm, and a fishbowl in his hand full of car keys. I see the boys have gotten smarter, safer.

"Of course. I'm a man of my word," I smirk. The old frat house is hopping, people funneling in and out of the house. Music blares from inside and into the street. How haven't these fuckers got the police called on them?

"The guys are inside waiting for you, I'll be there in a minute," he winks. "Oh, and hey Jules," he greets her, and she gives him a shy little wave. She's not much for these kinds of parties, and I don't blame her.

My hold on her hand tightens as I guide us through the crowd, and over to where Thomas is standing. I pull Jules behind me barely making it through without drunken people knocking into us. Someone screams right in my ear as they drunkenly fall into a group of people off to my left. I can't believe I used to love these kinds of parties. All I want to do right now is turn around and leave. I could name at least twenty better things to be doing right now.

Thomas slaps my shoulder when we finally reach him, and three more guys come sauntering up to us once they spot me. Every time I show up to one of these parties the entire university loses their shit. Everyone talks about Jules and me, how I'm whipped now that I've found the woman of my dreams.

They don't discuss the struggle we went through to get here. The pain that we both endured, the pain she endured. They only see what the gossip circle spreads. But the gossip circles can suck a dick because I've got everything I'll ever need.

Two of the guys I know. Vance and Clark, regular party guests at the frat house and overall fun guys. A little too cocky for my liking but as freshmen, I wouldn't expect any less of them. Vance gives me a head nod, acknowledging me, while Clark, his best friend, licks his lips, his eyes roaming over Jules with a predatory look.

*Fuck, to the no.*

I'm about to say something. Probably with my fists, but then his eyes move away from Jules and meet mine. He immediately sees me glaring and holds his hands up, while shaking his head. Good fucking choice.

"Shit, I need another beer, or twelve," Vance says, looking into his empty cup.

"You look like you are trying to drink your worries away," I tell him. "It's the end of the fucking year, what could you possibly have to worry about?" Not that I really care, the only thing I care about is right beside me, but I try to be friendly because in college appearances are everything.

"His dad is getting remarried," Clark blurts out. "And he's getting a stepsister."

"Oooh a stepsister," the guy I don't know chuckles. "How old is she?"

"Eighteen," Vance grits out, crushing the cup in his hand. Clearly, he's not happy about the situation and I want to tell him it could be worse, but I don't.

"Well, as long as she's hot... I mean she's legal so there's half your issue gone."

"Shut up, Mark," Vance warns, and there's a darkness inside him. A darkness that I understand all too well. "I used to know her, and I don't care if she's hot. She's a bitch and a liar, and that should be enough of a warning for you to stay away from her."

"Got it, you don't want to fuck your stepsister. Don't worry, I'll show her around campus...and around my cock." Mark lets out a bellow of laughter that causes Vance to snap like a two by four under pressure.

He moves so fast, Mark doesn't even see the fist coming. He's still laughing his ass off when Vance's knuckles smash into the side of his face. Mark's head snaps back and the smile literally gets wiped off his face.

"Here we go again..." Clark mumbles, bringing his cup to his lips. There seems to be a reoccurring theme with this kid. He's always fighting, using his fists like words.

Jules gasps and I tuck her behind me so she doesn't have to watch the violence taking place right before my eyes. Mark stumbles back into the crowd. His arms flailing as he tries to stay on his feet, but he loses his balance, the hit and the alcohol pulsing through his veins not helping him at all. He lands flat on his ass on the hardwood floor.

A circle forms around us, people start to cheer, there's an air of danger and for a moment I think that's going to be it, but then I see Vance stalking toward Mark like he's his newest target. He shoves drunken Mark backward and presses a knee to his chest to hold him down while continuing onward with his punches.

"It...I was jokin'..." Mark gasps, but his words don't stop Vance's assault. I'm not sure anything would at this point. I can hear his hits over the roar of the crowd. Mark doesn't stand a chance and I feel bad for the guy. He should've kept his mouth shut.

"Remmy, do something." Jules elbows me in the side, but I already know I need to intervene since Mark's body just lulled to the side, telling me he's passed out. Vance doesn't seem to notice or care, he just uses the fucker like his own personal punching bag.

"That's enough, Mr. Preston," Clark scolds as we move simultaneously. He grabs one arm and I grab the other, hauling him off of Mark before he kills him. As we pull Vance off of unconscious Mark, he punches two more times into the air, before finally letting up.

"Fine, I'll stop," Vance grits out.

We pull him back a few more feet before releasing him.

"Go get a beer and calm the fuck down," I tell him, slapping him on the shoulder. He shrugs me off but does as I tell him and turns to go into the kitchen.

"I'll take care of him," Clark tells me, giving me a grin before following behind his best friend like a lost puppy. I'm not sure that guy has a serious bone in his body.

Jules comes up beside me, snuggling into my side, making me forget what I was thinking.

"What was that about?" she asks.

"Not sure, but I'm guessing he and his soon-to-be stepsister have some kind of history."

"Oh really? Sounds a little like us?" She wiggles her eyebrows. I stare down at her, unbelieving that she is still mine, and that I haven't fucked this up again yet.

"I don't think there is any saving him. He uses his fists instead of his words. He's got an anger issue, and I'm pretty sure parental issues too."

Jules rolls her eyes. "So easy to judge, Mr. Miller, and here I thought you were all about helping others, being a better man?"

My eyes catch on the diamond ring that adorns her ring finger. I couldn't help but ask her, even though we agreed we wouldn't get married until after we graduated. I needed, no wanted to let every bastard on campus know that she was mine.

"I'll show you a better man... as soon as we get home."

Her cheeks pinken and I swear I'll never get over the way she looks at me, or the way she reacts to me.

"Kiss me," she orders, pressing up onto her tiptoes. Blonde hair framing her angelic face, with blue eyes that beam up at me.

And as if I could ever deny her what she wants, I press my lips to hers, relishing in the best thing that has ever happened to me.

∼

***Thank you** for reading The Bet.*
*You can find Sebastian's story in The Vow and Lex's story in The Promise.*

*The North Woods University series continues with The Dare.*

## ABOUT THE AUTHORS

**J.L. Beck** and **C. Hallman** are a *USA Today* and international bestselling author duo who write contemporary and dark romance.

Sign up for our **Newsletter** to receive **FREE BOOKS**, as well as sales and updates.

Join our Facebook Reader's Group Bleeding Heart Romance to interact with us, **Exclusive Giveaways** and teasers.

Check out our Website to order **Signed Paperbacks** and special swag.
www.bleedingheartromance.com

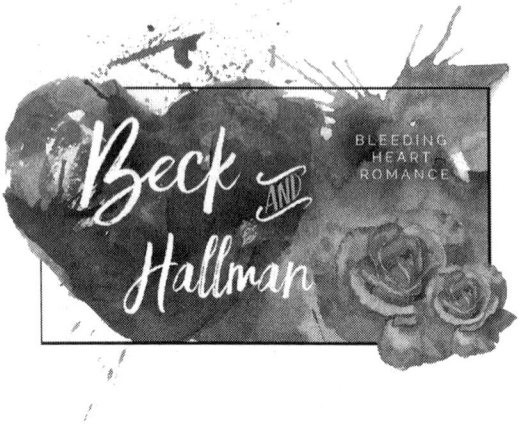
Beck
AND
Hallman
BLEEDING
HEART
ROMANCE

## ALSO BY THE AUTHORS

CONTEMPORAY ROMANCE

**North Woods University**
The Bet
The Dare
The Secret
The Vow
The Promise
The Jock

**Bayshore Rivals**
When Rivals Fall
When Rivals Lose
When Rivals Love

**Breaking the Rules**

Kissing & Telling
Babies & Promises
Roommates & Thieves

***

## DARK ROMANCE

**The Blackthorn Elite**
Hating You
Breaking You
Hurting You
Regretting You

**The Obsession Duet**
Cruel Obsession
Deadly Obsession

**The Rossi Crime Family**
Protect Me
Keep Me
Guard Me
Tame Me
Remember Me

**The Moretti Crime Family**
Savage Beginnings
Violent Beginnings
Broken Beginnings

**The King Crime Family**
Indebted
Inevitable

Printed in Great Britain
by Amazon